THE
TALLEST
LIAR

Books by C. L. Sulzberger

THE TALLEST LIAR

by

C.L. Sulzberger

CROWN PUBLISHERS, INC.
NEW YORK

Inquiries should be addressed to Crown
Publishers, Inc., One Park Avenue, New York,
N.Y. 10016.

Printed in the United States of America
Printed simultaneously in Canada by General Publishing
   Company Limited

Designed by Ruth Kolbert Smerechniak

Library of Congress Cataloging in Publication Data

Sulzberger, Cyrus Leo, 1912–
   The tallest liar.

   I.   Title
PZ4.S9534Tal   [PS3569.U36]   813'.5'4
ISBN 0-517-53141-0   77-5649

FOR

Clem and Jessie with a smile

CHAPTER I

Many people say I am the world's tallest liar. Karl Friedrich Hieronymus, Baron von Münchausen, was only six feet two whereas I am eight feet six, a growth already achieved by my sixteenth birthday. Nevertheless, although Münchausen, Lord of Bodenwerder, was famous for his highly embroidered falsehoods, I only report facts. Because a man is born in a stable, that does not make him a horse. My Mutterl brought me up with respect for truth.

As she often explained to me, my father was a tireless and imaginative talker. It is perhaps from him that I inherited a dash of fluency. Mutterl also swore repeatedly that Vati, a Prussian aristocrat named Karl von Snarl, was sick with love for me and had a passionate, exalted nature, as is often the case with criminals. Not that Father could be classified so basely: only a war criminal, ex post facto and posthumous, after his death heroically defending Hitler's Thousand-Year Reich.

Vati was the highest-ranking Negro in the Schützstaffel, or SS, in which he bore the rank of Sturmbahnführer. Of course, the Nazi high command, which cherished certain racial prejudices, was unaware that his own mother was an albino member of the Herero tribe in the former colony of German South West Africa.

When the Germans defeated them in 1904, the Hereros fled north to the barren Kaokoveld but some of them trickled back to Windhoek where Grandpa lived. Among these was my grandma who came from the clan of Johannes Oorlog, the famous Herero chief who had more than a hundred children. Oorlog is Dutch for war. She was allowed to become a domestic servant in the von Snarl family, a most lucky privilege. It was a fine house on the corner of Kaiser and Goering Streets and Sundays, in defiance of local custom, each of the servants was given a mug of frothy Windhoek beer.

Grandma was six feet without shoes (she possessed none) and pink-skinned with curly reddish hair and she wore the long graceful dresses which Rhenish missionaries had taught her to sew. Yet my grossvater never married her despite his admiration for her size and passion. Mutterl explained to me that even then, during World War One, the von Snarls had a snobbish streak. Grandpa feared her children might lack the albino heritage and come in a dusky shade. This showed his ignorance, Mutterl said. The babies of the handsome Herero women, no matter how black their mamas are, almost all arrive on this earth white.

In our family's case there was only one baby, Father, and he not only arrived white but stayed that shade, unlike the majority of his cousins. Grandpa, the Freiherr von Snarl, a famous brewer who was two meters high and nimble as a wolf, went east in 1914 to join General von Lettow Vorbeck's largely black guerrilla army. Eager for blood and greedy for fame, he fought the British and the

Boers all over Africa. When the First War ended he had achieved only evil and sorrow. Still like a wolf, but gone gray and gaunt, he died of malaria and sleeping sickness.

Mutterl learned this story from my father. He was sent as a child to Germany by an uncle who took pains to dispatch Grandma back to the Kaokoveld. He apparently feared that, despite her acceptable pigmentation, with her flat feet, trailing gown and strangely clicking accent, like a whale, she might not be tolerantly viewed among the Hochgeboren of Berlin.

It seems her caste-conscious tribe also looked down upon her. Therefore she sought refuge among the lowly Berg Damaras and Topnaar Hottentots in the Namib Desert. There she was known for her stature and albino coloring as the Great White Mammy and there she died. Kaokoveld means "lonely coast" among the Hereros. Often I think what a suitable place it was for my outcast Grossmutterl to end her days. Even had the Freiherr deigned to marry her I doubt he would have paid the customary tribal price: one ox, one ewe, one goat. He was known as very stingy.

My Herero legacy was, I am informed by doctors who have studied my impressive physique, a brand of syphilis that affected the pituitary gland. The Hereros were already an inbred dying race in Grossmutter's time, a people of yesterday who had ceased to pray for tomorrow. But the admixture of Grandpa's lusty von Snarl blood apparently conquered the Herero curse, impotence. At least this has been my experience, confirmed by my father's love clutch.

One might have thought this unorthodox heritage would have affected Papa's career after the Nazis came to power in 1933 and when he joined the SS. However, my father was a shrewd, well-educated man. He didn't just keep his eyes in his pocket. He managed to obtain an impressive, well-documented set of papers proving his descent from generations of Prussian nobility and the Oorlogs who, according to him, were a martial Dutch strain which originated near the Rhine.

Mama herself could boast unusual descent, especially for one who was approved by Himmler's breeding organization, Lebensborn, that was devoted to procreating the Nordic superrace. She carried this function out nobly by producing me, with Father's necessary assistance.

Mutterl's Austrian family, the Schumpeters, passed muster on her father's side. However, her mother, a von Josephi, came from a line of court Jews. They bought their title in the early nineteenth century in exchange for cancelling debts owed by the princeling who granted this prestigious patent. Notwithstanding, Vati, having already managed to obtain evidence of his own Aryan purity, easily satisfied the Lebensborn management with a beautifully engraved family tree he bought for Mutterl and which omitted even the remotest Semitic hint.

Since both my parents were blond, blue-eyed and exceptionally tall, SS General Gregor Ebner, Lebensborn's specialist on "problems of racial selection," personally signed Mutterl's admission papers. Ebner had been a university clubmate of Heinrich Himmler, his boss. The papers permitted her to enter the Lebensborn hospice at Steinhöring in Bavaria, where she was successfully impregnated by Vati.

Lebensborn means "fountain of life." Mutterl has often said to me: "Ach, what a man that Vati of yours was. The softest thing about him was his teeth. He had no foreskin, a mark unkindly viewed by SS experts, but how he worked his thing about. Wham, Wham, Wham, for the Führer," Mutterl used to recollect with proud affection.

I believe Father spent ten days in romantic production activities on behalf of the Herrenvolk, encouraged by Ebner's institution among the Bavarian Alps before he was sent off to the Eastern Front. There he eventually won

(4)

high decorations for his devoted services, first as a supervisor of racial purification among the subhuman Slavs, and then as the patriotic defender of Treblinka concentration camp, where he died a soldier's death.

From the time of my babyhood, still under Lebensborn supervision, I had dark skin and a great, hooked nose like a Cochin Jew from southern India, despite my kinky reddish-blond hair. I was enormous and growing like a mushroom. Mutterl had me named Kerl von Snarl. Kerl means fellow and I was already a lusty infant when the SS scroll had been duly attested by Max Sollmann.

Sollmann was an SS colonel and Lebensborn's chief administrator. It is just as well that this fine gentleman known to good Aryans as "handsome Max," never personally glimpsed me. As for Ebner, he surely might have had doubts about the purity of my genes. Ebner supervised the sterilization of kidnapped children from occupied areas, children who seemed insufficiently Aryan to his scientific eye.

My dubious appearance in no way affected Mutterl's adoration. "Was für ein Kerl," she used to boast of me: "What a guy." She had heard talk of another Schumpeter whom she claimed as a kinsman, an Austrian-born genius whose ambition was to become the world's best economist, greatest lover and finest horseman. "I think he failed," said Mutterl modestly. "I am not sure what an economist is, nor, I believe, is anybody else. Moreover, they tell me there were no horses at the university where he taught. Notwithstanding, like your father he was the world's greatest lover. For you, my Kerlchen, the future for you is boundless."

When I was seven years old, two years after the war, Mutterl heard from a friend that, because of his heroic death, Vati had been sentenced posthumously for war crimes. This distressed her but it did not restrain her adaptable nature which managed to climb to the top of

(5)

every successive human wave. She began to boast of her Jewish faith; she talked less of the von Snarls, even dropped the "von." Mutterl had an admirably tolerant personality.

At the end of 1947 she emigrated with me to America. The trip was arranged by a Yankee friend, Bill South, with whom she consoled herself in exchange for Hershey bars during that chilly winter. South had joined the U.S. Army straight from Ringling Brothers circus where he coordinated the freak show. A natural entrepreneur, he struck out on his own after being demobilized. Mutterl was his star performer.

Under the name of "Trabzi of Trabzon, last of the genuine Amazons," he billed her with great success, teaching her how to shoot a bow and arrow with sufficient accuracy to knock a pumpkin off my head. Mutterl had had her left breast amputated for cancer. Therefore she titillated her audiences by doing her archery stripped to the waist, about which hung a wolfskin, while South explained through a megaphone that proper Amazons always had one tit cut off to make them shoot easier and faster.

Mutterl, with no signs of regret for the ecstatic Lebensborn nights that spawned me, learned from a St. Louis newspaper that my brave father was considered only a mass murderer of Jews like herself. She shrugged her hips and promptly married a colleague, Borborigmi of Borneo.

Borborigmi was advertised as the smallest cannibal in history. Even then, a sort of kindergarten type, I towered over him. He was so tiny that, on tiptoe, his protruding lips could not quite reach that portion of my mother which they fancied most. Therefore Mutterl, with tasteful Teutonic sympathy, made for him a footstool covered with the face-skin of a tiger who had eaten his trainer. The trainer used to underfeed the animal and take his meat ration home for stewing.

The tiger choked on the trainer's pelvis and Borborigmi

rescued the remains, staking out a claim to the pelt. Into this my mother set a needlework panel of Leda and the swan whose godly amorous embraces must have been equally awkward to those of the Borneo dwarf. I was always fascinated that the swan on Mutterl's tapestry was black as the ugly duckling. Leda was, as to be expected of an artist-graduate from the Lebensborn, an azure-eyed platinum blonde. Even, I sometimes thought, with a hint of unnatural albino strain. By then I had been told of my Herero grandma and the Kaokoveld.

My affection for Borborigmi developed fast. We became very close because of our respective peculiarities. He was too small and I was too big. We had to buy our clothes at special shops and then get them altered. So we used to go shopping together hand in hand.

This pleased Mutterl, especially when we found one manufacturer who agreed to give us our clothes for nothing if we would spend six hours a week walking up and down wearing large signs on our backs and fronts, advertising his store. That was fun; it gave us a chance to see a lot of New York and exchange many interesting ideas.

Mutterl puzzled me as I grew older. Despite her resuscitated faith in Jewry and her pride in my Herero blood she still prattled to Borborigmi that "the Germanic race is superior to all others and the struggle against the stranger, against the Jew, against the Slav, against inferior races, is sacred." She treasured among her few souvenirs my own "Sippenbuch der SS" or racial passport which attested that all my ancestors had been probably Aryan as far back as the Thirty Years' War.

Borborigmi held me in much esteem when he analyzed my features with respect to the documents. "You see," Mutterl would often say: "Each SS man was duty-bound to choose a woman at least his racial equal if not his superior. That was laid down in the *Leithefte*. Both of Kerl's parents are certified as biologically without reproach. We women who passed through Lebensborn were awarded the Order of the Rabbit. The biological good breeders. We were told: 'all of you may not find a husband but you can all become mothers.' Those were the days, Borbo."

I'm afraid Mutterl's enthusiasm caused needless embarrassment when I was accepted in a New York public school after South died and the freak show broke up. He was gashed by the tusks of two boars while attempting to teach them how to draw a pony cart through Central Park.

We discovered that part of the requisite preliminaries to a U.S. education was a medical examination. Mutterl believed her personal experience could speed the process up. "You see," she advised the examining doctor and nurse, the former named Levy and the latter, Miss Booker, as black as obsidian, "he was born in the Lebensborn Eingetragener Verein near Munich and brought up in their crèche. I can show you his certificate of Aryan origin. Ach, those Germans, they were very scientific."

The doctor and the nurse listened in bewilderment and wholly forgot to examine me.

"The Nordic," said Mutterl, "is the jewel of the earth, the most brilliant joy of creation; not only the most gifted but the most beautiful. The Nordic has the perfect movements of the perfect body."

"What's this?" asked the nurse, fiddling with my behind.

"It looks like a tail. Well hidden. Fits between the cheeks," said Dr. Levy. "A vestigal tail. About eight inches long. Muscular."

"Maybe he isn't even human," said Miss Booker.

"Could be," said the doctor. "Just a primate."

Mutterl was furious. "Why, he is pure Aryan," she insisted. "The SS Sippenbuch proves this. So he must be human. Surely the SS word cannot be doubted. He has all the intelligence and skill of Aryans. But he has enough of the black man to have musical and rhythmic genius, thanks to his Herero grandma. And he is capable of great affection. Look at the size of his penis."

"But how can he be a black Aryan?" asked the nurse, measuring my calves and ankles with a tape.

"And I am a Jew myself," Mutterl insisted. "The only Aryan Jewess with a Lebensborn permit."

"Get her out of here," said the doctor. Mutterl punched him in the nose and there was blood all over the office. When she had been expelled, bellowing with rage, the two continued their examination.

"He certainly shows signs of being some kind of Mischling," said the doctor.

"What's that?" the nurse asked.

"Begging your pardon, I guess you'd call it mulatto. But I never heard of an albino Mischling."

"Mischling yourself," said Miss Booker, haughtily stalking after Mutterl and slamming the door behind.

Once I had been registered in P.S. 88 several things happened right away. My classmates started to call me Snarler. The boys looked up to me and held me in esteem because of my towering size. And the girls condemned me as a liar from the start.

I assured them that all I told them about my origins, my parents, my upbringing (and the newly acquired knowledge of my tail) was gospel truth. I boasted about my heroic father and also about his successor, Borborigmi.

"You know, Snarl," a girl named Mildred protested soothingly. "You'd be a good guy if you ever told the truth." I was sorry to hear her say this. Mildred was pretty; and she smelled very good.

"But the truth is all I know!" I shouted. "It has been fundamental in my upbringing. That is what my Mutterl says. It is the core of our Aryan credo."

Indeed, the tragedy of my life is that I have always—or almost always—told the truth as I was brought up to do by Mutterl. She was rigorously moral on this point if no other. "Think," she would console me, "you are not just an Aryan bastard reared in the holy Lebensborn crèche. You are also a proud Herero. And a learned Jew. How lucky can you get?"

Once I asked her: "When did you and Vati meet?"

"I was working in the Zentralfriedhof. Vienna. 1938. After the Anschluss. That's where they put dead Jews whose bodies weren't claimed. Such a clean place. Clean as a skull. I got the job through influence. My cousin ran a small hotel where some of those sentimental Nazis took their girls.

"Your Vati was one of them. And he also dealt with Zentralfriedhof affairs. When he saw me he fell head over heels. He took me on as his assistant keeping records. Then he got me my first set of false papers. Through Gildemeester. A Dutch Nazi. Partner of the Führer's nephew. Ach, they were a clever pair. The millions that they made."

I always thought it strange that such a brave and iron-disciplined Aryan as my Vati, with high connections like the Führer's nephew, should have told Mutterl so much about his African background. But he loved Mutterl even more than the Party, she assured me, and although he accepted his loyal responsibilities in Steinhöring and never breathed a word about the Hereros in his past, when they first met in Vienna he spoke often of them.

Romantically she remembered handed-down tales of my grandma: how the Kunene River flowed across the Namib Desert; the Oorlog soldiers on their donkeys by the omoborongbongo trees, the galloping ostriches and the sacred fire of the Maherero tended by the chief's wife.

By the time I was twelve and was graduated to Benjamin Franklin High School, I had become a basketball star. I was already over seven feet tall and, although awkward, unusually muscular. Ump Screwhill, the coach, decided he could fashion unbeatable plays around me because of my great height. It was only necessary to pass high into my hands which, when I was standing beside the basket, were able to dunk the ball easily through the hoop. Sportswriters for the New York newspapers began to write of me as the greatest schoolboy athlete since Lou Gehrig, a remarkable Yankee first baseman. Even the girls came to regard my "lying" as nothing but a subtle, teasing boast. Instead of Snarl or Snarler, they began to call me Curly from Kerl, not my hair I assumed.

My stepfather was unabashedly proud of my prowess. He was always on the sidelines during practice sessions, inventing new plays and then taking me home to perfect my passing and shooting against a backboard rigged in the cement-floored yard of our tenement. I don't think anyone before Borborigmi had ever realized it's as difficult to drop a ball through the basket from above as it is to push it in from below.

Mr. Parsnip, the principal, took a personal interest in me. He was a great sports fan but he was also very kind. He told Mutterl once when he had invited her to discuss my progress: "You know, Mrs. Snarl, your son's really bright. That boy's brain is fully big enough for his body. I think we can make something of him. Not just in the gymnasium. In life also."

There had never before been a twelve-year-old on the varsity team of any New York high school. The principal gave instructions to my teachers to promote me out of junior high so that I could technically qualify. And when my arithmetic teacher wanted to send me to reform school for trying to rape pigtailed little Mildred in a corridor, the principal expelled her.

He didn't punish me. I told him I was only feeling her panties. He explained to the arithmetic teacher that I was needed for the state championship. Mildred was white with rage. She was the only one who still called me Snarler when she spoke to me: "Snarler the dirty black-Nazi-kike."

Our team went through its regular season of games without a loss. Nevertheless, one day as I was practicing spins, turns, dribbling, lob shots, passes, I became so ungainly, not yet able to manage my vast size, that I lumbered into the coach and knocked him down. "You dumb nigger," spat Ump, a blocky little man who had once played quarterback for Brown.

I didn't know much about fighting. I wasn't even sure what nigger meant. But the way he said it, I knew it wasn't good. So I made a fist of my right hand, leaned over, and bonked him on top of his cranium bang, plunk, just like that. His head flattened and he sank to the floor. He never got up again.

Despite protests from the principal, I was expelled from school. While waiting to be heard in private before a judge, released on bail to my stepfather's care, I climbed through our back window, down the fire escape, and with the combined savings of Mutterl and Borborigmi in my pocket, disappeared into the Harlem night.

CHAPTER II

A reader of these recollections, impressed by the fact that I was already star of the Ben Franklin basketball team and charged with at least attempted rape, cannot easily realize that despite my immensity and maturity I was still but twelve years old, a powerful giant with the frightened soul of a child.

I made my way cautiously past the garbage pails down to the East River and then turned northward, hoping that direction would lead me away from a terrifying city. As I shuffled along in a half crouch, trying to look both innocent and small, I kept an eye alert for cops.

For the first time I realized the disadvantages of fame: many New Yorkers and every policeman surely knew who I was. So my relief was immeasurable when I passed a small barge with a shack built on it and saw an old man, an old woman and a large black dog sitting at the doorway, lighted by a kerosene lamp, eating together out of a single battered tin plate.

"Hi there," said the old man when he saw me staring. "Whaddya want? Speak up. It's dinnertime. Wanna eat? Come on board." His name was Pap Leezer and he was a retired tugboat captain from the Ohio River. The dog's name was Satan and Pap told him to shut up when he growled. "He's my best friend, my only friend, except for Inez here."

Inez turned out to be the aged former sweetie of a gambler named Canfield who had died years ago. He made a fortune playing all kinds of card games, some of which he invented himself. "But he didn't leave me a plugged nickel," Inez croaked. "Not a red cent. What a man. Made two million bucks and spent three. He had style. Real style. Say," she interrupted herself peering at me in the faint lamplight, "you're just a kid. How does a kid get that big anyway?"

I didn't know what to reply so, being hungry, I just began eating with the three of them. A large plateload of cold baked beans. There was one spoon, which Inez used. Pap and I used our fingers, Satan his tongue. It was very nourishing.

Whenever a boat or a police launch passed, the waves washed furiously against us, tipping the barge and its ramshackle hut. Pap would rush to the rail and shake his fist, a torrent of swearwords pouring from his toothless mouth. The dog growled and Inez just sat back huddled in amusement. Satan and I both sniffed her. She smelled like a mushroom.

"Never had such a good time since Canfield was alive," she mumbled. "I'll tell you, kid, he knew how to live. Things weren't the same afterward. Until I met Pap, that is. We lived in the same Steubenville boardinghouse those days. Then they run me out of town."

"Why did they run you out, Mrs. Inez?" I asked.

"Hmmph. They tried me for sorcery first. At a court near East Liberty."

"What's sorcery?"

"Witchcraft, young man," said Pap. "They said she was a witch."

"All I did was make wax figures for eight bits apiece."

"Yeah," said Pap. "And stick pins in 'em. Trouble was," he continued, turning toward me, "some of her customers died."

"Not my customers, you fool. Only them they didn't like. I always tried to please my clientele."

This was all very puzzling and I didn't know what any of it meant, not even the word clientele. But they were nice people and they let me spend the rest of the night and all the next day. However, when I told them why I was alone and wandering their welcome became less cheerful.

"On the lam," said Inez. "Better move off tonight," said Pap. "We have enough fuss with the dicks as things already are. Don't want to abet no childhood rapist-murderers. Don't want trouble 'cause of a kinky-headed young giant now."

So they told me what to do. I was to go across the city to the Hudson River railway tracks and, down near a Hundred and Twentieth Street where they shifted the freight cars around, I should ask for Pap's former first mate, Eat-em-up-Alive Jack Schmaltz. He was the watchman and wandered up and down beside the trains checking them for hobos and dusty-roaders. When I asked he explained that these were gentleman travellers who didn't buy their tickets.

"You got some dough, boy? Well, just give Eat-em-up-Alive a couple of simoleons and tell him Pap sent you. Tell him Pap said he should fix it for you to ride on up to Montreal. You won't need no ticket and you won't need no papers when Eat-em-up-Alive sends you off on your capers."

"What a wit," said Inez. "Just like Canfield."

That evening I bade the three of them farewell after sharing another can of cold beans. I walked across to Riverside Drive and then down to a Hundred and Twentieth. Sure enough, a big man with a gimp in his left leg and a cauliflower ear limped along the trackbed carrying a lantern. "Mr. Schmaltz?" I inquired. I paid him two dollars, he rolled open the door of a boxcar marked Canadian Pacific, shoved me in and set me along the road to high adventure.

I didn't know exactly where Montreal was because geography had never been my favorite subject but when the trainman dropped in to give me a sandwich he explained. He was a friend of Eat-em-up-Alive and suggested that I get off when we rumbled to a halt in the Canadian city because the train would be broken up at a roundhouse and my car would be inspected. If I just played Weary Willy for a while, panhandling my way, I might be able to run into some lively work. Montreal wasn't a bad town for that. So I became a beggar.

One day I saw a poster advertising jobs with the Spruce Falls Power and Paper Company in Northern Ontario. I applied at the address listed. They didn't ask questions, just gave me a ticket to Kapuskasing and told me to report tomorrow at the railway station where their recruiter would see I was set on the proper train. At Ontario we changed and another Spruce Falls official put us aboard for the long ride north.

It was a rattly old car with woven straw bench seats. Most of the passengers seemed to be part of the same group as me. I got the feeling they were no more familiar than I with what was happening because, although they were all strong, heavy-set men, few of them spoke any English. The fellow who sat beside me was a Lutheran pastor in a black suit. He wore no necktie and he was pleased to discover I spoke German. He was bound even farther, all the way to James Bay where, I soon learned, there was a colony of former Nazis.

"So," he said, "you are from Lebensborn. Funny, you don't look it. But you say Ebner himself sent your measurements to Himmler? Special, doch? Well, that must mean you were born on an October seven. The Führer's birthday. You must have been a spoiled fellow then. Eh? Didn't they give you a candlestick? Sure, I know. They were made by the workers of Dachau. The people who volunteered for our Greater Reich labor force. Fine work too. No, you don't have your candlestick anymore? A pity. Most valuable souvenir.

"Did your Mutti ever tell you of Frau Annie? She was part of my flock. No, not at Steinhöring. That is a Catholic region. Frau Annie was from Saxony. Lower Saxony. Champion milk donor of the Lebensborn. In one week she gave 27,800 grams. Best wet nurse they ever had. Fine German girl. Always pregnant too. Last heard of her at Kurmark hospice near Berlin. Shortly before the Russkis came."

I was charmed by this genial prelate and prattled happily to him about myself, about my Vati, my Mutterl, about the Oorlog Hereros and even about Borborigmi. He seemed more and more bewildered.

"My boy, there is something terribly wrong in what you tell me. You know, I come from Bodenwerder in Hanover and our proudest citizen was Freiherr von Münchausen. When I was your age I had already read the 'Vademecum für lustige Leute.' I still remember his picture in the front of the book: tall, thin, with three-cornered hat and powdered, braided wig: slim lined face with broad cheekbones. Not much like you, and so much shorter. And, now I'm beginning to think, without your native genius. Yes, my son, I believe you are the greatest and the tallest liar ever heard of."

With that he shut up. His mouth snapped tight and remained determinedly so. He didn't move, just stared glumly out the window. I looked at the other passengers. They were all speaking strange tongues. Later I learned:

Ukrainian, Polish, Lithuanian, Finnish, Norwegian. Almost all had been forest workers in their homelands and almost all had collaborated with our glorious Wehrmacht at one or another time.

We knew when we got to Kapuskasing because the conductor came through our car to make sure everyone understood this was the end of the ride. I said goodbye to the pastor who didn't seem to hear. Then I climbed down. Unlike the others, I had no suitcase or paper bundle. A man checked us off a list, asked for our documents but didn't seem to care about those who hadn't any.

We were taken through a modest little town to the head of a broad river where thousands and thousands of long and short logs and entire tree trunks were floating downstream together in a solid jam. There we got aboard a boat with a blunt nose and powerful engine that forced a passage through the drifting wooden obstacles and finally broke into clear water rushing down upon us from the south. To the side, carefully controlled by booms, the endless log jam drifted heavily, slowly toward the Kapuskasing sawmill by the tracks.

I looked out over the rail. It was summer but windy and chill. Near Kapuskasing itself I saw a few grainfields shivering. From there on it was nothing but forest and more forest. Despite the noise of the turbulent flowing water and the chugging engine, you could hear the trees creaking in the wind like the rigging of old sailing ships in the stories they sometimes read to us at Ben Franklin.

Three men seemed to be in charge. There was a handsome fair-haired youth named Buck. There was an Indian (a Cree I was later told) with flat cheekbones and skin the color of tobacco juice. He spoke some kind of language called French and he wore a round, broad-rimmed felt hat. He was called Vincent.

And there was another Indian with huge round shoulders and enormous hands from one of which the little finger was missing. I later learned it was chopped off by Vincent in an axe fight. I also learned that he was part Nez Percé, his name was Tawis Geejumnin, and that this means "Horns Worn Down Like Those of an Old Buffalo." He was a very mean-looking Indian and he and Vincent obviously hated each other.

When I got to know him better Tawis told me: "Him sorriest son bitch ever breathe. I lost finger fighting that man. But he lost something more important. You ever seen him in the shower? No? Well, ask him why he squats to take piss."

We were four hours on the boat ride. Our group became more and more silent as the new migrant workers dozed off and their many-tongued conversations ceased. Finally the boat pulled up by a board pier and Buck ordered us all off, mainly by signs. At the foot of the pier was a small cross of sawn slats on which somebody had burned a date and the words: "Three of us killed this son of a bitch."

Just beyond was a narrow-gauge track and a two-car little train into which we piled. Everyone jammed together along the benches that lined the cars except for Vincent and Tawis Geejumnin who stood at the exit, facing each other with eyes glittering from their impassive faces. They were there to see that none of us escaped.

It took all night to complete the journey, first by train and then by tubby motorboats that carried us over an enormous, whitecapped lake to the camp that was our destination. Once more we unloaded and were marched to long frame cabins that were our living quarters. I discovered that apart from Tawis I was the only inhabitant of our hut who was neither Ukrainian nor a Finn.

"O.K. boys," said Tawis Geejumnin in a surprisingly shrill high voice. He had a gamy smell. "Dump your stuff. Anyone wants piss or crap, do so. Then we go for breakfast." There was a shithouse on the way to the mess hall. They were both long, low buildings, but the shithouse had no windows; only rows of holes, side by side along one wall, and a sheet metal urinal along the other. I was struck by the fact that the holes were all occupied by Ukrainians and the urinal by Finns. Tawis and I stood by and watched in silence. I had peed by a tree when we first got off the boats.

The mess hall impressed me as being very strange. It was breakfast time and there were plenty of eggs and pancakes, not of the sort Mutterl used to give me, filled with apple jelly, but thick, soggy and covered with a brown sweet syrup; yet there was also a splendid assortment of pies, tarts, cookies and even plates of candy.

Tawis Geejumnin saw me staring at them. He leaned forward, reaching for the pie plate, and murmured in my ear: "No booze this camp. Therefore plenty sweet things. Hard work here. Big men work hard need plenty sugar. Now don't speak at all," he continued muttering as I opened my mouth. "Not allowed speaking. Only pass bread, pass jam, pass pie, pass coffee. Speaking waste time, waste energy. Speaking just make trouble. This big rule. You follow, boy, and you stay clear trouble." Then he added: "Cook not much good. But he needs the money."

So I dug in silently with the rest: four eggs, thick slabs of ham, half a pie, two cups of extrasweet coffee. And all this time a whispered rustle: "Pass bread. Pass jam. Pass pie."

Buck explained to me later that lumberjacks are traditionally hard drinkers and go mad if they don't have the additional sugar when their liquor supply is cut. I found out it wasn't always cut as completely as Buck and Vincent pretended. Lumberjacks aren't bad smugglers.

We kept a few heavy workhorses at the camp to drag out big logs from difficult swampy country and undergrowth where tractors didn't like to go. There was a large oat bin behind the shithouse and many of the jacks managed to pass by it even though it seemed out of their way. Most of them were Finns and most of these had flat white bottles of moonshine whisky hidden under the oats. I guess that's why the Finns were always pissing more than the others.

Some of us were given double-bladed axes and some of us were given two-handled saws which we worked in couples. There were only a few power saws, allotted to the favorites of Buck, Vincent and Tawis Geejumnin. I soon found out the reason why. The favorites paid a cash rental fee each week for the automatic cutters. They could chop much faster than any of the rest of us and so, under a complex pay system based on a small salary and a piecework bonus, the chain sawyers made extra even after taking into account the bribes.

Every Sunday we had time off. The lucky ones, usually for a tip to those in authority, were able to get off Saturday afternoon and take the long trip in to Kapuskasing, getting there before the last bars closed. They lay around all Sunday sobering up and caught the evening boat-train boat back in time for Monday morning logging. The rest of us just lay around, sometimes listening to the radio which specialized in Eastern European songs.

I didn't like that much. So I often went fishing with Tawis on Lake Opazatika, a long slate-colored body of water mirroring the lowering dull sky. Tawis Geejumnin, who said he was also part Ojibway, told me Opazatika meant Lake of the Poplar Islands in their language. There hideous, huge pike lay like timber in the weed beds, peering malevolently at the upper world through evil eyes, much like the alligators Mutterl and Borborigmi used to take me to see on our occasional expeditions to the Bronx Park zoo.

Above, arrowheads of geese were already commencing their weary course southward from the Arctic tundra belt. Ducks scooted across the marshes, wings beating upon the chilly air with only the shadow of a sound. Beaver and mink scuttled along the banks and, in the bush, tubby black bears scooped pin cherries from the trees while partridge pecked at the late seasonal berries. At night, in anguish, rutting moose screamed to each other beneath a cold moon.

Tawis told me how the northern Ojibways trapped unwary martins and laid wire snares for wolves. He showed me how to call up moose through a horn made of rolled tar paper. He whistled back to the mocking Canada jays which all the men knew as whisky jacks.

One Saturday Tawis said to me: "You look something like Indian to me, kid. Like Indian you can live and think as something other. You can live and think as deer, fish, heron. You can live and think as moose call. You not just human. You part everything. You sure you not part Indian? Like Vincent," he said with a sour look.

"No, I am not just human, I am a primate. I am only an Indian because I am Aryan. I have a certificate that proves it. But I have the ambitions and beliefs of other things as well. Maybe a heron or a fish."

"Okay kid. I don't understand. You Aryan Indian come with me tomorrow and I take you our Ojibway Indian encampment. Nobody know tribe there. We moving south. Winter come soon and we have games before we leave."

So, early next morning, he took me off in our usual fishing canoe, which had an outboard motor, and we glided miles down the lake. On the shore of a small bay, wholly cut off from view in this desolate, uninhabited area, we disembarked. I strode through tangled roots and swamp, following in Tawis Geejumnin's footsteps, until we broke through a screen of alder trees into a flat place ringed by branch and tar paper shacks and canvas teepees. Canoes were hidden under the alders. Everybody seemed to be drinking moonshine corn. "Here we make rodeo," said Tawis.

To my astonishment the tribe had not only assembled several scrawny-looking horses but also some steers and young bulls. They had built a corral and a chute where riders climbed aboard their animals before they were released. "You Indian, you ride," said Tawis drunkenly. I clambered on a bony steer and managed to stay on him by walking swiftly, my long legs straddling him on each side, while he bucked up and down between them. "Hah! Hah! Hah!" the Ojibways screamed hoarsely. An old man, all bowed over and his neck stiff from boozing came over and clapped me on the back.

Tawis took me to a cage of thick logs set around a pit dug down to water level and in which stood two sullen, savage bears. "Very fierce," he said. "This where we put our enemies. Keepers see they never eat enough. So eat people we don't like. One day Vincent end up here." His eyes gleamed darkly. "Him and his tapeworm. Him got tapeworm ten foot long."

I asked him why he and Vincent hated each other so. "Hah," he grunted. "He didn't like it when I called him a breed. But he's a half-breed, that's all."

"That's what I am. Tawis," I pointed out. "Negro, Jew. And Herrenvolk."

"What's hearin' folk?"

"The lordly people."

"But Vincent was angry because I called him part red Indian. Surely we are the lordly people."

"Maybe. But the whites killed almost all of you. I read about it in school. Maybe Vincent wanted to be white in order to survive."

One of the fellows who shared our bunk was a bald Ukrainian named Smielnicki. I never did like him much and one day, when we were in the shower at the same time, I saw him staring hard at my middle. Finally he couldn't contain his curiosity. "Vat's dat?" he asked, pointing at my short vestigial tail. "Oh, that. It's a tail. You see, I'm a primate."

"Vat you mean you a primate? I primate. I primate of Ukrainian Church for Podkarpatskaya. Vat kind of primate you be?"

"I don't know, Mr. Smielnicki. I'm just an ordinary primate I guess. Not really a human they say. If you're a primate, where's your tail?"

Smielnicki snickered. "Haw, haw," he sneered. "I show you." With this he sidled up to me and made a grab. But he wasn't grabbing for my tail. He got the front section instead and began to pump it.

"Listen, Mr. Smielnicki, you've got it ass backwards. Or ass forwards."

"Don' gif me none dat stuff, Curly. You like what I do? Da? You pretty big for chust young boy. Da? Bogami, I don't want tail."

"Bugger me? Bugger me, you say? I warn you as one primate to another."

Smielnicki continued, unruffled, muttering: "I will wring your . . ."

"This hurts you more than it hurts me," I said, bonking his cranium so hard with my right hand that it fllattened out like a mushmelon. He said nothing. He just slipped to his knee, rolled over on his face and stayed there.

Right then Tawis Geejumnin came in. "Hey, kid, you plenty trouble now," he muttered. "You come with me. Quick. Get dressed, take your money. I hide this fairy bastard in oat bin. He got donkey nature anyhow." So saying he picked up the late primate, slung him over his shoulder, and walked out into the night.

When I was dressed Tawis waved to me. There was nobody around. It was Saturday night. Many of the Finns and Poles had gone to Kapuskasing. Most of the others were in the clubroom, listening to the radio or playing cards. There was a log fire by the landing where Tawis had drawn up his canoe.

I followed him down there and, as we pulled the boat

into the water, one of the Norwegians stood up by the flames. "Where are you two going?" he asked drunkenly. Tawis saw a frying pan full of fat where someone had been cooking bacon. He hurled the grease into the fire so it exploded in the dazed Norwegian's face, immobilizing him for several moments. Then we shoved off.

"Keep mouth shut now," he warned. He drew out a hunting knife and before I knew what he was up to, sliced a long gash in my left forearm. "See," he said. "Don't hurt much. But if any questions you bad injure and I taking you Kapuskasing go hospital. You say nothing. I answer all questions. You just let me be doctoring."

He flicked the engine rope and off we putted over the greasy surface of the Lake of the Poplar Islands.

CHAPTER III

B y the time we finally reached town in the snub-
nosed boat Tawis commandeered, I began to
calm down. The Indian had taken a torn towel
from the train and wrapped it around my arm, then
squeezed it hard enough to soak the bandage in blood. I
guess I must have looked pretty bad and, when we drew up
at the sawmill, I was ready to play the part of a badly
injured, frightened youngster.

There was a man standing on the jetty, a sturdy fellow
with leather bindings around his legs, dark pants, a gray
shirt, and a broad hat whose top was pinched in from four
directions. He had a silver badge glittering on his chest.

"You Curly von Snarl?" the man asked.

I looked at him. Then I looked around for Tawis. He
had vanished.

"Royal Canadian Mounted Police," said the man.
"We've been searching for you. Lucky to find you that
easy. There's a man here to see you."

Good God, I thought. Everything is against me. Where's my Mutterl? Now they'll get me for Ump and also on that charge by Mildred. And for running away. "I am no baby," I said. "But I cannot go up against you for I respect the law."

"What's the matter, kid? Oh, the affair in New York? Don't worry. It's been dropped. The girl withdrew her complaint. Says you're too young to do anything anyway. Doesn't look like that to me, though. As for the coach, judge called it accidental manslaughter. That's another way of saying justified homicide. Black judge, wasn't it?"

I thought I hadn't looked too young to Mr. Smielnicki either. I hoped Tawis Geejumnin would get him out of that oat bin before he was found by a drunken Finn. Mr. Smielnicki would make a fine dinner for those Ojibway bears. I wondered if there was a black judge in Kapuskasing. More likely Ukrainian.

But it didn't seem the Mounted Police knew anything about the other primate. On the contrary, this policeman was very friendly. "Call me Jack," he suggested. "What'd you do to your arm, pal? You ought to get sewn up at the hospital." He took me there in his car, with the siren blaring loud although there weren't any other autos in sight and the street was broad and empty.

While a young doctor in a white smock was stitching me like Mutterl making Borborigmi's tiger stool, a short, pudgy man, badly in need of a shave, came in puffing the wet end of an unlit cigar. He didn't ask permission and he didn't say anything, just chewed the dead butt. Later I found he was a nonsmoker. When the last stitch had been snipped off, he said: "Abe Saperstein. I've come to get you. Plane O.K. Take off in the morning. This goddamn field is for the birds. Birds, yeah, not moths. Not enough light to attract a moth."

Mr. Saperstein took me and Jack to a large, swell hotel where he bought Jack a whisky and me a Coca-Cola. "This is the real article," said Jack approvingly. "Aged in the keg." Then he said goodbye—"Look after your arm, pal"—and the two of us went to a suite upstairs and ate large steaks. "I used to weigh a hunnert ten," said Mr. Saperstein, rubbing his bulging belly. "Now look at me."

I was very interested to know why Mr. Saperstein had come all the way to Kapuskasing looking for me and finally I said so. "First of all," he replied, "stop calling me mister. The whole world knows me as Abe. Second of all, I run the Harlem Globetrotters and we're going on a tour. I need you."

I said I didn't know what the Harlem Globetrotters were and he looked amazed. "Well, well, well. And a New Yorker too. From Harlem. And with a rep as a player himself. Hmm. Listen, kid, the Harlem Globetrotters are the finest damn bunch of basketball players in the whole wide world. The whole world. And we're going on a world tour. And you're going with us.

"Ya think I come up here for pleasure? Well, let me tell ya I din't. I come up here when I read in the papers your case had blown over. I put out tracers for ya because ya had somewhat of a name already. See? And when that fellow Leezer said he'd told ya to come to Canada, the police sent a message to the Mounties. They put out tracers too. Now here ya are and here I is.

"Brother, I wouldna believed it. How old are ya now? Thirteen, ya say. Well ya must be almost eight feet high. And still growing. Wow! How much do ya weigh, because you ain't skinny neither? Two hunnert fifty? Wow! Wow again! Ya really got some muscles in them arms. And what a neck. What legs. Wow again!

"Now lemme tell ya something, kid. I got permission from ya school principal, Parsnip, to take ya along wit us. In return I promised we'd keep a good eye on ya."

"Oh, if Mr. Parsnip said so why of course I'll go along. How about the Spruce Falls company though?"

"Forget it. What they don't know won't hurt 'em. Ain't ya innerested in what we pay ya?"

"You mean I get paid for playing basketball?"

"Sure ya gets paid. Fifty bucks a week an all expenses. But tell me. It's true yer a Negro, ain't it?"

"Oh, yes, Mr. Sap—Abe—my grandma was from the Oorlog Hereros and my Vati was the highest ranking Negro in the SS."

"What ya mean, SS? Ya must be crazy, kid. Now don't ya ever mention that word again. Not in New York. Not around my Globetrotters. They're all black and they'd kill ya. Not nowheres to nobody. See?"

"All right, Abe. I'll try and remember. But certainly I'm colored. I'm also Jewish, through my Mutterl. And I was born in an SS ..."

"Ya just forget that word. Starting right now. I'd be murdered if that leaks. But I sure am glad yer black, boy. Ya see, all my players is black. Anyone plays ball as good as you is black. No matter what his color. I decide who's black and who ain't. Got it?"

"Oh, yes sir. I see. And I'll be proud to be a member of your squad. Can I see my Mutterl first, when we get back? Does she know all about this?"

"Yep. Parsnip put me on ta her and she's delighted. But tell me, boy, who's that little creep with her? The broad-nosed one. He's even shorter than I am."

"Oh, that is Borborigmi. He's my stepfather and my coach."

Next morning my arm was feeling pretty good and we had a fine breakfast with Abe's assistant, a man named Dave Zinkoff. Zinkoff paid the bill and drove with us to the airfield. It really was a field, grass everywhere. There we three got aboard a plane.

I'd never flown before and I clung to the seat with both hands when we took off. I hadn't needed to do that because even without a safety belt I was jammed in so tight that a nice young lady who came down the aisle to look us over asked if I had used a shoehorn.

On the trip Abe and Dave explained to me that the Trotters weren't just star basketball players. They played the game for laughs. They knew all kinds of tricks. Some of them could shoot baskets sitting down. Others specialized in doing it from piggyback. I'd have to learn my own specialty and they'd think something up. But there wasn't much time. Our tour was starting pretty soon and we intended to visit more than thirty countries.

From then on I was prouder than before to live in Harlem. Borborigmi used to come around each day when we were practicing and listen carefully as Abe, who had once been a player himself, if almost a midget, taught me to spin a basketball for half a minute on my fingertip and how to give it so much backspin that it would bounce right back if you threw it across a room. To Mutterl's fury, Borbo made me do this twenty times a night in our own little parlor. "Practice makes perfect," he would say. "Just shooting baskets is not going to take him anywhere."

All the fellows on the squad were very friendly and they treated me like their son. They were delighted that, because of my tail, I had to wear two jockstraps, one covering the rear. And gee, they were good. There was Goose Tatum and Sweetwater Clifton and Rookie Brown and Babe Pressly, Joshua Grider and J. C. Gibson and Pop Gates.

Every day I'd form an eight-man circle with this group and, while the others watched, we'd whip the ball around at each other while a loud phonograph played "Sweet Georgia Brown." I got as good as the others soon. Borborigmi told me he had a hard time following the ball, it moved so fast.

Of course, none of them was nearly as tall as me. But they were real artists. Goose would sometimes take his foul shots bouncing the ball off his head. He could drop-kick it through the hoop from the middle of a court. He was only six foot three but I'll swear his arms were nearly as long as mine. He was always teasing the spectators, borrowing their hats without asking then shooting a basket, or grabbing the spectacles off an onlooker's nose and handing them to the referee when he disagreed with his decision.

Before I joined, the tallest men on the squad were Tarzan Spencer and J. C. Gibson who thought they were big at six foot eight. Tarzan and J. C. were famous for their jump shots. Sweetwater Clifton was six foot six. Abe had built most of his plays around these three and not even the Celtics, the team against which we played most often and which worked with us on the global tour, were able to hold them when they got going.

But now Saperstein decided he'd develop a brand-new strategy focussing around me. I was billed as Curly Snarl, the Boy Monster, "Look at him and watch him grow." The fans had used to holler "Go, Go, Go" at the Trotters when they wanted a score. After they'd got used to me they changed this to "Grow, Grow, Grow." I don't know why but this delighted Dave Zinkoff almost as much as Borbo.

I got to really understand the game. When to switch, when not. When to pass, when to hold the ball. When to help out, when to shoot. Dave helped Abe dream up some joke plays for me. I'd chew a big wad of gum and then, standing by the basket, I'd take a pass and drop the ball into the hoop. That was billed as my dump shot. But sometimes before I received it I'd slip the gum into my hand and the ball would stick to it instead of falling through.

Other times I'd lie down on the floor beneath the backboard and then get up slowly when there was a scramble for the ball, if somebody failed to score. I'd stand, stretch, and then just reach over, grab it, drop it in, lie down again and pretend to go to sleep. Still, other times I'd just pick off the ball from the basket and, instead of making an easy goal, hand it down to one of the six-foot shrimps and watch him while he registered, clapping my big hands as the net swished.

All this went down fine with the crowd. Borborigmi would explain these plays in detail to Mutterl but she didn't understand a thing, just shook her head slowly, saying, "School's where my baby ought to be, not being paid to make a fool of himself."

When we took off from Idlewild Airport in May, Dave had completed the arrangements for our tour. He had shipped a seven-ton hardwood floor, split up in sections, to be used in European cities where they had no basketball courts. He had bought two large buses and sent them to Marseilles to carry us around with our baggage.

Each of us was allowed only eighty-eight pounds, and Saperstein insisted I include some schoolbooks in my allotment because he had promised this to Mr. Parsnip. So I took only two pairs of shoes instead of three like the others. My shoes weighed more. Also, as Zinkoff pointed out, I was still growing and by the time we got to Egypt or Asia I could have another couple pair made overnight as soon as my swelling feet were measured.

We played in France; we played in Germany; we played in Italy. When we were in Rome, two months out of New York, Dave fixed it up for us to see the Pope at Castel Gandolfo, out in the Alban Hills. We gave him a basketball all of us had signed. Then the eight of us who passed the ball best, whistled "Sweet Georgia Brown" and zipped it around in front of the pale old man who sat tapping his foot in rhythm with the tune. "I don't know much," said Goose Tatum as we drove back into town, "but I'll bet that little pointy-head never had a black-Nazi-Jew like you, Snarler boy, banging around in front of him before."

We played in Greece, where they had to hose water over

the baking August asphalt on the court, until it rained and we then played in bare feet. We played in Egypt and in the Philippines and Singapore. When we went back home Abe said he was proudest of everything when Mr. Parsnip told him I'd passed my exams and was moving up from junior high school. But I stayed with the team, refusing basketball scholarships at Yale, Stanford, Osceola and Bob Jones University.

I got to be so much a part of the team that Abe took me on our second Grand Tour and that's where the trouble started. That year Saperstein got ahold of Wilt Chamberlain, the seven-foot-two Kansas University boy who liked to be called the Dipper. And that year, also, we revisited Egypt where Colonel Nasser had taken formal charge and bounced our old host, General Naguib. But when we reached Cairo there were headlines in a newspaper, *Al Ahram,* saying: "Jews Who Call Themselves Black."

What was that all about? Well, someone had worked on Nasser, who'd been clobbered two years earlier in a war, and the paper said: "A Jew by any other name is still a Jew. Curly Snarl claims to be a black and he stupidly also claims to be a Nazi. But the truth is that his mother's an Israeli agent."

"Well, well, well," said Saperstein when all this was translated to him after the first game we'd ever played where we were booed. The crowd had hollered "Schmo, Schmo, Schmo," not "Go, Go, Go," or "Grow, Grow, Grow" every time I took the floor. "They know I'm a Jew," said Abe. "And they know Zinkoff is a Jew. Why the hell pick on you, kid?"

"But I can't fight it. There's something behind all this and the ambassador has told me they got plans to boycott us in all them Moslem countries. I've got to make back fifty thou we paid out already, kid, so I guess we better send ya over to Parsnip. He says anyway we owe ya a real education and there's a wide field to pick from. Maybe ya'd get more dough from Osceola but Parsnip votes for Yale. He claims it's better known.

"How the hell do I know, Curly? But I think the time has come. You ain't getting any taller. Guess eight foot six is high enough. Old Wilt there can handle the plays you been featuring; even if he is a dwarf. And you won't lose by it. Tony Lavelli's a pretty fair forward; yet he went to Yale."

"But that's not fair, Abe," I protested. "I can prove I'm from the Lebensborn. Mutterl has my Sippenbuch. Do you think the SS coddled Jewboy niggers?"

"Yeah, you're the living proof of that, kid. As rare as a basketball with tits. Beats the hell out of me but you're it. They got something on ya I don't know about. Me and Zinkoff, why they just say we're descended from the Lost Ten Tribes so we're O.K. We're not like you. We can't produce Nazi certificates saying we're pure Aryans. But when someone starts out on ya, the game's up. Next thing ya know they'll be challenging the color of your black grandma. Then you'll even be cooked in Harlem."

"But Abe," I said, "I've got all the documents. Mutterl even has a Himmler paper. Where is the liberty, equality and fraternity that you and Mr. Parsnip talk about?"

I suppose that just wasn't my lucky year. I stopped growing. Chamberlain came on board and he was big enough to handle my plays. The Arabs took out after me. Abe was financially in the hole but he was such a decent guy I felt he had begun to waver. Then there was another *Al Ahram* headline: "Zionist Agent Involved in Canadian Murder." And what was that?

Dave got a girl from the embassy to type out a translation. It said, as I remember: "An Indian suspected of pro-Israel sympathies has just been arrested on a charge of murder in the Canadian province of Northern Ontario. Tawis Geejumnin, often referred to as Davy Goy-killer, has been taken into custody in the long unsolved Smiel-

nicki case. Taras Smielnicki, a Ukrainian priest, had been
sent on a cultural tour of North America by the Moscow
Ministry of Religious Affairs.

"Geejumnin is an Indian version of 'Goy-Bumper'
which means Christian-slayer in Yiddish slang. Smielnicki disappeared near Kapuskasing a few years ago. It is
notable that Smielnicki was believed to be investigating
anti-Soviet plots in the emigration. His disappearance
more or less coincided with that of Curly Snarl, the well-
known American basketball player and pro-Zionist, who
is now in Cairo with a so-called black team called Harlem
Globetrotters.

"Snarl, to mask his Israeli ties, even has the effrontery
to boast of his high connections with the late Adolf
Hitler's National Socialist Party. It is reported the Goy-
killer has made a full confession to the Royal Canadian
Mounted Police. Ottawa is understood to have asked the
authorities of the United Arab Republic to make further
inquiries concerning the said Curly Snarl in order to as-
certain whether he played any role in the alleged murder
of the innocent priest."

"There is more," the girl said. "About his sexual habits.
It does not translate well into English."

"Whew," said Abe. "That's torn it." At Zinkoff's sugges-
tion he took me over to the U.S. Embassy and asked for
my protection. The embassy said they couldn't do anything officially. But it just so happened the Portuguese
Government had requested the State Department to send
a delegation of athletes, preferably part white and part
black, to their overseas province of Mozambique in order
to help sell racial peace.

Lisbon wanted to stress that all "civilized" peoples
could live happily together as brothers. Our ambassador
was ready to certify me as "civilized," of mixed blood,
and sufficiently near the area in question to save the State
Department money if it should decide I might be a useful

(35)

propaganda asset. He also said I was big enough to be considered a "delegation." He cabled Washington, adding that the Portuguese ship *Torres Vedras* was in Port Said and proceeding down the East African coast two days hence.

Dave Zinkoff was allowed to drive to Port Said with me and a U.S. Marine from the embassy, wearing civilian clothes. I took my 88-pound Trotters bag of belongings and was placed in the care of Senhor Mario Cunhal, captain of the *Torres Vedras*, a down-at-heels vessel loaded with machinery for Beira and Lourenço Marques.

We idled through the Suez Canal, which was baking hot. Then we stopped briefly at Djibouti, in French Somaliland, and again at Moroni on the French island of Grande Comore. We spent some time in Moroni, and Senhor Cunhal took me ashore with him to swim and eat while the seedy port serviced his ship with water, fresh fruit, dried fish and other stores.

Grande Comore is a large island with small, seeping volcanoes whose chocolate-colored lava inches imperceptibly over the jungles down to the sea, past coconut, banana, pepper and vanilla farms. I didn't know what language the filthy population was speaking but the captain seemed able to make himself easily understood in Portuguese.

The first afternoon we left the *Torres Vedras*, Senhor Cunhal invited me to a restaurant in Moroni. He ordered dinner and then took me on a long walk to give them time to catch, clean and cook fish for us. While we were trudging on a path through the jungle, the dusk suddenly descended. Huge fruit bats with bodies as large as rabbits and wings almost a yard wide came wheeling out of the sky to hang upside down in trees, attached to branches by their claws. Maroon-colored birds flopped by vanilla plants as the sun slid through them into the sea.

Senhor Cunhal had a large drink before dinner, something he called absinthe, which turned milk-colored when he put pieces of ice in it. First he told me about his long and adventurous life and travels. Then he began to ask me questions as they brought us a fish called wahoo.

"I don't understand why your embassy in Cairo ordered you out and placed you aboard my ship. Simply because you're Jewish. For all I know I may be Jewish too. Almost everyone in Portugal is. Anyway, it is obvious that David Zinkoff who brought you to Port Said is very much a Jew. Yet he is of the party left behind."

"Oh, yes, Mr. Cunhal. Dave is a Jew. But he and Abe Saperstein are supposed to be from the Lost Ten Tribes."

"That makes a difference to the Arabs?"

"Yes, Mr. Cunhal. They like anything that's lost."

"But if you're Jewish, then how are you a Negro? I thought yours was a Negro athletic team."

"Yes, of course it is. All the Trotters are black. And so am I. My grandma was a Herero from South West Africa."

"Oh. Then your grandfather Snarl was Jewish. And your father is half and half?"

"No sir. It is my Mutterl who is half Jewish. My father, who died the death of a war hero, was the highest-ranking Negro officer in Hitler's Waffen SS."

"A Negro in the SS! Why that is impossible."

"Oh, no. And my mother, who is just as much Jewish as Vati was black, produced me in an SS Lebensborn clinic."

"You mean the free love hospices where the SS made Aryan babies?"

"Yes, that's it. Perhaps that is one reason I am so big. We were supposed to be Herrenvolk, the lordly people."

"Well, well, well. Now I've seen it all. So you are a Nazi assimilated into the Negro and Jewish communities. This is assimilation in reverse of how we Portuguese understand it."

"What do you mean Senhor Cunhal?"

"Well, as you will learn in Mozambique, my boy, we

have our own way of handling racial matters. Not that there's any problem. That is the basis of our policy.

"You see, our law makes no distinction between Mozambique and the provinces of Portugal itself. They are just far away from each other. And our law makes no distinction between the white people, black people, brown people, Indian people, Chinese people and Malgache people, who live in Mozambique. They are all equal. Except they all have to prove they are civilisado, which means civilized, or assimilado, which means assimilated. This is easy for the whites because they are automatically certified by their color. But there aren't many whites."

"I don't understand," I said. "Why aren't the others civilized or assimilated? And what does it matter if they aren't?"

"Well, to be assimilated you first have to prove that you are civilized. And to be civilized you have to be educated. But to be educated it is far easier to get admitted to a school if you are already accepted as assimilated. As for what it means, you can't get a decent job or live in a decent house or even eat in a decent restaurant if you aren't both civilized and assimilated."

"How does one know? Do they wear a sign?"

"The trouble is one doesn't know. I confess I know many people in Lourenço Marques who have white skins and dirty characters. But they have the power to say who is civilized and who isn't."

"Oh, it's like in Germany. Mutterl tells me the Führer could decide who was an honorary Aryan."

"Such as the Japanese," sneered Senhor Cunhal.

"Yes, that's so. Like me, too, I guess. And like my Vati and my Mutterl. But they helped their position with false papers. That's what Father did. He was very clever. A Kerl, Mutterl used to say. That's where I got my name of Curly. Not from my hair."

"I see," and the captain nodded his head and called for

another absinthe. "I'd offer you one of these, Curly, but I don't think it would be good for you. It's illegal, even in France. Too strong. And it makes your prick shrivel up. And it's like putting a thief in your own mouth to steal your brains.

"But I want to drink your health. You have shown me a formula that may yet save Portugal from its folly. If we civilize the whites and assimilate them among the blacks, why then there won't be any problem. We must make Mozambique a nation of Curly Snarls. Then everyone will be happy."

"Oh, no, Senhor Cunhal. By the time that happens, they will find something else wrong. Also, like me. The Germans were always worried that I mightn't be pure white. The Americans worried that I had an SS certificate of origin. The Jews didn't like me being black and now all the other black Trotters are applauded in Cairo but I'm thrown out because I'm Jewish."

"Yes, that is a very interesting problem you pose to the world, my boy. And Mr. Saperstein and Mr. Zinkoff are approved by everyone because they stem from the Lost Ten Tribes of Israel—which probably never existed. The way to exist in this world, Curly, is to prove you don't exist."

CHAPTER IV

S enhor Cunhal told me if I wished to appear
civilisado in Lourenço Marques I must stay in the
Hotel Girasol, so since I had two thousand dollars
in traveller's checks saved from my Trotters pay, I moved
into that curious round building. Then I went to a shop
and bought the largest pair of socks available (which were
too small), the largest shirt (which was all right at the
neck but nowhere else) and two ties, one bright blue and
one bright red. I didn't have much to wear in my basketball bag.

Then I had a taxi take me to the American Consulate
where the consul, a nice soft-spoken man named Kidd,
received me pleasantly. He told me he had nothing else to
do and that someone in the Cairo embassy had sent him a
message to expect me.

Unfortunately, he added, the propaganda scheme in
which I was to figure had been called off. The U.S. Congress had, as usual, reduced the State Department's

budget. There wasn't enough money left to finance the display of my civilized, multiracial qualities. The Portuguese had indeed been interested in the idea, but not so interested that they wished to pay for it themselves. They were too commercial to actually pay for civilization.

Mr. Kidd said he hardly ever saw an American face, except when sailors jumped ship or got into trouble with the police over bar fights. Therefore he would be glad to have me for dinner in the evening, together with his own wife and that of the vice-consul who was away. They would come by my hotel to pick me up and take me to a restaurant along the shore. Meantime he would devote some thought to suggestions about what I should do with myself.

We went to a pleasant open-air place under spreading trees, with soft waves rolling in below us, and ate very peppery shrimps that Mr. Kidd called piri-piri. Mrs. Kidd explained the other guest's husband was out shooting. Both he and Mr. Kidd loved killing things. They belonged to an organization called World Wild Life which preserved game so there was more to kill.

Mr. Kidd shot nothing but big animals, which he killed for the Smithsonian Institution in Washington. The vice-consul shot nothing but birds, which he killed for the Museum of Natural History in New York. The Institute and the Museum paid their expenses, including ammunition, and helped finance the cost of preparing skins and other trophies for display.

This made an ideal arrangement, she said. Mr. Kidd would go off for two weeks as soon as the vice-consul returned. Then, when his next hunt ended, his assistant would return to the field. It kept them both busy. Each looked after the other's wife when her husband was away. There wasn't enough work for two men at the consulate so the State Department, which didn't know that fact and received enough reports to remain content, seemed pleased with the system. The two consuls had requested a second tour of duty which they were now serving together.

The ladies were interested in me. They said they had never seen anyone so large. I told them about my unusual family and at first they thought I was joking. Then Mrs. Kidd remembered that when she was in Germany right after the war, visiting her father, an army officer, she had seen Trabzi of Trabzon. So now she believed everything I told her. It gave us a kind of mutual bond, like being related.

From then on all three kept firing questions at me. I told them a lot about the Globetrotters, about Mutterl and Borborigmi, about Vati and the Schumpeters, and also about my Oorlog Herero grandma. I didn't say a word about Mildred or Ump or Kapuskasing or the primate. I was beginning to learn there are some things you don't talk about.

I had never spoken so much, except perhaps to Borbo, and I got to feeling pleased with myself, having drunk three cokes. So I was startled when Mr. Kidd brought me back to reality and the fact that I had no idea of what to do or where.

"You know, Curly," he said, "the U.S. Government never gives us money to pay for a passage home by citizens temporarily stranded in foreign places. Although your case is different from the down-and-outer seamen who get dumped on my doorstep, and I know from what Jane says that your mother would happily pay us back, I can't advance you money for an airplane ticket. And you might have to wait a long time before you got passage on any ship heading even approximately in your direction. Of course you are fortunate to have two thousand dollars in traveller's checks. But that kind of money doesn't last here very long.

"So I have an idea. There's a train to Johannesburg in

South Africa. If you go to Johannesburg I am sure our people—and I will call them—can help you get on a plane for South West Africa. I know the name von Snarl is still held in high repute there although the Afrikaners have been in charge more than forty years. I believe your family is still involved in the brewing operation. Therefore they must be prosperous.

"It would certainly please them to meet their American relative. They are in a position to help you out. If I were you, I'd take a chance and go. You don't really have much to lose. You'd probably have to go to South Africa anyway to find transport back to the States. And I guess you must have some kind of sentimental feeling about seeing your kinsfolk and where you came from.

"As for me, I'm certain I can get you a visa. You just leave your passport with me. Also that document proving you were created in a Lebensborn institution devoted to producing Aryan babies. Aryan babies are much in favor with the South Africans. I'll have a photostat made of your Sippenbuch. I recommend you always keep it with your passport in your pocket once you get there."

"Gee, Mr. Kidd," I said. "That's a wonderful idea. I've never met any member of my family but Mutterl. I sure would like to go there. And maybe I can see the Ka-okoveld and visit my Oorlog Herero relatives."

"Well, maybe," he replied with doubt in his voice. "But I shouldn't think the von Snarls will go out of their way to help on that. I wouldn't mention it to them until the end of your stay. Oh, and by the way. You bring over your passport and that SS paper first thing in the morning. No, it would be better not to take it to the South Africans yourself. They are strange people. You never can tell what kind of impression they'll get. In your case it's better to leave things in my hands."

I was very excited when I woke up early next morning. Mr. Kidd had said I could come at eight o'clock so I did, bringing the papers. He said he'd get in touch with me next day. If I didn't hear from him by noon I should ask the man at the hotel desk to call. We shook hands. I squeezed his so hard by way of thanks that he winced with pain. Then I started to walk back to the Girasol.

On the way I saw a small open-air coffee shop where they were also selling pastry like the jam tarts at our old lumber camp. I went in, ordered one with a large cup of coffee (pointing at what I wanted) and sat down to watch the people pass. But the people stopped passing. They just stood in a crowd that got larger and larger and their mouths gaped as they watched me. I got all red in the face as I sometimes do. Mutterl calls it a flush and says it proves I have lots of von Snarl and Schumpeter blood even if my skin isn't exactly pink.

At first I didn't pay much attention. I fingered the fuzzy beard I was starting to grow. Then I realized they had never seen anything like me. Finally a chocolate-colored young man came up and asked if he could sit down. "I am studying English," he said in very good English, "and I can tell from your clothes that you are American. Will you talk with me?" I didn't know if he meant my Harlem clothes or my Mozambique clothes. Yet he wanted to know what I was doing in Lourenço Marques so I told him. I explained I had been sent here for a job that had never worked out. Now I was waiting to go to South Africa and then on to South West, which is where some of my family came from.

"Afrikaners?" he inquired.

"No. Part German and part Herero." This interested him so I explained.

"But you have no way of knowing if your father's family still exists or, if it still exists, whether it will help you? No, well, perhaps I can give you an idea. You will permit ...?" Then he signalled to another young man, dressed in torn pants, torn shirt and torn leather sandals. "I am

João," he said. "And this is my friend Joaquim.

"I am civilisado. I am even assimilado. But Joaquim is indigena. He is considered a native but I am considered Portuguese. We each play our part. The Portuguese like this kind of game and we find it quite amusing. I am supposed to do everything like a white man. Joaquim is supposed to do everything like a black man. So officially we hate each other."

João ordered me another coffee and then he bought two glasses of red wine for Joaquim and himself. "Joaquim," he said, "is my cousin. He speaks MaRonga and Shangaan. I speak Shangaan, Portuguese and English. Together we can help you. For our family is famous for its shikwembos. Shikwembo is soothsayer, witch doctor. Have you ever seen a witch doctor?"

"Not exactly. But I knew a sorceress once. Her name was Inez. She got into trouble with the police for casting spells."

"Quite so. The police are always making trouble for shikwembos too. But we have a relative who still practices. Her name is Mahigo and she lives in the jungle to keep away from the police. It is a long time since we have seen her. We could take you there if you like. Mahigo will tell you if it is wise for you to go to South Africa and South West. It will not cost you anything and it will give us pleasure. We have nothing to do. Joaquim speaks her language. I can translate from Shangaan into English. For you it might prove interesting. For us it will be fun."

João had a rickety Ford and drove us out of the city, down a sliding sand road through manioc plantations until we left the cleared country and began to go from one patch of thick jungle to another, passing through low underbrush areas in between. He let Joaquim drive as soon as we were well away from Lourenço Marques. "Now," he said, "no one will see to criticize him as an *indigena* for driving. And this way I can talk to you more easily."

He explained that for as many generations as anyone could remember, his family had always boasted at least one shikwembo. For some reason no one understood these were always women. The majority of shikwembos are usually men.

The greatest of his family's shikwembos had lived several generations ago and was named Mwagulane. She was famous all through southern Africa. People used to make long long journeys to consult her. She knew much about love and had sex potions. She was also especially known for her ability to exhort demons and to apply long-range curses. She was famous for the high prices she charged —and it was risky to default on payments. But she never failed to carry out promised commissions. Mahigo was a direct descendant and had an excellent reputation. Like her ancestors, she too knew much about love.

João wasn't sure just where his esteemed cousin was working. He had not seen her in many months, so we stopped off at a village called Shamankulu to consult another soothsayer, named Mafumo, on her whereabouts. Mafumo was an ordinary, modest practitioner, an Inyanga who deciphered the occult by throwing bones. He had a bad left eye, a wispy mustache and a practical business sense. He made Joaquim put ten escudos on a low table before he went to work.

Mafumo was sitting on the floor in his undershirt. As soon as he had verified the payment, biting each coin thoughtfully, he opened the wicker basket where he kept his equipment and took out a divining stick, some flat bone chips with holes in them, two old dice, several seashells and a bunch of wild goats' teeth bound by wire. He made a pattern of these objects scattered around him. Then he leaned forward and shook the dice exactly like the older boys at Ben Franklin High. Suddenly he began to mumble.

"That is Shangaan," said João. "I understand. He says

Mahigo is near Mefalalla. It is a village not far from here. She has been there only a short while. Her magic told her the police were looking for her in the place she used to work."

We all said goodbye to Mafumo and thanked him for his speedy, efficient help. Then we piled into the Ford and drove off for Mefalalla. This proved to be a tiny hamlet, even smaller than Shamankulu, with just a few houses made of branches and woven reeds. When we asked for the shikwembo an expressionless old man pointed toward the surrounding jungle. He murmured a few words to Joaquim who led the way into the underbrush.

We found a well-hidden path at the end of a sandy alley. We followed this through tangles of trees and bushes and past occasional cashew orchards. Once or twice we passed small clearings surrounded by palisades and filled with corn patches with ten-foot stalks. There was a sweet smell which João told me was fermenting cashew wine.

After a sweaty walk of more than an hour we came to another clearing containing five cassava trees and a neat wood and reed hut. Mahigo was lying on a mat in the shade watching her small, very black grandchildren throwing sand at baby chickens. Two of her daughters, Maria and Isabel, were sitting with her, talking in low voices. Both of them wore headscarves and all three wore colored blouses and skirts.

Mahigo was very friendly. She embraced Joaquim and João and shook hands warmly with me. She was a large woman, rather elderly but vigorous, with a bald spot in her close-shaven peppercorn hair, and generous, unrestrained breasts. She had an oddly penetrating, curiously female animal odor about her. It was strange: an ugly old lady, she made me stir.

"I knew you were coming," said Mahigo in MaRonga which Joaquim translated into Shangaan and which João then translated into English. "I could see you. First you visited Mafumo. Yes?"

I was astonished. I glanced around to see if there was a telephone wire. My two friends were not surprised.

Mahigo said she was prepared to foretell the future or to cast spells, and would do anything I wished out of respect for her cousins. But, she explained, the greater part of her work was devoted to curing aches, pains and fevers with various herb concoctions. She was also very good at setting broken bones. Each treatment was accompanied by prayers addressed to the god Kulukumba and to the spirits of her ancestors, the Unguluve, especially the previous shikwembos. "I can be either Tagati, and bad, or Sangoma, and good," she explained.

She then asked my two friends to explain in detail just who I was and what I wanted. While they did this, she eyed me speculatively, as if trying to read my mind, interpret my past actions, assess my qualities, before getting down to the prediction business. She glanced briefly at my palms and scratched the earth.

Finally, after an hour squatting in the hot sun, João turned to me and said: "My kinswoman now wants to be left alone with you. She has asked Joaquim and me to go off into the jungle with Maria and Isabel. We are to come back when she sends for us. It will be some time. She has means of letting us know. And you need not fear anything.

"She does not know your language any more than I know hers, for I cannot understand MaRonga. But she knows how to transmit her own ideas and to understand yours. After all, that is what language is for, is it not? So we will now say goodbye. Later, when we come back, we can tell you whatever Mahigo decides we should tell you. Now, good luck, Curly."

I watched as Maria and Isabel herded their children before them and walked out into the underbrush, flouncing their pretty behinds, followed by Joaquim and

João. I wondered if Maria and Isabel were the reasons for their wish to make this lengthy trip.

Mahigo turned and beckoned me into the hut. It was quite cool and pleasant in the dark shadows. I had to bend over almost to my hips and finally, following her instructions, I lay down on a reed mat which was smooth and comfortable.

Then, paying no attention to me, Mahigo prepared herself for the consultation. She carefully picked out of a cardboard box a necklace that seemed to be of fragile snake vertebrae and thrust her head gently through it. She rubbed some ochre-colored mud on her cheeks and drank deeply from what João later told me must have been a gall bladder. When it was empty it sagged so she put it to her lips and blew it up. Then she put on a monkey-skin kind of hat. She picked up a whisk broom made of some sort of animal's tail and held it before my eyes, saying "Eshoba, eshoba." She used it to drive an aardvark anteater out of a cage in the corner and then hung a lot of red, white, black and blue beads over the monkey cap. It made her look silly. Why should Mahigo wish to look silly? I thought.

Finally she came and sat beside me, crooning a soft, tender song and rubbing my temples with her soft hands. Then she made me open my mouth and placed on my tongue what looked like a tiny bean pod, gently saying "zilongo, zilongo" as she did this.

For a moment I neither tasted nor felt anything. Suddenly it began to get hotter and hotter and bigger and bigger. My whole mouth felt on fire. I became more and more sleepy. The last I could remember was Mahigo stripping off my shirt, pulling off my shoes and trousers, and caressing my eyelids with fluttering fingers. Her animal smell was overpowering.

I knew I had been asleep or unconscious a long time when I awakened. João later figured it was more than two hours. I felt that I had been dreaming but could remember nothing. I opened my eyes and suddenly, amid a haze, saw Mahigo peering into them, a smile on her gentle, kindly face. She was saying something in a kind of croon and I had no idea what it was about but felt a tenderness oozing from her and a lazy feeling of relief all over me. I was wet and cool and relaxed. She had removed her regalia, the ochre, and the aardvark which I heard scratching behind me.

In a moment, just as had been forecast, João and Joaquim came through the bushes accompanied by the two girls and their children. With no hesitation they went right up to the doorway, pushed aside the curtain flap and entered, leaving Maria and Isabel outside. They squatted beside us and smiled at Mahigo. I had a strange belief this was not the first time they had done this sort of thing for the shikwembo.

Mahigo began talking in a low voice, looking at me all the time. Joaquim translated, from MaRonga to Shangaan, I presumed, and João repeated phrase by phrase in English, his face without expression.

"She asks how you feel. Fine? She is glad. She says you are very large. You are like a white snake. She is fond of white. And of snakes. You give her pleasure. She didn't know you had a tail. Do you really have one, Curly? She has never seen a man with a tail before. She used your tail also. She tried it with your tail. She had great pleasure from you.

"You are a nice boy, she says. She is going to do you a big favor because she has never heard of anyone like you before. And all the magic secrets have been passed down since Mwagulane. Mwagulane was our first shikwembo. Also the greatest. Not since Mwagulane has anyone spoken of a boy like you. You are big and strong, she says. But your real strength is luck."

Mahigo kept talking in snatches and pauses, allowing

time for the double translation. Both Joaquim and João seemed intent on their work. I had a feeling that Joaquim spoke with more assurance. Perhaps an *indigena* felt more *assimilado* here, in the hut beneath the cassava tree.

João continued: "She says you will have great experiences where you are going. You will see a member of your family you never saw before. But it will be most curious. You will have high adventures. There will be death; but you will escape it. And there will be near-death which she will help you to avoid. There will be many grave risks. But in the end you will triumph and you will be happy you have gone there. Now she is going to give you something.

"And I must interrupt here," João said. "I have never seen Mahigo give anything to anyone before."

At this point Mahigo reached beneath her blouse and, from between her large, hanging breasts, pulled out a string to which was attached a brass amulet shaped like a heart, quite thick and at least two inches long. She pressed one end with her heavy thumbnail and it sprang open. From inside the amulet she extracted a dark, rubbery-looking ring. It seemed very old but still flexible and firm. It was made of some strange, stretching, black-gray substance.

She held it up in the air so we could all look at it and talked rapidly to Joaquim with new, peculiar-sounding words, sometimes like the noise of grasshoppers and sometimes squeals and high-pitched clicks like the language of dolphins I had heard at Coney Island with Borborigmi.

The odor grew more clinging. It was present everywhere, a special kind of female odor, I thought. I remembered in our biology class at Ben Franklin one teacher said smell was passed through invisible nerve endings behind the nose to the most sensitive centers of the brain. If the nerves were cut, you couldn't smell anything. The

teacher also said smell was connected with sex. Mammals, that is creatures like me with warm blood, were stimulated by certain smells.

Mahigo held the rubbery ring in the air so all of us could see it. Then she leaned over me and, as she did so, much to my embarrassment I saw my penis get larger and stiffer, rising toward her as she bent forward. I had never allowed anyone to see my penis do this before. I wanted to cover myself with my trousers but she had taken my clothes away.

Mahigo grabbed my penis with one hand and, with the other, worked the ring down over it. It was tight but it stretched quite easily as she pushed it down toward the base. She looked at me as she did this and then began speaking again.

"This is a magic ring," João continued. "When you put it there and make a wish, no matter what you wish will come true. But only three times. You can make three wishes and all of them will come true. But beware. Never make the mistake of wishing a fourth time, when it is in the wishing position. Then Kulukumba will punish you. If you do that it will bring you disaster.

"She has had this magic ring for years. It has been handed down in our family from one shikwembo to another. I have never seen it. Only when the new shikwembo has passed the fullest tests, showing she is ready to carry on the magic and knows how to enlist the spirits of the Unguluve and of Kulukumba, only then does she receive the ring. Usually her predecessor dies soon afterward."

I wondered if this meant Mahigo soon might die, after giving me the wishing ring. But I dared not ask. She continued talking, clicks, strange rasping noises. Joaquim and João translated:

"You should not worry. This does not mean she is going to die right now. But neither Maria nor Isabel wants to be a shikwembo. Nor have they any talent for that. Mahigo knows. The strain dies out with her. She has seen on the streets of Lourenço Marques what will happen to her grandchildren. Also she is afraid of the police.

"So she wants you to take the ring and make good use of it. You are an unusual boy. She can see strange mixtures in your blood. Much of your blood comes from this part of the world. Your grandmother. You are not *assimilado* anywhere."

"Is that true, Curly?" João interjected. I nodded.

"I guess so," I said. "I'm beginning to find she's right."

"Now Mahigo says you must go. You will have good news tomorrow. Very soon your trip will start. She thanks you. You have made her very happy. She thanks us for bringing you. Never before have we brought anyone like you. Or so nice as you."

I was pleased. Mahigo got up, a bit wearily, and brought my clothes from where she had put them under a pillow. She pulled the ring off, put it back in the amulet and hung it around my neck. My penis was still stiff and swollen so, without an instant of thought, she jerked it off in her hand, watching it as she did so. The boys watched also, fascinated. "Now, is that better?" João asked, as she hauled up my trousers and tucked me in.

I didn't know what to say. I crawled out the doorway on my arms and knees, scraping against the sides, and finally stood up, dazed, in the gathering dusk. Mahigo followed, shook hands gravely and then commanded Maria and Isabel to do so as well. I went over to shake hands with the children but they ran into the jungle when they saw me coming.

"There is one question I want to ask," I said to João and Joaquim. "I believe everything Mahigo told me. Of course. And I am lucky she has helped me. But I don't understand magic. Is she allowed by Kulukumba to tell me what the ring is made of? It is so strange. It is of a material as strange as its purpose. It is soft and it is strong and it seems indestructible."

This was translated to Mahigo. She didn't smile. She simply looked at me with understanding and then spoke a few words. When Joaquim had interpreted to João, he told me.

"Yes, she says. Maybe it is good you asked. It may help understand the magic of the ring. It is made of the vulva—is that what you call it? The woman's. What man wishes in woman. The vulva of Mwagulane, the first and greatest shikwembo of our family, many, many, many years ago. Pickled," he added. "Pickled in the salt of human blood."

CHAPTER V

When I went to get my passport back next morning Mr. Kidd asked me: "Did you ever hear of the Makondes?"

"No sir. What are the Makondes?"

"Well, they're a tribe in Mozambique who survive by exporting men to South Africa where they work in the mines. Mainly gold. The chiefs are perfectly willing to send them off because otherwise they'd starve. Their families are happy for the same reason. The Portuguese are delighted because they get a percentage payment on each man provided. And the South Africans wouldn't be able to keep some of their mines going without this source of cheap labor."

"Yes sir. That's very interesting, sir."

"The point is my friend the South African consul was impressed by your certificate of origin from the SS. He not only gave you a free visa. But when I told him you had a money problem because the job you were promised had fallen through, he asked if you'd like a temporary job. It has something to do with the Makondes and the mines in the Rand. That's the area near Johannesburg where you're going anyway."

"Yes sir, Mr. Kidd. That would be very nice."

"I thought you'd be pleased. I'll call him and tell him you are willing. And he told me he'd have you met. There'll be a man named Lessing looking for you at the railroad station in Jo'burg tomorrow morning. You go by train you know. Lessing is tall, he said—of course, not by your standards. He has some function in the security organization. Security and recreation are his fields. Seems peculiar, don't you think? That combination."

When the train pulled in at Johannesburg, after a pleasant all-night ride through a wild animal park where I saw nothing, although there was a full moon, I took my Globetrotter player's bag and started to walk to the end of the station. A thin fellow, as tall as one of our substitute forwards and with large, long hands, came ambling along the platform.

"I don't have to ask who you are," he said with a friendly grin. "I'm Tiny Lessing from Anglo-American. That's the mining corporation. This here's Piet Burger of BOSS." A barrel-chested man with brick red face, light blue eyes, no neck and tight thin lips, came up and shook hands—less warmly than Tiny.

"Oh, you're Mr. Lessing's boss?" I wondered.

"No, Curly," said Mr. Burger. "BOSS means Bureau of State Security. Something like your Gestapo used to be."

"It wasn't my Gestapo, Mr. Burger. You see, I'm American."

"Well, no harm meant. We here at BOSS sometimes help Tiny and the others to coordinate their work. We don't like trouble with kaffirs. Or," he added with a glint, "troublemaking agents with the kaffirs."

"You have trouble with your coffee? I don't understand."

Lessing chuckled. "Bantus," he said. "Blacks. Come along. Give me your bag. There'll be plenty of time to educate you on all these new things. What we want right now is breakfast."

Among us we three ate fifteen eggs and two piles of flat, skinless sausages. So I felt pretty good when they put me between them in the front seat of a small British truck and Tiny drove us through the city.

There were lots of tall buildings, like Montreal but not like New York. There seemed to be many more black people than white people in the streets. The black people didn't look happy. I don't know what it was, but they moved around and talked and shopped like the white people but their eyes mirrored no pleasure.

While we drove along Mr. Burger told me in gruff, short sentences about the kind of work I would be expected to do. He said one of the most important jobs at the mines was to keep the visiting tribal workers from Mozambique happy. After all, they were away from their families and from most of their friends. Although the pay was good and the food was better than anything they'd ever had and they got extraspecial medical care, they also had to have amusement. Sports. Things like that.

"Oh, that's the sort of thing I understand. You want me to teach them to play basketball."

"Not that," said Mr. Burger, "although we've been told at BOSS that you are a professional. I don't know anything about basketball. It's not a game we play here. No, we like them to feel at home so we let them work off steam by means they are used to. Not English-type games, silly games with a ball and a stick of wood. No, more African style. We let them fight."

"Fight? Is that an amusement here? Or where they come from? It doesn't seem like an amusement to me. I don't much like to fight."

"That won't be your job," said Mr. Lessing. "You'll be part of the staff of supervisors—under me. We fix the rules and make them observe them. To be sure they don't hurt themselves too badly."

"Too badly? I thought the idea of fighting was to hurt."

"Well, yes. Up to a point. But the company can't afford to lose its labor force through injuries. Costs too much to replace them. A few broken heads every now and then. For those who have too much steam to work off. But not more than that."

"Broken heads?" I commented. "That hurts badly, doesn't it?" They didn't answer. I didn't much care for their cruel manner.

When we got into the area everyone referred to as the Rand there were great tan piles of what they called "tailings"—the leftovers after the ore is separated out. They took me to a wooden dormitory where I would sleep with the other security officials. "All big fellows," said Mr. Lessing. "We like them big. So they can stop the Bantus from beating each other to death when it becomes necessary."

"But not big like you," Mr. Burger added grimly. I began to realize why the South African Consulate had suggested me for the job. Size. And maybe the implied SS connection, the Sippenbuch.

"We pay you well," said Mr. Lessing. "You'll see when you get your pay book. If you translate from rands you'll find it amounts to about thirty U.S. dollars a week. And that's all profit. We feed you, clothe you and take care of you." He sounded very proud of this.

Tiny took me down into a mine "so you can get the atmosphere," and Mr. Burger left. The elevator was just a platform without real sides and dropped so fast I wondered if the rope had broken. I had to crawl around, even in the hallway spaces where the miners could stand and rest. They were all, every one of them, glistening, sweating black men.

Tiny, as he kept asking me to call him, took me to a

mess hall where we ate lunch. The only black people in the room were waiters. Then he said: "We are going to have a weekly fight this afternoon. It's late so it doesn't interfere with the work shifts. You can go and take a rest now in your dormitory. I'll drop by and pick you up. I'll come early to give you some clothes. We have Indian tailors here and I think they can stitch out a shirt and pants in time. Eight foot six, aren't you? Your passport says so" (a modification, I noticed, made by Mr. Kidd). "Are you still growing? And nineteen-inch neck? Better wear your own shoes and socks. Can't drum those up in a hurry."

When Tiny returned a few hours later and I put on my new clothes he gave me a pay book, pointing out that I'd been charged already for the shirt and pants. Wow, I figured, if clothes cost this much in South Africa my two thousand dollars won't go far. Was everything that expensive? I later found out it was just everything around the mines. I guess the company wanted to earn back most of what it paid the workers.

Tiny took me to a special arena the company had built and introduced me to more than a dozen tough-looking white men, each of them carrying a club. Soon I realized that not all of these men were any more South African than I was. They seemed to be a kind of white equivalent of the black tribal workers recruited abroad because they were cheap.

I saw Mr. Burger sitting in the center of the rows of seats on one side. "He's not regular. Just on inspection," Tiny said. "I don't know why BOSS is so interested in you."

Suddenly there was a lot of noise. About fifty black men wearing feathers and not much else, small skirts or shorts around the middle, and carrying spears with blunt points, sticks and long thin shields, pranced onto the fighting field and began to hop up and down, shouting, singing

(59)

and screaming. When they opened their mouths, I noticed their teeth were filed to needlepoints. "Boao-oo," they shouted.

"Makondes," said Tiny. "From Mozambique. Very fierce. But not the group who were sent in yesterday. They won't travel as fast as you. In fact they'll walk most of the way. And they come from far north. It'll be some time before they have any steam to work off. They are tough people. You must teach them fear. Not love or respect. They have a funny language and much gusto."

At the other end of the arena a gate opened and perhaps seventy other blacks came pouring through, dressed and equipped about the same but with strange marks painted in white on their faces and with different sorts of feathers. "Shangaans," said Tiny. "Mashangaanas. They don't like the Makondes. But they're not so tough. Therefore we balance the sides numerically."

The he blew a screeching police whistle. Immediately the two teams rushed toward the middle and began to beat each other up with very loud shouts.

"You see how happy they are?" said Tiny. We called it something else among the Trotters.

"Now you watch the other protection guards. You'll learn from them. Don't try and break them up too soon. We've got to let them work off steam. But if you see someone you think is being killed, you move in. Just bang anyone around you. That's the only rule. Break it up—before they break each other up. You get to know them soon. Wait'll you see the Xhosas fight the Fingas. Or the Basotho fight anyone at all."

I learned a lot that afternoon. There were several broken bones but it was evident, from what Tiny told me, that they enjoyed this recreation and were grateful for the chance to release all that pent-up energy they hadn't been able to get rid of in the mines. They had so much happy exercise they were blowing like men with asthma. How lucky they were that the company thought of their recreational needs. I could also see, from the enthusiasm they brought to bear in this sport, that the Makonde and Shangaan people at home obviously didn't care much for each other.

"O.K.," Tiny finally hollered, blowing very hard on his whistle. "That's enough, boys." Promptly all the other guards stepped into the fray and began swatting everyone around with their clubs. "Go ahead. Join them. Get in there," Tiny ordered me. So I did. I think I did a good job but it was rather tiring.

When we were all through and the Makondes and Shangaans had thumped out, some of them carrying their bleeding teammates, I asked Tiny where there was a toilet. "Eat something bad in Mozambique?" he asked with a grin. "All that grease. Sure, there's a loo over there." He pointed to three tall, small buildings of wood set on concrete foundations about eighty yards away by a clump of trees.

I got there in a hurry. It wasn't that I'd eaten too much grease. I just felt sick to my stomach. I don't know why. Maybe it was the sun. Anyway, when I arrived at the three buildings I noticed each had a well-printed sign on the door: "Europeans Only"; "Africans"; "Colored." Naturally I entered the one called Colored. It stank bad and I vomited all over the place.

I had just finished retching when there was a furious knocking and shaking at the door. "Come on out of there," said an angry voice which I recognized as Mr. Burger's. I opened the latched door and staggered out, surprised to see the rage in his cold blue eyes.

"What's the idea, Snarl?" he asked in a rage. "Can't you read?"

"Yes, sir. I can read. I went to Ben Franklin High."

"Well, don't you see that sign? Colored. You ought to have enough brains to use Europeans Only."

"But Mr. Burger, I'm not European. I'm American."

"Don't you try and get funny with me, you clod," he roared. "If you want to stay on the right side of BOSS you follow the rules. That's rule number one around here. You watch yourself, Sonny, or I'll kick your arse so hard you can wear it as a hat."

I decided not to say anything. I vaguely realized that European meant white. I also realized that Mr. Burger wouldn't be favorably impressed if I explained that my father, the aristocrat from Windhoek, might not be so classified if they knew he was African or Colored. Only later did I become aware that Colored meant people the color of coffee with lots of milk in it. And Asian was still different; more milk.

"It's not that we don't like you," Tiny told me that evening over a beer for him and an orange soda pop for me, "but we've decided perhaps you aren't experienced enough for this kind of work. You're the right size. But maybe you haven't been around enough." I figured Mr. Burger had been complaining about my using the wrong toilet.

He handed me my pay book. There were a lot of deductions checked off in addition to my shirt and pants. Tiny also gave me an envelope. I opened it up and found some coins. "Severance pay," said Tiny. It came to about thirty cents, U.S. I didn't know whether the company was always very thrifty or whether Mr. Burger's BOSS was showing who was really boss around here. In any case, I didn't think they were loose with their money. It stuck to them like they say sweat sticks to a Bantu.

I put the money in my pocket and Tiny took me down to a company bus stop where he said goodbye and I climbed in with my bag. "Be sure and stay in a hotel for Europeans. You've got to learn the rules, Curly." My thoughts turned to my happy life in Harlem. Our rules were different with the Globetrotters. That was the line of my thinking.

Naturally I was sad that things hadn't worked out the way I thought they would and that South Africa was proving to be not just a complicated place, difficult to understand, but also very expensive. I went to a small, old-fashioned hotel the white bus driver recommended to me, and I automatically gave the man at the desk both my passport and the Lebensborn document, as Mr. Kidd had suggested. While I stood leaning down over the desk, I saw an elderly gentleman with a little black string necktie, rimless glasses and a well-trimmed triangular beard, staring at me openly.

When I came down from my room, expecting to go out for supper to a cheap restaurant, the elderly gentleman was still there. He arose from his chair and walked over to me with very short, precise steps. "Beg your pardon," he said. "But news travels fast here. Aren't you the young man BOSS pushed out of Anglo-American's recreation program this afternoon? Bully for you, young man. We've got to show BOSS who's boss around here, don't we? Why don't you sit down and join me for a drink?"

So I sat and he bought himself a beer and me an orange pop and he introduced himself as Bram Jonker. "Confidentially," he said, "I think you should know I'm a broer."

Thinking it best, I explained: "Oh, my father's family were brewers in South West Africa."

"Well, I didn't mean brewer. Not a brewer of beer. We have a word in Afrikaans that is broer. It means brother. But, as a matter of fact, I knew a lot about your grandfather. Old man von Snarl. He was a big war hero with Vorbeck.

"When Botha's men attacked South West in 1915 my father was along. And he moved up there after the war and took me as a boy. Your grandfather had died by then, of course. But everyone spoke about him. He was much admired, even by the kaffirs. And you know, I sometimes think of him still when I drink a mug of this fine Windhoek beer. It's the best beer in the world."

I didn't say anything. I was beginning to feel uneasy about talking to people too freely in South Africa. There seemed to be many persons who had authority to push me around.

"Well," said Mr. Jonker, "I thought I'd tell you a bit about the Broederbond. That's the secret organization the broers are in. Then you'll understand more about BOSS and about Burger, the man who gave you trouble. You see the Broederbond really runs this country. And it runs BOSS. And Burger works for BOSS. And he does what he's told—by the Broederbond.

"The broers look down on the English-speakers, and they look down on the Asians, who look down on the Coloreds, who look down on the kaffirs, the Africans. The Africans looked down on the Hottentots and Bushmen until they almost all died. And the Broederbond just runs everything. To be a broer you have to be a Protestant Afrikaner, like me. And now almost the entire cabinet and two-thirds of the government party in parliament and most of the department heads are broers. And that's above all true for the army. And even more so for BOSS. Through BOSS the broers intend to put their foot on the neck of every other community in South Africa. They're well on the way to doing so. Hence, Burger.

"Now you might ask why I'm telling you all this and how I dare, since it's a secret organization as I told you. Indeed, a broer risks being murdered if he exposes the Bond. But everyone in this country knows where I stand. And they know what I'm saying all the time.

"The broers also know that I have a lot of papers exposing their private dirt all locked up in a safe abroad; they just don't know where. And I've warned them that if anything happens to me—anything at all—the dirt will be spread thick. Maybe they can stop it from appearing in their own press. But even the bullnecked broers know they don't control all the papers in the world.

"What I'm getting at is just this, young man. You've got, to watch your step. Whatever you do is known by BOSS. Make no mistake about that. And we, the handful of rebels in this country, know plenty about what BOSS is doing.

"So just take the word of a renegade broer. Watch your step. Keep your ears open and your mouth shut. And if you ever get into any trouble, call me. I'm a lawyer." He gave me a card: A. A. Jonker, attorney-at-law, plus a telephone number. On the other side, same thing, in Afrikaans.

I was so worried by what Mr. Jonker told me that I went out for a walk. It was still quite early, about eight o'clock, but the streets were fairly empty. Oddly enough, I saw hardly any black faces. I kept looking behind me at corners and by the streetlights reflected in windows to see if there were any strange persons following me, agents of the mysterious BOSS. But there was nothing.

I walked on and on. Finally I came to a restaurant where there were lots of people and they seemed to be happy and laughing so I went in to have some supper.

The pleasant lady who was serving asked me if I wanted a whisky. "I do not drink whisky, but you are kind," I explained.

"Well then, what do you drink?"

"I rather fancy root beer," I said.

"We don't have none of that," she answered. "Better have a real beer, mate."

"OK, I'll have a Windhoek."

She went to a long bar and pulled a lever and so for the first time in my life I drank a beer in order to wash away the worries left by Mr. Jonker's conversation; and also, to give me a feeling of family pride, I specified Windhoek beer. I saw quite a few women giggling and drinking beer also.

A man and a girl sat down at the table with me. He was an amiable, tough-looking sailor. At least I was sure he was a sailor because he had a wind-burned face, clear eyes and tattoos all over his wrists and the backs of his hairy hands. The girl was pretty, with plump hips and long golden hair. She hoisted a large glass of beer in a toast to the sailor and said: "Drink up, sport. Money flows like water in Jo'burg. You just have to know how to get it. Do you think I know?"

"Yeah," he said with a chuckle. "You sure know." He spoke with an American accent.

At this point, emboldened by the beer which had my head pleasantly spinning, I introduced myself to the sailor. "Please, sir," I said. "I'm American too. My name is Curly Snarl."

"Well, well, well," he said, looking me over carefully. If you ain't somep'n. You're the biggest kid I ever did see. What d'ya think about him, Liz?"

The girl rolled her eyes at me and winked. "I'll bet he's a terrible fuck-about," she said. I felt myself blushing.

"Say, boy," the girl continued. "Want to get a little poontang?"

"I don't understand, Miss. What does poontang mean?"

"That's a word he taught me. Old Sinbad there."

"If big boy here wants poontang," said the sailor, "he'd better go to the zoo. Or buy himself a kaffir. A dinge."

"Now don't you be so mean, Sinbad. Let's take him along with us to my place. I'll telephone Yumyum and get her to come down with a bottle of you know what. Got any money, boy? All right, that's fine then. And Yumyum can take anything you can give her, big boy," she added, looking approvingly at the front of my pants.

We lost a good two hours of pleasant doing nothing while Sinbad got started drinking seriously and, when the girl asked him if he didn't want to do something more serious he replied: "I'd rather screw a manatee than any woman in this godblasted place. There's more response to it."

"There he goes again," said the girl, who told me to call

her Elizabeth. "Whenever he gets tiddly he's like that. Come on." She led the way out and Sinbad and I followed. We walked eight blocks to a small apartment house and she took us up to the third floor where she let us in with a key. She went straight to the telephone. All I could hear her say was: "This one will really give you some fun. He's awful innocent and young. But, baby, wait till you see him."

A moment later there was a rap on the door. "Lives only two floors above," Elizabeth explained. She opened up and in came a well-shaped girl with straight black hair cut in a fringe across her forehead and pretty, squinting Chinese eyes.

"Yumyum. Curly." Elizabeth introduced us. "Yumyum's from Macao. She came here from Lourenço Marques. She's half Chinese. That's honorary European here. She's also part Portuguese, part Korean. Koreans are considered Asians. Depends which half you sleep with if you break the law, I suppose."

"Holy damn," said Yumyum, looking at me with admiration. "Is all of him that big? I'll take him in my better half."

"Yumyum's a nymphomaniac," said Elizabeth. "She needs a lot of loving. She can't sleep if she doesn't come ten times a day. She gets hysterical if she comes less than six times."

"Yep," said Yumyum happily. "And I can't come unless I'm paid for it. Love may be important but it's not enough. You know, I'm half Chinese, after all. We need a little masquerade and theatre."

"She should have been a hyena," said Elizabeth with a grin. "You know a hyena can both sire a litter and produce one. There's a vet in Natal who has proved this. Think what fun Yumyum would have fathering and mothering her own children."

"Great idea. But what would the family live on?"

Yumyum asked. "Anyway, I got to be paid if I'm going to come. I'd go broke paying myself, wouldn't I? That reminds me. You've got some cash, Curly?"

I told her I had some traveller's checks. Sinbad warned me not to get carried away by too much generosity.

"Hmmph," said Yumyum. "Don't listen to him. What are you boy, anyway? I mean what kind of a hodgepodge are you? Funny-looking American. Funnier than a Eurasian South African type like me."

"Well, I am certified by the SS as being Herrenvolk. Herrenvolk means Aryan. Aryans are Indian, I think."

"You mean brown? My style?" Yumyum asked.

"No, brown my style."

"Well, let's call it Asian," said Yumyum. "Then there's no breaking the law. Against mixing races in bed. Could be honorary Asian. Or dishonorary. Take your choice."

Yumyum took a bottle filled with dark fluid out of her large handbag and poured drinks into two glasses, set the bottle down, looked at Elizabeth, then grabbed me by the hand, holding the two glasses in her other hand, and led me into a bedroom. "We'll get out of your way, chum," she shouted gaily over her shoulder. "We've got work to do as well." She slammed the door and locked it.

She put the glasses on a small table beside a quite large bed and promptly began to get undressed. She wasn't wearing much and it took no time at all. Then she looked at me, standing there. I felt embarrassed. "Come on, Curly," she said in a soft voice. "Don't be afraid. I'll give you a good time." Then, without waiting for me, she began to pull my clothes off. "Let me at it. Let's see what I'm getting."

"My God," she continued, "you're only like a goat. A giant like you and only a billygoat. I hoped you'd be a donkey."

"How do you know what goats and donkeys are like?"

"How do I know? Why, I've done it with goats. In

shows. Sometimes with donkeys, too. Even on a few occasions with horses, but that's hard. Me! Why I could take a fire hydrant, Curly."

"But isn't it against the law with goats and donkeys and horses?" I asked.

"Oh, no. Only with different races of humans. You can do it with a brown, black or white donkey. But you can't mix the humans. The law says that."

"Well, I'm not human," I told her proudly. "I'm a primate. See my tail." She regarded it with admiration. She suggested an act with her and Elizabeth that seemed impossible even with my exceptional physical construction.

Yumyum really was very pretty and just looking at her produced the results I had learned about with Mahigo. But this time I wasn't embarrassed. She watched me with approval. Then, as she was drawing me down beside her on the bed, she noticed the cord around my neck and the brass amulet.

"What's that?" she asked. She opened the amulet with her thumbnail and pulled out the magic token. "Why, it's only a prophylactic. An old condom. You don't need that with me, boy. I'm clean as a shark's tooth."

"No, Miss Yumyum," I explained. "That isn't a conundrum like you think. That's a wishing ring. Please, I must put it back." I tucked it carefully inside the brass heart while she watched me with a puzzled look. And then we went to work. Somehow I knew most everything to do. But she taught me more.

After about an hour and a half I was tired and felt pleasantly drowsy. I lay beside her soft, yellowish shape feeling happy. There was again that kind of perfume of woman which I found I liked. I heard buzzing noises and suddenly Yumyum swatted her round, long thigh. "Did you ever notice, Curly, that the smell of sex brings mosquitos around? Didn't you know that? Well, stick with me and you'll learn plenty of things. Yop. And you're a pretty good subject, too. It'll be fun teaching you.

"Too bad I've got that thing on money, not being able to come without it, and having to come in order to sleep. I guess you're going to have to pay for your lessons, Curly. But, brother, you're going to learn a lot."

I was just thinking over what she said when I heard a series of loud knocks on the front door, echoing right through the outside room. There was a scuffle on the sofa on the other side of the thin wall separating the two rooms and, amid whispers between Elizabeth and Sinbad, there came a rough voice: "Open up. Open up quick. Police. If you don't open right away we'll break the door down."

"It's the coppers again," whispered Yumyum, a frightened look coming across her face. "And there's no way out, except through that other room. Why not even the bathroom opens here. I guess we've had it."

I could hear the door opening so we rushed into our clothes, unlocked the door and walked in just as a hard-faced policeman in uniform was handing documents back to Elizabeth and Sinbad. Another tough fellow in ordinary clothes looked on frowning. It was Burger.

"All right, you two," said the policeman. Yumyum produced some kind of paper; I couldn't see what. While the civilians were studying this I handed over my passport with the photostat of the Lebensborn Sippenbuch attached.

"Well," said the cop, after he'd finished looking at the document. "Lucky I read German. Well again. Well, young fellow. I must admit you don't look much like an SS type. But there's no better proof than this. And although you shouldn't be sleeping with non-Aryans, under our law, I guess the fact that you're an American excuses you. But don't do it again. I know you've already been in trouble with our security people."

I looked at Burger. It must indeed be BOSS who was

responsible, I thought. One of them certainly had followed me—us. And I'd have noticed a uniformed cop.

"Now you," said the policeman to Yumyum in a rasping voice. "I can see by your permits that you've been here long enough to know better. You know damn well you can't sleep with Europeans and get away with it. It's a bit of pokey for you, my girl."

"But I'm not European," I protested. "I told you people that once. I'm American. Mr. Burger knows."

"Listen, you clot. You've already been told at Anglo-American that in this country European means white. And you've a certificate that you're white."

"Well, I'm not really. That's to say my grandmother was from South West Africa and the Oorlog Hereros. My Mutterl . . ."

"Stop that nonsense, sonny. Don't tell me the SS didn't know its business. And the SS didn't issue race testimonials to Bantu."

"I'm also part Jewish. Anyway I'm a pri . . ."

"You'd better shut up, lad. Or we'll lock you in the madhouse. Don't tell me about the SS. My brother died for them in Jugoslavia. They knew what they were doing. Now, my girl, come along there and we'll take you to the lockup. And none of that honorary-white stuff, Chink. You, son, you can come along too and ride in front. We'll drop you off at your hotel. Don't worry, we know where it is."

With a bitter, frightened look but always avoiding my glance, Yumyum walked between the two and when we came out in front they took her into a kind of cage that served as the rear body of a small truck. The policeman got in beside her and locked the door. Mr. Burger motioned to me with his hand and I climbed in next to him on the front seat. Sinbad and Elizabeth stayed behind in her apartment. But somehow, I think, the bubbles had gone out of their party.

When we stopped at a red light Mr. Burger turned and looked me in the eyes. "I'm going to get you, sonny," he said. "I'm going to get you good. Just you remember that."

CHAPTER VI

Thanks to Mr. Jonker I was able to get permission to visit Windhoek so I bought a round-trip plane ticket, packed my Trotters bag, paid the hotel bill and boarded a bus for the airport. I began to think about what Mahigo had told me of Vati and his Herero mother. I also remembered what Mahigo said about seeing a member of my family.

All this set me to thinking. After I had checked in at the ticket desk and left my bag I went to the toilet, entering the door marked "Europeans." I took out the magic ring from the amulet around my neck. When it was adjusted in position I wished secretly to myself, shaping the words on silent lips: "May I see my nearest relative on Vati's side before the sun sets today."

The mere fact that I had made the wish excited me. I rolled the ring off carefully and folded it back into the brass heart. Then I buttoned my pants and walked out, somehow expecting things to happen right away. I thought I would feel different but nothing happened. Soon I became disappointed. First I suspected it was only a fake or a bad joke at my expense; but then I forgot the entire matter in the excitement of flying off all by myself on a fantastic voyage.

At last we were called for the Windhoek flight and were led past a large Lufthansa aircraft. I guessed it had just arrived from Germany because it was still unloading. Officials stood by the baggage hold checking off on lists of paper each bundle or crate as it emerged. As I came level with it a forklift was starting to lower a long wooden box to the ground.

The lowering apparatus seemed to get stuck and we all looked up as an employee in overalls scrambled atop the lift and then climbed to the platform. My eyes wandered idly along the gear and ratchet and over the unpainted boards of the awkward box. To my sudden astonishment I saw, painted along its side in heavy black letters:

VON SNARL
WINDHOEK

(FOR REBURIAL. DISPATCHED BY ODESSA, FRANKFURT A.M.,
B.R.D.)
HOLD! HOLD! HOLD! TO BE PICKED UP AT AIRPORT.

The man on the platform pushed the crate toward the outer edge in order to make room for himself. Then he squatted and began to fiddle with some tools, testing the machine's greased steel teeth. When he arose, he did so abruptly and seemed to kick the box. For a moment it teetered on the edge of the forklift. Then, very slowly, it seemed to groan, wobbled off and crashed heavily to the ground.

With a crack the lid smashed. A coffin inside sprang open exposing a skeleton clad in a few vestigial rags. Its skull, tan and not very clean, rolled out on the ground with a scary grin. A white airline worker laughed uproariously. "Welcome, Fritz," he said, giving the skull a hard kick. It disintegrated at the touch of his shoe.

I was almost blind with rage. Rushing at the man, I lifted my right fist and bonked him hard right on the center of his head, shouting: "He broke his skull; he broke my Vati's skull." I didn't mean to kill him but I did.

Before I even realized what was happening a pair of airport guards rushed through the horrified crowd, seized my arms, pulled them behind me and snapped a pair of handcuffs around my wrists. They were a very tight squeeze and pinched me so hard I bled, which didn't improve my temper. Then they led me to a small room marked Bureau of State Security. There, sitting on a leather sofa, calmly smoking a cigarette as if he had been waiting for me to keep an appointment, was Mr. Burger.

"Curly," he said, not trying to hide the satisfaction on his face, "I thought that for a while at least you'd watch your step. And now you've gone and killed a man. Well, well, well. Who'd of thought that?"

"But you saw what he did to Vati!" I shouted. "I had my father's honor to attend to. I wished at least to see him buried properly at Windhoek in a new SS uniform. And he was smashed. Ask these men. These guards." I strained unsuccessfully to break the chain link of the handcuffs and one of them rapped my funny bone with a baton. They slammed me down next to Mr. Burger on the sofa.

All I could think was: So this is what Mahigo meant. To see a member of my family I'd never seen before. No, I had never seen him. Nor would I. A grim joke. The wishing ring worked, perhaps. But in what a strange way.

"So," said Mr. Burger. "You fell right into my hands at that, didn't you? You can't say Piet Burger doesn't smell a bad character from the start. Curly, you're as green as an avocado pear. But you're not going to stay that way. When I've finished with you you'll be a different color.

More like your father, I'd say. And maybe before that you'll need a touch or two of the sjambok."

"Better make it a real one and of rhino hide," said one of my guards, rubbing his chin and seeming to measure me with his eyes.

I was driven off in the same kind of wired-in vehicle that had taken Yumyum to her fate, a policeman sitting on each side of me and Mr. Burger in front with the driver. We seemed to be going north, as far as I could tell from the bright sun warming up the piles of tailings. Finally we stopped on a hillside in front of a great big brick building surrounded by strands of barbed wire.

"All right, lad," said one of the cops quite amiably as he hit me on the ear and shoved me, crouching, through the rear door of my cage. "Here y'are at your new hotel. Hotel Fort. Yes sir, this is *The* Fort. National Monument of Johannesburg. Did you ever live in a monument before? Well, you'll have lots of company here, boy."

I was hustled past uniformed sentries with rifles, all of them white, and could see at each far corner of the brick wall small towers on steel legs with other guards inside them. Then I was pushed through a huge double doorway of brass and old wood. Inside two warders took over but Mr. Burger stayed with me until I had been registered, photographed, stripped, examined and all my personal possessions including my belt and necktie taken away.

"Guess we can't fit him out with a uniform," said one official. "Least not yet. Not his size. For a few days he can wear the clothes he's got. Give him a thin string to keep his trousers up. Thanks, Burger. He's all ours now. This'll be the biggest one that didn't get away. He'll be seeing you at the trial."

I was jammed into a narrow cell with two little cots but there wasn't any prisoner with me. "You're big enough to have a room to yourself," said one of the accompanying trusties as he slammed the door with a clang. "Room with a view," said the other. I looked out the small barred window, and over the wall of a gloomy courtyard I could see a grass-covered bank.

"Don't worry, kid," said the first trusty. "This Fort's been dug right out of the hill itself. And you won't get away. Better not try or we'll dig you into the hill."

I found it was impossible to stretch out on the bunk allotted me; it was almost a yard too short. But when I pointed this out the guard said: "What do you expect, tailormade cells to fit every murderer we get?"

"You're in the monument, mate," someone shouted from the cell across the way. "Only monument in the country where you can't get your picture took—except by the police. No one else allowed. We're a secret national monument, national secret. Architectural apartheid."

"Hey, shrimp," his cellmate called to me. "What you in for?"

"I don't really know, mister," I said. "I became very angry when a gentleman broke my father's skull. So I bonked him. But I suppose that's understandable, isn't it?"

"Man, you mean you really killed someone! You're sure in for it. Why man, they give me ten years just for busting up a pub. I was completely broke, man, when I walked in there. I had only one cent in my pocket. And when I get broke I do crazy things. But killing, man, that's different."

"Oh, no, sir. I didn't mean to kill him."

"Well, if he killed your father, maybe . . ."

"But my father was already dead."

"Look, man, don't make fun of me. If there's one thing I hates more than anything in this world it's people laughing at me. I have a terrible inferiority complex, man. When people laughs at me I want to hide. But since I can't hide here I want to hide 'em. See. The only thing I laughs at is when I tells a joke. Not no one else's."

"But mister, I wasn't laughing at you. What I said is . . ."

His cellmate interrupted. "Don't you worry, youngster.

Janny here is around the bend. Every day he goes to the psychiatric clinic for examination. He's a nice chap, ain't you, Janny, but you shouldn't take him serious. Don't you worry. It's nothing to any of us how many dead men and dead dogs you killed, youngster."

The first few days I wasn't allowed to see anyone except the warders and my fellow prisoners. I found out the Fort was an old military garrison and that we were all sort of mixed inside, white, black, colored and the tan people they call Asian. Except they kept dividing us up to do things.

The whites were in cells together and only two in a cell. They kept treating me as white, even leaving me alone because of my size. I suppose that was the value of my Sippenbuch. The black and tan folks had to sleep four in a cell. They ate apart and when we were all let out to walk in the stone courtyard for recreation under the watch of uniformed riflemen, we had to do so according to our color registration.

Everybody complained that the food was awful but I didn't mind it. There was lots of corn, although they called it mealie. I told them that was a treat in my country. They looked at me as if I were even crazier than just the attacker of a dead man's murderer.

One day, after I'd been fitted out in a prison uniform by an Indian tailor, like in Johannesburg, one of the trusties who had first taken me to my cell showed up accompanied by Mr. Jonker. He opened the door and let him in, locking it again when he'd entered.

"Well, Curly," said Mr. Jonker. "How are you, my poor boy? It has taken me time but I have now been granted permission to handle your case. I have assembled a team of consultants. You need not worry about the cost. This is an interesting problem—or set of problems.

"They are charging you with murder under the 1955 Criminal Procedure Act. Obviously this is not a case of murder but of accidental death, unprovoked homicide or unintentional manslaughter at the most. Moreover, it is perfectly apparent that Piet Burger and the BOSS apparatus are out to make a sacrificial victim of you.

"It is intolerable for them to be made the victims of a joke. Yet you are certified pure white by the authority they most respect, Himmler's SS. At the same time you are now established to be one quarter Herero. And they know that's black even if it doesn't show much on your skin.

"Finally, they don't much like Jews (except in Israel where they are fighting Arabs). Yet they find you also part Jewish. And American to boot. Americans aren't too popular either—ever since one of your ambassadors was photographed shooting a harmless antelope from a jeep. The antelope was standing still.

"So, Burger, the BOSS man is after you on several counts. He doesn't care about innocence or guilt. But he also doesn't dare to mix himself in this affair too publicly. He has secured the services of Colonel Ulf Dutoit, one of South Africa's best-known and shrewdest criminal investigation officers, to make certain enough evidence is obtained to try and bring conviction and a death sentence. And they are spreading allegations all over to make headlines in the newspapers. This is quite intolerable and I can guarantee you the best defense that is humanly possible in this benighted land.

"As for the cost, it's no problem I assure you. Your government can't help because it's against U.S. law, although they promise to provide a character witness named Kidd and to send the necessary documentation. But a basketball entrepreneur from New York has volunteered assistance on legal fees. And the Johannesburg Jewish community is very liberal—both in politics and funds.

"I expect to make a good thing out of this anyway, even

if I don't earn a single rand. Just think of the fun I'm going to have with the Broederbond. Your friend Burger's a broer, I told you."

While I was awaiting my trial I became friendly with my neighbors. One of them was a very nice, quiet gentleman with pale, steely blue eyes and thin white hair. He told me he had once been a predikant, which is a preaching man in the Dopper Kerk. He explained that the Dopper Kerk is a very strict branch of the Dutch Reformed religion. It believes that white men are much better than men of any other color, who aren't quite human.

My neighbor, whose name was Chris, had been married to a young woman from Capetown who was less rigid in her beliefs. She liked flirting and dancing, both of which are regarded as sinful by the Dopper Kerk. Chris beat her up regularly with a sjambok. That is a kind of stiff leather whip. She put poison in his homemade druppels so he tapped her on the head with a beer bottle and she died.

Chris shared a cell with a very friendly fisherman called Maritz who came from Vis Hoek in the extreme south and always talked about the good life by the seashore which he had left. Maritz was also waiting trial. According to Chris, he was accused of carving up a girl he did not even know, using a fifteen-centimeter scaling knife.

Maritz enjoyed talking about this unfortunate occurrence. He explained to me that he was homesick so one day he wanted to get his mind off the sound of the rollers at Vis Hoek and he thought the best way might be to murder someone. But there was no one he particularly disliked. He thought about the problem seriously and decided there were enough people in the world to kill even if he did not hate them. That is precisely what he did.

"I wanted to do something real important," he explained in a low rumbling voice that commanded attention from all the nearby cells and also from the warder standing in the corridor. "So I opened a bottle of beer and by the time I had finished drinking it, very slowly, it came into my mind that murder was a real important thing. So I figured I'd kill the first girl I saw that day. Just for the fun of it.

"Naturally I didn't rape her. That would be a dirty thing to do. I just watched her walking down the street and I followed and when she got to her house I got her talking. She was very nice and we talked for twenty minutes on the stoep. Finally I pushed her through the door and into the house and I killed her, without thinking whether it was a good thing to do or not. I just knew it was important. I thought, this is something real big and I left her to die. I just walked away. So here I am."

"They're going to plead insanity for Maritz," Chris explained. "But I'm not insane," said Maritz. "How crazy can people get?" asked Chris.

All of us, by then including me, had to wear a kind of drab prison uniform and the more dangerous criminals had leg irons linked by a chain above the ankles, so they would not be able to escape. I was included in this group, thanks to Mr. Burger, Bram Jonker told me. We were not only chained but our warders were always armed.

The European dangerous criminals were allowed into the exercise yard at the same time as the black dangerous criminals but we weren't allowed to talk to each other. I had a feeling the black dangerous criminals weren't in the least bit eager to speak with us. They had a club-like way about them, somewhat like the Globetrotters.

The prison warders seemed to get back at the blacks by profiteering. Some of them were regularly marched outside the Fort for special work forces in the neighborhood compound including the cleaning up of the white officials' quarters, maintaining the sporting facilities which were marked "Europeans only," and even on unknown assignments we never learned about.

The regular warders were all white and included

women as well as men. They wore khaki uniforms and the women wore berets instead of the peaked caps of the men. There was also a special body of black warders. But they were regarded as inferior and given second-class duties; they even had older rifles than the whites.

All of them, however, had whistles around their necks, tied to white lanyards, so they could summon help in an emergency. Also, most of them carried truncheons and they were not timid about using them. I often felt quite large noggins on my head. One warder explained to me that my skull made a special clanging noise when it was properly rapped.

Mr. Jonker told me that I would be examined by a group of doctors and experts from the main city hospital to see if I was considered legally mad. "Of course, I don't think you are mad," he assured me. "This is simply a procedure that must be applied. It is always possible you will benefit from it."

I did not understand what this meant but I was taken three times to a group of people called psychiatrists, headed by Dr. Aubrey Hartogh. They asked me foolish questions and did strange things to my body. They spent an unusually long time examining my tail, although I asked them what that had to do with a legal process involving the accidental death of the man who broke my father's skull.

"You yourself say you aren't really human," said Dr. Hartogh earnestly. "You say you are a primate. So we must investigate the angles of this unusual situation and see how they may juridically apply."

I was taken for trial before Mr. Justice Dorp at the Rand Supreme Court on Kruis Street in the heart of Johannesburg, near the main post office. It was a grim, gray building with lots of steps and an enormous number of pigeons that seemed to find plenty to eat in those sad surroundings. I was very interested to watch the people who came to watch me being judged.

There were several lawyers in black robes and officers of the court dressed in gray suits. Messengers kept bustling in and out with envelopes for people sitting in the audience. There seemed to be groups of people of almost every color—white, black, tan and brown—and they all were assigned to places in separate sections so it was something like a racial checkerboard.

I was brought up into the courtroom from a tier of cells below and as two warders escorted me in, hobbling because of my irons, a gasp like a great sigh of wind echoed. Everyone admired my large size in astonishment. Mr. Justice Dorp rapped his desk with a wooden gavel and called for order.

Mr. Jonker had warned me before the trial began that the prosecutor who would be seeking to convict me was an extreme and heretical Dutch Reformed Afrikaner who sought to prove that his people were true Herrenvolk, like my Vati, by bossing all the rest and convincing them they were inferior humans.

The prosecutor, who was named Mr. Malan, was a very fat gentleman with a red face and a shining pink bald head. He had a peculiar trick of rolling his light blue eyes right up into his head so that only the whites stared frighteningly at you. The blue part would stay up under the lids for a few seconds and then roll down again but none of this interfered at all with his presentation. He simply talked and talked without interruption and with savage emphasis as he pounded a square fist from time to time against a square palm with a flat, cracking noise.

"The main issue is not who committed the murder," he said. "There is no reasonable doubt on this. The evidence is not circumstantial. It is direct. The main issue is not whether there was a murder. I shall demonstrate with witnesses that the accused deliberately and slowly, if with anger, proceeded to beat the late Jan Rupert to death and with the intention of beating him to death.

"And I shall also demonstrate with witnesses that the

accused has deliberately violated the law of the land on prior occasions by flouting the national custom known as apartheid although it is legally called separate development. He has been seen to do this with evident intention to affront the law in such various circumstances as ignoring the plainly marked provision of labelled toilet facilities or deliberately violating the statutes stipulating separate racial congregation for social and sexual affairs.

"Therefore, Your Honor," he said, turning to the judge and rolling up his eyes, "we are left with only two issues to resolve before this court. First there is the question of motive, which is related to the matter of whether there was deliberation in this vile act. And secondly, after I have demonstrated that there was indeed a direct motive, the anger at Jan Rupert because this good man was a white Caucasian, there is the question of the mental balance of the accused. In other words, could there have been a variety of extenuating circumstances by reason of psychiatric incapacity? I shall prove that the answer to this question is in the negative."

Mr. Jonker was at last able to make a speech in my defense. He explained that I should legally be entitled to classification as of mixed ancestry, in other words colored, because of the known fact that my grandmother was a Herero of the Oorlog clan. This fact wholly negated and rendered void the type of evidence planned by the prosecution with a view to demonstrating my violation of racial statutes and the assertion that this could have been related to the question of a motive for the killing. "The killing, I shall contend in my presentation, was unintended, wholly accidental, and done in a moment of acute psychological tension," he concluded.

With that the trial began. The prosecutor summoned a psychiatrist, which by then I had learned is a kind of mental doctor. He testified: "I am able to say that at no time did this prisoner, whom I have examined and observed for a considerable period, display the least remorse. It is clear that his was a very aggressive act.

"Perhaps it may be argued that his emotional state at the time of the aggression was influenced by his feelings of rejection because of some confusion concerning the racial origins of the accused. It might be adduced this was an aggression that originated because the subject felt he was being rejected. I cannot testify on this."

Another psychiatrist was then brought to the stand, a gentleman who had amused himself for some days by sticking pins into me and knocking my joints with different kinds of hammers. He testified: "Of course the prisoner is not entirely normal in the usual sense. This is evident from his size and also from the fact that he possesses a vestigial tail. I believe photographs, X rays and other evidence concerning this have been submitted to Your Honor.

"If he were entirely normal he would not have perpetrated this assault, this crime. It is not normal to kill a man simply because he has kicked a fragile, dry skull, no matter to whom that skull originally belonged. But I do not wish to suggest that such abnormality as the accused man may possess represents a mitigating factor in this case. No doctor can decide a problem of this nature.

"Our team of examiners has concluded that the accused is not addicted to abnormal drugs such as dagga, is in no sense an alcoholic, cannot be considered a sufferer from schizophrenia and has a good level of intelligence."

Mr. Jonker then addressed himself to the judge. "Mr. Justice," he said. "There are many unusual aspects to this case and I have reason to suspect that my distinguished legal adversary" (here he nodded to the prosecutor who dutifully rolled his eyes up into his head) "would like to further inflame racial tensions in our lovely country by using the sad case of this unhappy boy as a tub-thumper's sounding board.

"I would call your attention to the fact that the accused can in no sense be fairly charged with either *dolus directus* or *dolus eventualis* as these instances are defined and understood within the meaning of our laws.

"Now *dolus directus*, as we recall, attests to an actual intent to kill. *Dolus eventualis* attests to an act resulting in another's death and perpetrated by someone aware of that possibility but nevertheless persisting in the recklessness of said act. Clearly either such *dolus*, and this has long been the ruling of our courts, represents what the law calls murder.

"However, it is perfectly evident that my client, the defendant, cannot in any sense be charged with *dolus directus* or *dolus eventualis*. His was but an act of hasty anger and no criminal *dolus*. The boy was simply emotionally upwrought and for a moment forgetful of his own extraordinary strength. Any worthy citizen of this great nation will sympathize with the natural instinct of a son to resent a deliberate insult to his father, even to the corpse of his revered parent.

"As for the question of race and of violating restrictive legislation with which, as I believe is well known, I have no personal sympathy myself, I offer the following sworn photostatic documents. They have been taken from the records of Windhoek and from the witnessed testimony of native affairs agents in the Kaokoveld district and also the Namib area.

"It will be seen, Mr. Justice, that this boy appears to be legally within what is known as the Colored racial category. He is not European nor Bantu African. Therefore the allegations brought before the court by the state prosecutor and including the testimony of Mr. Piet Burger are clearly demonstrated to be inapplicable and out of order.

"But I insist, as a matter of personal conscience, on adding that my client, the defendant, in fact belongs to only one race, that to which we all belong, the human

race. Is that not right, Curly?" Mr. Jonker inquired, looking straight at me.

There was a loud murmur in the courthouse and the
judge rapped for order. "You may answer," he told me.

"No sir," I replied. "I am not human. I'm a primate as
Mr. Jonker knows. Dr. Levy told me so years ago. I'll show
you my tail if you want."

Great roars of laughter swept the court and again the
judge rapped his desk with a kind of wooden mallet.

The prosecutor protested. "If you please, Your Honor,
the defendant strikes me as being nutty as a fruitcake. I
do not, however, know whether you consider this
disqualifies him as being legally insane. Upon reflection
and with due respect to the testimony of those psychiatric
experts we have heard, I don't see what one has to do with
the other, apparent insanity and legal insanity."

"No," said the judge. "Nor do I. In this state I do not
see any reason why these factors should disqualify the
defendant from trial and judgment and sentencing. Just
the reverse, I might add."

At that point I was taken downstairs to the cells, clanking along in my chains and stooping beneath each door-
sill, while the judge deliberated on my fate with the two
assessors assigned to join him in making that decision.
When I was conducted back into the courtroom after
waiting for three hours, the judge was sitting behind his
desk wearing his red robe. He looked at me sternly and he
said:

"Kerl von Snarl, it is normal in this country that in a
case such as yours the bench should deliberate a day or
two before arriving at its final conclusion. However, in
this case I have found a remarkable unanimity of opinion
as between myself and these two associated magistrates.

"This unfortunate man, Jan Rupert, was most brutally
done to death. And there is no faint doubt that you were
guilty of that crime, you alone. In our country a dozen or

more murders are committed weekly in African and Colored townships and a halt must be put to this sordid situation.

"Your defense counsel has made no submission proving the existence of extenuating circumstances and on the balance of probability there is no indication that such exist. There is, therefore, but one conclusion to be drawn.

"You have been found guilty of murder without extenuating circumstances and without mitigating factors. Consequently there is only one sentence I can pass upon you. By law there is only one sentence that can be passed: that you be returned to a place of custody and hanged by the neck until you are dead. Kerl von Snarl, you will so be taken and there hanged by the neck until you are dead."

CHAPTER VII

I was conducted back to Pretoria Central Prison in one of those wire cage half-trucks that are so small I had to sit on the floor instead of the bench and to hunch my head between my shoulders. "There you go, Curly," said the friendlier of my two guards as he shoved me, chains and all, below and through the door of my cell and clanged it shut. "Death Row for you," said the other with satisfaction. "Next chap you see will be here to measure your collar."

The cell was small and low and, although it had three bunks, I was alone in it. Later I was told by one of my colleagues along the Row that this was not so much because of my large size and for the sake of my comfort as because the authorities had not managed to decide whether my roommates should be white, black or brown.

There was still official confusion about the shade of my skin in terms of racial classification. Moreover, if I had been officially placed in the white category I would have had only one companion; but as nonwhite it could have been up to three and there simply wasn't space for that. Apartheid was very much the rule in Death Row and Toto Croome, one of my neighbors, pleasantly assured me such was even the case when the corpses were subsequently buried.

Pretoria Central was where they executed people in the northern part of the country called the Witwatersrand and I learned that it had a frequently used gallows widely reputed for its efficiency. Toto said he was glad of this because he was bored with life, which he found very difficult. He appeared to have had an interesting career that was marred principally by the fact that he almost always managed to get caught after each adventure.

He knew the inside of all the South African jails from Brandvlei to the Cape. He had been flogged many times. Sometimes, he told me, the police would tie his arms around his knees, put a broomstick through and set its ends on two tables. Then they beat the soles of his feet as he dangled upside down. He did not like the police, he confided to me so I told him about Mr. Burger. "I've heard of that BOSS bastard," said Toto. "If I can get word from here to one of my pals maybe I'll have him killed for you yet."

Toto had a cellmate everyone called Nutty Natty. Natty had been convicted of murdering one girl with a Zulu battle-axe, severing the jugular vein of another with a long knife and drowning yet a third after she called him mad. He insisted this was an unfair affront to his character and intelligence and objected when the judge pondered aloud whether insanity should be considered in meting out his sentence.

"I am not insane," Nutty Natty had protested, hollering in the court. "It is just that I have not had a fair trial. Everyone is prejudiced against me and nobody has even for a moment mentioned the unbearable provocations I suffered."

Ntimane, a strong and very agreeable Zulu, lived in another nearby cell with three black colleagues. The guard along the hall was very generous about letting us talk. He seemed fascinated by our conversation. Ntimane told me: "I have had every opportunity and I even went to school but I didn't like it so I started killing people. Especially women.

"It wasn't that I had a special grudge against the women I killed. I never saw them until I cut them up. They had done me no harm and I didn't want to go to bed with them. I just killed them in protest, I suppose. You night call me a protest killer. When the judge asked me why I murdered them I told him it was none of his business.

"I guess I don't much care that they are going to hang me. Most people seem to get cross at me for nothing so it's pretty much the same to me whether I live or die. But it is sort of bad luck, Curly, that I have to leave this place. I like this prison better than any place I've known and I have the nicest companions I've ever known. Real friends. I get good food and I sleep fine and everyone is kind. I'm happy here but I guess it's rather late for that."

One of Ntimane's room-mates was a Basuto who used to hide in the thick tambookie grass in the low mountains there and, wearing a brown balaklava knitted cap over his face as disguise, would shoot the local farmers because he didn't like them. He was a very good shot and always managed to escape the police until they took to using dogs. They tracked him down after he murdered an Indian storekeeper in a lonely farming village.

He explained to me that he only started killing all the white people when he got married and had no money left after paying the lobola or wife tax to her father. When she fell ill the doctor in the district, a white man, refused to treat her because the Basuto had no money. So she died. He swore that she would have plenty of company wherever death took her. The very first companion he selected was the doctor.

" 'Baas,' I told him just before I shot him, 'you have not been very kind.' Baas is what we call the white man in my region," he explained. I noticed he pronounced the word just like BOSS and I told him so. "That's right," he replied with pleasure. "And all I wanted to do was kill the bosses."

The Basuto confided to me that his other room-mate originally from Zimbabwe, was not a criminal but really a very patriotic gentleman just dangerous to those who disagreed with him. He was an ardent African patriot and therefore disliked the white people in charge of the country. Even more he detested the black people who did not share his opinions. He had been sentenced to death for a quite unpleasant action against one of his neighbors who made a public speech in a black township favoring the Afrikaner system as better than anything in Zimbabwe.

With admiration in his voice the Basuto told me: "He surely knows what to do when he is angry. He went to that neighbor's house one night and, at gunpoint, had his wife tie the neighbor up. Then he hacked off his ears, nose and lips with a knife and made her cook them in a mealie pot. And then he made her eat the pieces while he watched. That's some man. I never disagree with him. He is a great patriot."

I found those days very interesting and even quite amusing as we talked, stumbled around the exercise courtyard in our chains, and ate the prison food which I liked although the others grumbled. But one day Mr. Jonker appeared at the door to my cell and the gruff guard let him in. Mr. Jonker seemed embarrassed.

"My boy, I have bad news," he said. "My appeal to the higher courts has been rejected because it is claimed there are no extenuating circumstances. I have done my best, Curly, but I fear it was a grave mistake on my part to serve as your counsel in this terrible case. Clearly the prejudice against me of my fellow Afrikaners and above all of the Broederbond has redounded against you. What we have as a consequence is a serious travesty of justice. The gravest I have ever encountered; indeed, the gravest of which I have ever heard.

"My poor boy, I have no word with which to console you. This is a terrible fate for you to find, and in a terrible country. You must confide yourself to deep and philosophical reflection about life's purpose. And you would do well to write to your mother. I assure you that your letter will reach its destination even if I have to take it there myself. I shall, as is my moral duty, attend the final leave-taking ceremony. And you, my boy, I am confident that you will bear up courageously with all the resolve and tranquility you have already displayed so far."

Mr. Jonker left after stretching up on tiptoe and hugging me, embracing both my cheeks as I stooped down over him. I could still hear him sobbing down the hall when a very thin man came to the door of my cell, which had been locked tight again. He looked at me a long time, taking down some notes with a pencil on the back of an envelope. He had still, cold, gray eyes and his hair was smooth and shiny, seeming to point up a certain cruelty in him. Finally he went away with light, silent footsteps.

"That's the hangman, Curly," muttered Toto. "Figuring out your neck size and strength. Already has statistics on your height and weight. Hard for these bastards to handle a case like you, pal."

I said nothing but began to think more and more about the wishing ring in my brass amulet which the admission authorities at Pretoria Central had refused to give back to me when I arrived and it was handed over by my accompanying guards in a bundle with my other personal possessions.

Two days later, as I was thinking about this strange place where I was about to end my life and wondering whether there ever would have been any Globetrotters if the Dutch had beat the British in the Battle of Nieuw Amsterdam so that it would have been spelled Haarlem and not Harlem, I had another visitor. This was a somber, ashen-faced gentleman dressed like a preacher with a collar that turned backward. He introduced himself as the chaplain of Pretoria Central, a dominie of the Dopper Kerk.

"I do not know what your faith is, young man, but ours is a tolerant religion. I wish to help you make your peace with God and thus to ease the load you carry on the road to your departure. May I suggest, to start, that together we recite the Lord's Prayer. Now, after me, phrase by phrase."

He bowed his head, clasped his thin, bony hands, and said in a low voice: "The Father which art in Heaven . . ."

"But, chaplain," I protested. "I know that prayer. My Mutterl taught it to me when I was a little boy. It doesn't go that way. It starts: '*Our* Father which art . . .' "

"But you are of mixed racial ancestry," said the dominie. "You cannot claim Him as your own Father. Only as a world Father."

"But he's my Father three times," I objected. "White, brown, black. He's your Father only once. Surely you have less right than I to claim him."

"Heavens, you cannot believe that God is colored," he complained.

I decided not to argue with him for I needed his help. I told him I had a special amulet which I wished to take with me to the gallows. Then Mr. Jonker could send it to my mother as a keepsake and a proof that I was thinking of her at the end. I explained that this was among my few belongings held by the prison authorities. Would he have the kindness, despite my ignorance of heavenly matters, to obtain this for me and help console my final moments.

"Yes," he said. "I will do this. If first you recite the Lord's Prayer properly with me." So I obliged him with the apartheid Father of the white people. With a gleam of satisfaction in his eyes, he then shook my hand disdainfully and departed. A half hour later he returned holding out the amulet by its string as if it were a poisonous snake. He handed it to me through the bars and left.

As soon as I received the amulet I unsnapped it and extracted the wishing ring. Then I opened my trousers, took out my poor frightened organ, and rolled the ring down along it. "Oh, shikwembos," I whispered to myself, "Oh, Mwagulane, if ever you came to the help of anyone please help me now. Let me survive. Don't let them kill me. Please."

As I was about to tuck myself together again inside my pants and put the amulet back around my neck a guard came in and asked me what I'd like for my final meal. I thought a long time and then I said: "Could I have some sausage. It will remind me of the good hot dogs we used to get near old Ben Franklin High. And also I'd like some mealie. That's like corn on the cob you know. And finally, I've only had one glass of beer in my life. Do you think, sir, that I could have a glass of beer?"

The man seemed surprised. "They usually ask for steak," he told me. "But I guess we can handle this." I was so pleased that I forgot to remove the wishing ring and I was so flustered I didn't close my fly when I hung the amulet on my neck. In a short while he was back with my meal and it was very good. I settled down with a little tray and ate it all up. The beer was simply delicious. I wished I could live a little while longer in order to drink some more beer.

At this point four guards, two of them bearing short guns, arrived at my cell together with the dominie, carrying a small Bible, and an authoritative-looking man with white hair and stern face who appeared to be in charge. I guess he was the prison warden. Anyway, they came right into the cell, clamped my wrists behind my back, and shoved me through the door.

As I clanked down the hall past the cells of all my friends they began to kick up a fuss. Toto Croome and Nutty Natty started to sing "Abide with Me" in very loud, off-key voices. Ntimane and the other blacks chanted "Nkosi Sikolele Afrika," their special anthem, in beautiful harmony. And several of the prisoners farther down the hall, the ones I didn't really know well, rattled metal objects along the bars of their cells and stamped their feet so that really it sounded like quite a joyful and musical occasion.

In the back of the prison, as far as I could tell, there was a door which opened into a small room where I saw the gallows platform. I recognized it immediately because I had often seen gallows in book illustrations and in some of the comic strips I used to read.

There was a kind of reception party awaiting us inside the little side door where we entered: the grim hangman and a white assistant, a man who appeared to be the superior of the warden as the latter nodded to him with respect, and a fellow wearing a white smock whom I took to be a physician. There were also about a dozen ordinary people standing in solemn rows. I saw among them Mr. Jonker, tears rolling down his kind cheeks, Mr. Malan, the prosecutor who succeeded in having me condemned, and Mr. Burger, who quite clearly was moving his lips in a way designed to send me a message. "I promised to get you," no doubt.

I didn't have time to think. Hands pushed me rapidly forward under the gallows bar and I saw the dominie sidle up and open his holy book. The last thing I remembered was the way the prosecutor's eyes were rolling up into his head and then a black cloth covered my face. The dominie appeared to be muttering something in Afrikaans and there came a loud bang. I dropped suddenly into space.

My heart stopped. I was certain I was dead but I realized I could hear a wooden creaking and then I found that I was standing on my toes and, while the noose around my neck had tightened somewhat, I could still breathe all right. I just stood there and was pleased that all my years of playing basketball had given me very strong and springy feet. I felt the shock of almost being hanged had given me an erection and, intensified by the shikwembo ring, there was nothing my fettered hands could do to disguise it.

Naturally I couldn't see anything because of the black cloth. I couldn't even tell if the people who had come to watch me get hanged were able to understand exactly what had happened. There seemed to be a great fuss and much discussion. At last I heard Mr. Jonker shout:

"I refuse to countenance another attempt. This poor boy has been duly punished for his alleged crime and the good Lord himself, by a miracle, has confirmed his innocence. It is against the law of this country that a man be punished twice for the same crime. That the executioner made a mistaken calculation is his fault, not that of Kerl von Snarl. I demand he be taken back to his cell and held there safely and well treated and protected until I can obtain a writ from the highest court deciding on the judicial position.

"I insist on the correctness of this procedure and surely anyone here present with the faintest understanding of legal precedent and legal practice must agree with me. I shall hold the governor of this prison and all present here responsible in the event of any miscarriage of justice with respect to this boy."

Again there was a hubbub. Sometimes I thought I heard Mr. Burger's voice barking out angrily, but eventually some people came and took the rope off my neck. One of them said with undisguised admiration: "Did you ever see such a hard-on, man? And look at his open fly. The fellow even wears a condom to get hanged. And, by God, he busted it." They led me stumbling around what I took to be the gallows, conducted me outside so that I shouldn't see any of the people still arguing in the execution chamber, and there removed the black cloth from my face.

Rather to my surprise I was taken to an entirely new section of the prison and there, far from Toto, Ntimane and my other friends, was placed in another cell. I guess the authorities couldn't bear to let any of the tenants of Death Row know that it was ever possible to escape their scheduled fate.

They tell me that the final trial, or retrial or nontrial in the same first dreary courtroom at Johannesburg made legal history in South Africa and even in other parts of the world where English is spoken and precedents are established for the future interpretation of common law. In any case, a friendly guard had shown me copies of the *Star*, the *Daily Mail* and other newspapers I could read. They were full of the case, even discussing in guarded language certain of the more private and embarrassing aspects of the hanging that didn't come off.

"You're quite some hero now, Curly," said the friendly guard with every sign of admiration. "And you won't be lacking girl friends if you ever get out from behind the bars. That fellow who took the rope from around your neck, why he's still getting free drinks from one end of the Transvaal to the other end of the Rand. Just for describing what you look like. Or part of you, at least. He even swears that famous tail of yours was sticking out behind."

My second trial was very interesting and I felt proud when they brought me into the courtroom still chained, and some of the people stood up and clapped. The judge, who was a different man, rapped his hammer on the desk for order. I hadn't realized how nice all the old wood in the place smelled, and also the well-scrubbed people. It was quite different from the sour, acid stink of jail and the even worse and putrid odor of the little chamber where the Pretoria gallows stood.

After a good deal of argument that was barked back and forth between the various lawyers and police and technical experts, the new state prosecutor began a long speech which was very hard for me to understand.

"This man," he said, looking at me with a severe stare, "had been properly investigated and held for weeks of preliminary hearing before he came up for trial in the Rand Supreme Court. There all aspects of the case were fully and impartially assessed by the state."

At this point he made what appeared to be a favorite gesture. He fingered the side of what would have been his nose if he had had one. Instead, he wore a kind of leather apparatus on a band that covered the space between his eyes and upper lip and that served to obscure what might have been an unpleasant scar. Later I was told he had been a great war hero. I never found out just whom he fought.

"This man, as you can easily see if you study his stature, his sullen expression, his distorted features," he said, apparently forgetting his own ugliness, "is clearly of a criminal type and unsafe to be permitted circulation in a free society like that of our own great nation. Twice already he has been involved in cases that resulted in deaths from some form of homicide. I think there is no need for me to recount once again the instances of Mr. Screwhill and of the Ukrainian Primate with which this honorable court is already quite familiar, thanks to documents produced by my distinguished predecessor in a previous trial.

"Nor is it worth my recalling to you, Mr. Justice, that prior to the murder of Jan Rupert, of which the defendant

was convicted by a due and final verdict, the murderer
—for such he is by legal decision—was twice involved in
deliberate offenses against the various separate development statutes by which we protect the purity and vigor of
our nation."

Here again he rubbed the edge of that strange, bulging
leather patch and I forgot what he was saying because I
was so fascinated by the possibilities of what lay beneath
it. He continued:

""As everyone knows, Mr. Justice, Kerl von Snarl was
duly convicted and then duly sentenced for the crime of
murder to a punishment which is mandatory under our
laws, as we are all aware, except in the case of a woman
killing her newly born child or in the case of persons
under the age of eighteen and in extenuating circumstances. The convicted person, and there is ample evidence
of this, is not a woman. He is over eighteen, and the court
has ruled that there were and are no extenuating circumstances.

"Now it is laid down under Criminal Procedure Act
Number 56, which became the law of this great state in
1955, we accept in our free society the principle of *autrefois acquit* and *autrefois convict*. That is to say, if a
person has already been charged and acquitted or
charged and convicted of a crime, he cannot be charged
and acquitted or convicted again of the same crime.

"Moreover, as is the case with the legal precedents of
English Common Law and accepted in most civilized
societies like our own, a man cannot be sentenced twice
or punished twice for the same crime. But such is not the
issue here.

"I would remind you, Mr. Justice" (and here he deliberately pointed to his non-nose) "that we South Africans
fought and suffered and many of us died for the freedom
which we now possess. I well remember how, on distant
battlefields, I thought back to my mother here on our

farm along the Vaal, an excellent woman of a most delicate temperament, a good woman as the Predikant said when he wrote me of her death.

"And I thought on that distant battlefield what we were fighting for: a peaceful, tranquil, just society, such as we have indeed created. And it is that justice I ask you for today. This man should not be sentenced twice. He has already been fairly and duly sentenced under our laws. This man should not be punished twice. All I ask is that he be punished once, only once. That he be properly punished as the law intends.

"The stern and immutable course of destiny shall not be permitted to be deflected by an accident, deplorable as it may be. Sir, I thank this court." The prosecutor sat down and there was a ripple of applause from the grim, stern-faced people jammed into the courtroom. I noticed among those clapping Mr. Burger. Again the judge rapped.

When Mr. Jonker rose to defend me once again it seemed to me that a cold and hostile atmosphere greeted his opening remarks. But he was very smart. Clasping in one hand a folder of documents he often tapped for emphasis, he said: "Mr. Justice, some of my client's friends have expressed fears about the severity of this court but I have reassured them to a man that no one in this splendid republic loves truth and mercy and justice more than the honored judge presiding on this bench or is more familiar with the niceties and traditions of our law or more respects the unshakeable meaning of that law.

"And now we are faced by an issue adroitly posed but also adroitly confused by the distinguished prosecution, namely that no man can or should be sentenced twice or punished twice for one and the same crime. He claims that Kerl von Snarl should—and here I quote him—be punished once, only once. But is this truly a fair statement of the issue? Mr. Justice, I ask but that.

"Surely, when he stood upon the ghastly gallows in Pretoria, this boy was placed in jeopardy of his life. And surely when he dropped into what must have seemed endless space, he was in jeopardy of his life. Under law it is accepted by custom, tradition and by specific statute that no man convicted of any crime shall be placed in jeopardy of his life again, and deliberately, for that same crime.

"This is true no matter what the nature of any additional evidence that might be produced, no matter what the caliber of any conceivable new witnesses. But there are no new witnesses; there is no new evidence. Even though Kerl von Snarl were now to confess before this court that he had deliberately done Jan Rupert to death, the State would not, it could not, legally reindict him.

"Of course that hypothesis is ridiculous for he is truly innocent. But the point is simple, we are talking about one crime and one punishment; and that this punishment, which I respectfully submit was most unjust and upset only by an act of providence, has already been meted out. That it failed of its purpose is surely not this boy's fault. He has suffered enough already.

"And I would turn to another aspect of this tragic case. Here is a young man who has been accused this very day of being twice involved—and here I quote again—'in deliberate offenses against the various separate development statutes by which we protect the purity and vigor of our nation.' Our great nation, I might add.

"While this is not the specific issue before us, Mr. Justice, I crave your indulgence to digress since emotion and bias have indubitably marked this case and since the matter was deliberately introduced by the esteemed prosecution.

"This boy has been slurred and tortured for racial reasons. He has been depicted in an earlier session of this very court as what we would call of Colored blood. Therefore it cannot be claimed that he was transgressing our statutory distinctions when involved in one or another act with non-Europeans or using non-European facilities.

"It has been said that he is descended from the Herero people, on his father's side. And we South Africans well know that the Hereros developed a strong hatred for the Germans during their period of colonization northwest of us, and that this hatred translated itself into an antipathy generally toward all white men. The Herero nation came to think, it is said, that all white men were enemies of their nation.

"And only two percent at most—this being a generous figure—of the Herero people are literate. And in many stations scattered throughout their tribal land their men, accused of offenses we might regard as petty, are shackled with leg chains. And in the Kaokoveld, where it is said this boy's grandmother originated, the proud remnants of the Oorlog Hereros still attempt to maintain their dignity, exchanging gift for gift, and even wearing what white man's clothing they can muster in order to emphasize their self-respect. We are now, in all our gracious wisdom, seeking to protect and civilize these poor Hereros who suffered so long as a consequence of a cruel German occupation.

"If this young man sincerely believed that, according to our standards, our definitions, he was a non-European, he was morally and legally correct to behave as a non-European. And according to the complexities of our social system this placed him within the category of a Colored man and that is what he accepted, in all sincerity. Why then should his actions in that capacity be dragged before this court with every intention of demeaning his name by implying a deliberate intention of lawbreaking?

"And at the same time we have been told, in an earlier process which now again becomes moot, that Kerl von Snarl's mother was of Jewish descent, a statement that appeals, in certain cases, to narrow-minded prejudices.

For, despite the admiration of our Government for the small state of Israel, there is a decided limit to the admiration of our populace for Jews, as such; for South African Jews. The preference is not for Jews at home but for Jews abroad. And all these prejudices, of color and of religion, have been appealed to, indirectly I admit, throughout the tortuous proceedings of this two-stage case.

"Thus this boy, I maintain, has been victimized at least in part because of emotional bias on racial and religious grounds. He has been in that sense made to suffer for alleged descent from two suffering peoples. But I would contend before any tribunal, on earth or in Heaven above, that God as a Trinity at least unites all people symbolically in one. As Saint Francis of Assisi pointed out, all creatures, not just human, descend from God. There is no apartheid in Paradise.

"There is even a question of aberration, of affliction. All of us," said he, staring straight at the prosecutor's dark brown leather nose "can suffer similarly and this warrants sympathy, not affront. My client, my friend, claims quite rightly to be a primate because of a slight physical deformity. But we are all primates. Human beings are primates. And he is of the human race, primate species, as are we all. Nor is this a lesser matter.

"Moreover, each race has its gifts, its special talents. One may have an eye for beauty, for color, for shape. Another may have an ear for harmony and rhythm, a voice for loveliness, for poetry, for song. Another may have a heart for tenderness and courage, a touch for gentle kindness and for heroism. Another may have a body for sinuousness and strength.

"We all share these gifts in one or another way and to one or another degree. And my young friend, Curly von Snarl, has been unwittingly depicted by those who would malign him, as actually indeed more fortunate than others because, it is said, he can draw on three special founts of human ardor and vitality. For this he should be blessed, not cursed; honored, not maligned.

"Yet he tells me the worthy dominie who came to comfort him just before what was intended as his final moment on this earth—an event he miraculously survived —indignantly assured him: 'God is not Colored. He is not your Father. You may address Him only as *the* Father.'

"Prove it, I say. Prove that God is not Colored. With all His variegated genius for creation, how can He be anything else?"

There was a roar of disapproval in the courtroom. I felt a wave of hostility whirling through like a cloud. The prosecutor looked satisfied and fingered his leather patch. Even as he rapped for silence, the judge was frowning his displeasure. But Mr. Jonker continued undisturbed.

"The point I wish to make," he said, "is not that miscegenation is sublime, or even desirable as such. The point I wish to make is how our prejudices may often lead us to incorrect conclusions. In a court of law it is obvious that logic and intellect must decide, not emotion and sentiment. Now I would wish to recall to you certain salient facts.

"Blackstone teaches we must accept as valid evidence the confirmed truth, regardless of source, regardless of whether or not we admire that source, so long as we know it is valid. And what is the real truth of Kerl von Snarl's racial origins? There is one unchallenged, if detestable and reprehensible source on this question.

"It is based upon the sworn and attested evidence of so-called, self-proclaimed and (by their adherents) much-admired experts. That source is the racial purification branch of the National Socialist Party of Adolf Hitler's Third Reich, a party which had its moment of popularity even among some of our more prominent fellow citizens in this fair land.

"This young man was born in a kind of hostel at

Steinhöring in Bavaria. It was operated by the National Socialist organization known as Lebensborn which, in turn, was a 'racial selection' branch of the famous SS. Indeed, SS General Gregor Ebner, its acknowledged specialist in such matters of race, personally signed the admission papers to Steinhöring of Kerl von Snarl's mother, certifying that she came of what is known as pure Aryan descent.

"Likewise, the boy's father was not only similarly certified; he was actually a high-ranking officer, a Sturmbahnführer of the SS, an organization—I would remind you—that prided itself on the untainted purity of its white, Aryan blood. And there is unchallengeable evidence that Kerl von Snerl was born of the union of these two untainted people in an untainted hostel supervised by the SS. I even have an attested, photographed copy of Kerl von Snarl's SS Sippenbuch or SS certificate of the purity of his origin. I shall submit it as an evidential document if the court so wishes."

"That will not be necessary," said the judge, his eyes gleaming with fascinated interest. The whole room was hushed.

"I need not tell you that the National Socialists of Hitler Germany, the Nazis as we know them, were —whatever their devilish shortcomings—obsessed with the question of racial purity and less likely than any people I can think of to make mistakes in this connection. Especially, gross mistakes. Biology for them was more important than love. Political biology, that is.

"And in the main office of the Lebensborn on Herzog-Max Strasse in Munich, teams of experts assured themselves that no Jewish or Negro blood had entered the families of those admitted to this SS breeding institution, as far back as the Thirty Years' War. The Thirty Years' War, I need not recall, ended in 1648. This is a finer breed even than that of our own late and unlamented Ossewa

Brandwag to which I believe, distinguished members of our government once belonged.

"Now, how is it possible that Kerl von Snarl could have been so grossly misjudged in every respect by the courts and people of this splendid land of ours? First he is wrongly charged with infringing the racial separateness code when, at the same time, he is charged with being himself Colored—and therefore patently innocent of the charge.

"Then he is damaged by public prejudice aimed at his 'Colored' blood when it is demonstrably and legally proven that his racial strain is more white than that of anyone in this courtroom.

"Then he is slandered by the slur of having been 'involved' in two homicidal cases. Yet I have herewith evidence—which I shall submit in attested documents if the court so wishes—that each of the cases referred to was adjudged wholly accidental.

"And, finally, we have the tragic instance of what has happened in our own lovely land. This man has been hanged—wrongly hanged, I submit—for what was adjudged a crime according to the sentence of a legally constituted court. And that hanging is punishment, even if through no fault of anyone except an incompetent executioner, the hanging failed of its purpose, namely death.

"And I agree with the learned prosecutor. *Autrefois acquit* and *autrefois convict*. This man cannot be convicted again of the same alleged crime. He cannot be tried again for the same alleged offense. Nor can he, in justice, again be punished. Furthermore, he should not be smeared again by slurs deliberately foisted to damage his reputation. He is as demonstrably innocent as he is demonstrably white."

Mr. Jonker sat down amid an ominous silence. I felt hostile forces were summoning themselves in a storm. But then there was a curiously odd break in tension, a lightening of atmosphere.

Suddenly there was a loud clamor of applause. Soon everyone in the courtroom was weeping or even stamping their feet, everyone, that is, except Mr. Burger and the prosecution's legal staff, who hurried out of the chamber.

The judge beat uselessly on his desk with the wooden hammer. People began to shout: "Good old Curly." "Triumph for Curly." "What a smash for the Broederbond." "Jonker has plenty guts, what?" "Ho, Ho. How that former Broer can twist the law around." "Get yourself another hangman, BOSS."

As for me, the guards took me downstairs swiftly before any verdict was announced and I was still clanking in my chains. But, even though I couldn't hear the judge's decision, I knew from the milling about outside the guardroom that things were going in my favor. Instead of rushing me back to the cells and the cage-truck, my protectors sat me on a bench and gave me a cup of coffee.

A few moments later Mr. Jonker burst in with a broad smile, embracing me. "All right, Curly," he said. "We made it. You're innocent. That is, you're finished with these courts. No more trials. All over. No more persecution. They're just going to take you back to get your belongings and wind up formalities. Then you're free. The only thing is, you are being deported. By government decree. I shall not challenge this. Have to leave as soon as possible. But don't worry. You're in my recognizance. I'll arrange everything.

"Meanwhile," he added, turning to the guards, "unlock his chains. From now on Curly von Snarl is free."

I took my first unhindered steps in weeks and weeks. My stride was unfamiliar, long, as if I were going to take off any minute.

CHAPTER VIII

I t was four o'clock in the morning when Mr. Jonker's car arrived at the airport. I had a feeling it was a different field from where I had the dismal encounter with my father. The only planes I saw seemed to be military and every person was in uniform. All luggage, including my Globetrotter bag, was put straight on board without labels and without inspection.

Our airplane was a long four-engined model with no markings on it at all and a gleaming silver color. "It is chartered," said Mr. Jonker, following my glance. "The Israelis charter from private American airlines to handle secret missions and also to handle certain types of weapons shipments. You see, we have a kind of informal alliance. The Arabs are openly against both of us, which throws us into each other's arms."

"The enemy of my enemy is my friend, I was told in Cairo," I said, glad of a chance to show how wise I was.

When my turn came to climb aboard Mr. Jonker went

up the gangway with me. "I have special permission," he explained. "And I'm taking no chances with you. Nothing is going to go wrong again." He walked me down the aisle toward the front, past piles and piles of sealed, wooden packing cases crammed into the fuselage, and past about twenty very tough-looking gentlemen who had a military air about them.

As I went by them, an American voice with a New York accent called out: "Hi there, Stretch. They couldn't stretch your neck after all, could they? Nice going, keed."

Everyone laughed as the voice began explaining his joke in what I took to be Hebrew.

At the end of the aisle there was an empty seat where Mr. Jonker deposited me beside a short, bulky man with strong hands and arms, big features, blond hair and a sunburn. "You may call your neighbor Arik," he said. "He is returning to Israel from a State mission. He has undertaken to look after you. Now goodbye and good luck. You've had such astonishing luck already that you may need my wish. Luck has a way of changing when you least expect it."

I thanked Mr. Jonker for all he had done. He was a brave, honest man. Also I began to realize how true it is that honesty is the best policy. Mr. Jonker was openly opposed to everything in South Africa, his country, and he told that to everyone. So he had no secrets and no one, not even BOSS, dared touch him because of the private files on key leaders which he had accumulated and locked up in inaccessible places abroad.

He leaned over abruptly, as I was trying to work my behind into the rather narrow chair where I was seated, and he placed his bristly cheek beside mine, tickling me with his beard and hugging my shoulders. "God bless you, boy, and maybe some day you will come back again, back here to a better South Africa." His eyes were glistening as he turned and rushed from the plane.

(110)

Mr. Arik told me to fasten my seat belt. I pushed myself into my place as hard as I could and tried to get the belt around me to snap at the farthest loose point. He also had difficulty, short as he was, and the two of us together were almost bursting the light chairs where we sat together. The plane began to move and rickety, rickety, all the packing cases in the fuselage seeming to crack and squeak, up we strained and turned into the faint pink of predawn forming over distant Mozambique.

I looked across and out a tiny window at the sky as the sun crept into it. It was the flattest, widest, deepest sky I had ever seen, like the road to heaven, paved with soft flat clouds. It went on forever and unchanging except for the colors painted on it by the sun.

Mr. Arik was very friendly but he wouldn't talk about what he had been doing or about the packing cases or about the other, tough-looking men aboard. However, he seemed to know a lot about me.

"Yours is the most unusual case," he said. "Under South African law you are Colored—and that fact helped in a paradoxical way to make you a free man in a land where it makes others like you slaves. Under the Nazi Nuremberg law you are a Jew because of your mother's mother. Despite the fact that you are certified Aryan by Nazi and SS jurisprudence. And under our law you can be an Israeli anytime you want to be. If we accept the Nuremberg law's definition that your mother is a Jew. For us anyone with a Jewish mother is a Jew. And therefore automatically eligible to be an Israeli citizen. But we despise the Nuremberg law. What does that make you?"

"I am an American," I said.

"Yes, you are lucky. Imagine being an American citizen after starting life in a Lebensborn hospice. Only in America can you be a Jew and a Negro and not be too much bothered by either fact—or both. You could even be an Israeli and a U.S. citizen. Did you know that?

"There are many choices in life but there are also many combinations you can make. As for me, I am an Israeli and I am a Jew. There are no combinations. That's what makes Israelis tough. One might almost say desperate. There are no choices. No alternatives."

Mr. Arik looked at me curiously and then said: "I am glad you are coming to Israel. You should know it is not just a question of doing Bram Jonker a favor. Or of helping a mixed-up kid like you. I have heard about the strange bonking blow of yours. How it just squashes and kills immediately.

"Now we don't have anyone in Israel who is anywhere near your size. Nevertheless, I want our commandos to watch you operate. To see you use it—on a dummy of course. We always want to learn new tricks. If we can adjust your bonk to silent, unarmed combat it could prove very helpful. So now you see. You need us and we need you. Almost like Israel and South Africa."

For a while both of us dozed. We didn't take our seat belts off because it wasn't worth the trouble. We were tightly jammed in anyway. After a time an American steward in a dark blue uniform came by and served us breakfast. I caught a glimpse of a willowy girl, also in a dark blue uniform, passing trays to the men in back.

"They go with the plane." Mr. Arik nodded with a grin. "Charter job. We don't have enough of our own available for long flights like this. Not yet, at any rate. This is a regular U.S. civilian aircraft. The company just paints out its markings. But they leave their own crew on board. All we have is our security men."

"You mean Israel has a BOSS too?"

"No, Curly. It's not like BOSS. Thank God. We're a real democracy even if South Africa is our ally. Our cobelligerent, let us say. The Arabs want to destroy both of us. Wipe us off the face of the earth. I think you know what I mean. Wasn't there an incident in Cairo?

"Of course, we have no alliances in the technical sense. Nothing written. But we have friends—like America because the others have different ideas and will help us only so long as it's convenient for them. But your second President, John Adams—you've heard about him, of course. He was the very first to proclaim that the Jewish people would come back and build their own state in Palestine. And in 1922 the American Congress supported the idea of an Israel. You probably didn't know that, did you?

"Our first big loan came from the U.S. and the U.S. was the first land to grant us recognition. But in terms of defense it's France. France saved Israel in 1956. Without French aid Nasser would have overrun us, eventually. And South Africa is the same, in the same boat. We help them and they help us. On defense. But the day either France or South Africa feels they can do better by dropping us, they will. Mark my words."

Mr. Arik was very curious about how I felt, being all mixed up among Nazis, Jews and Negroes. I told him I really didn't know. It was too strange. Did different kinds of humans feel more or less human? Anyway, as Mr. Jonker pointed out in court, I was a primate.

He said: "We have a new generation in Israel, a new type of Jew. There are immigrants from the Arab world who lived under foreign rule dependent on others for mercy. Then there are the survivors of the Nazi ovens. Many of our young people don't even really know what happened in Germany. It comes as a shock when they are told. What men like your father did.

"I'm sorry, Curly, but that's the truth, isn't it?"

"My Vati was a war hero," I said. "He was decorated. He was brave."

Mr. Arik said nothing. He continued as if he had not heard me.

"The SS killed Poles and others. But the people it wished to destroy totally were the Jews. It is only when our young people realize this that they are shocked into reality. Even I didn't understand at first. I'm a farmer. The son of a farmer. I was born in Israel before it was Israel. They call people like me Sabras, prickly pears."

I asked him what a Jew really was. Mutterl hadn't brought me up with any true religious feeling. Was it only religion to be a Jew? If so, I wasn't a Jew. But if it was race, I was part German, part Austrian and part Negro also. Albino Negro, I added. Albino primate?

"That's a good question. You are by no means the first to ask. It's something that puzzles every Israeli at one time or another. Every Jew I guess. Our great founder, Ben Gurion, told me once: 'My own adjective is Jewish. I refuse to be called a Zionist now. A man who feels himself a Jew is a Jew. No one knows why he is something—but he knows that he is. I have no quarrel with American Jews, only the American Zionists. If they are real Zionists they should come to Israel.'

"A Jew, under our law, is someone with a Jewish mother. Any Jew by that definition can come and live in Israel and be a citizen whenever he wants. Thus you can become an Israeli. Because, as I said, under the Nuremberg law, your mother is Jewish. It's odd that Hitler's laws make you eligible for Israeli citizenship.

"But don't forget this. We are all human beings. Arabs, Jews, whites, blacks. Even, maybe, primates. The first man was not a Jew. He was just a man, made by God, neither black nor white nor red nor green. Faith made the early Jews strong and they believed in redemption.

"I am not myself observant in a religious way. I do believe there is a higher principle above all things, a principle of justice. This was a unique belief in ancient days and it was the teaching of our prophets. They taught that you should love your neighbor as yourself—but no more. They did not speak about turning the other cheek. As Christians now preach but never practice.

(114)

"And our people cannot understand destiny. They believe in the freedom of human choice. Human beings can make their own fate. All history proves this and most recently and specially the history of Israel. The history of Israel is a remarkable history, above all because the Jews survived for two thousand years even without Israel. That was due to their book, the Bible.

"There is no abstract fate or destiny involved. We don't believe in fate. Our greatest asset is our people, with a great purpose in life. We know what we are doing and what we have to do. I think we have this feeling more than any other people in the world. And in the end, we count on ourselves alone. Not on the French. Or the South Africans. Or even the Americans. You will see for yourself, Curly, when you get there."

We were served lunch by the American crew. Again I noticed the slender, pretty girl in the dark blue uniform passing trays in the back of the plane while a smiling, quiet young man took care of the front seats.

I told Mr. Arik the slender girl looked like someone I had known in high school but who had not been very nice. I thought I loved her but she had turned against me nastily.

Mr. Arik hitched his trousers up over his broad, heavy belly. "There is no generosity in women," he said. "They resent being part of us. Only a rib. That's what Eve was, you know, Adam's rib. They want everything coming in and nothing going out. They will not trust you. I have had bad experiences too.

"They hate to acknowledge your generosity. You must not expect too much unless you have your brains where your bowels are and vice versa. I have often had cause to wonder if the story of Cain and Abel isn't wrong. Should it not have posed the question: 'Am I my sister's keeper?' "

I was puzzled by his bitterness and I also kept trying to decide whether the stewardess was really someone I might have known or not. While I was thinking and after we had finished lunch, the quiet young man came back to us again and told Mr. Arik that in not quite an hour we would be stopping at Dar-es-Salaam. The captain wished to discuss something with him first. Would it be possible to follow him into the crew compartment. Grunting, Mr. Arik pulled himself out of the narrow seat and moved up front with a waddle.

While he was gone another of the crew stewards dropped by and said: "Hi, I hear you're American also, pal." He sat down in Mr. Arik's place, adding, "I'll only stay until he comes back. But thought we could have a chat. Understand you've had all kinds of adventures back in Jo'burg."

I learned fast that he didn't want to ask me about my adventures so much as he wanted to tell me about his own. "Is it true they picked you up with Chinese Yumyum?" he asked. "Boy, that's some doll. I've taken her out several times now. Almost every time we make one of these hush-hush flights for the Jews.

"Boy, and are they hush-hush too. We don't have any idea what or whom we're carrying in either direction. Just cases and cases and people and people. Always false manifests, both cargo and passengers. Those Israelis sure are full of secrets. And it's always men we carry. Military specialists I guess. Enough to make a Women's Libber out of you."

"What's that?" I asked.

"Good grief. And you an American too. Where've you been the last few months. God, before Yumyum I was having a go with a Black-Is-Beautiful Women's Libber back in Boston. No wonder I was ready for Yumyum. Say, that's a piece, isn't it? When she's done with you for the night you're like a wet washrag, aren't you? I think Yumyum's boyfriends should start a Men's Lib movement.

"Well, anyway, Women's Lib is an outfit that thinks women haven't had a fair shake. They want total equal rights. Same pay. Same jobs. Same rights in bed. You know, my Black Libber said it was a disgrace the women were always underneath the man. I said Baby, I'll do it any way you want. Or you do it any way you want. Underneath. On top. Inside out. Backwards and forwards. Any way with you's a good way.

"But she still wasn't happy. Called me a sexist and male chauvinist pig and a bigoted honky. There wasn't any way you could make her happy. I said, listen, doll, as far's I'm concerned you can get any job in the world. Even strong man in a circus. But I don't know how you're going to make a wet nurse out of me. Or a chorus girl either, as a matter of fact.

"And what's wrong with my prick anyway? You've given me pretty good indications that you like it. In between lectures. Would you rather be clutched by another Libber? Do you want to become a Lesbo to prove your point? Or do you want to be grabbed by an octopus? All it could do is give you a good feel. Hah! Jeez, I just couldn't take it anymore. But when she forgot that Libber business, she was a pretty good piece of tail."

I asked him how he met Yumyum. I also told him the security people didn't take well to sleeping across the zigzag color line. That had been one of my troubles.

"Man, do I know. I was warned and warned on that score. Even by Yumyum. But she's an honorary white, you know. At least the best part is. I used to wonder what'd of happened to us both if I'd met my unsexist Black-Is-Beautiful baby in Jo'burg.

"As for how I met Yumyum. Why that's easy. Did you ever walk along that street behind the main post office around midafternoon? Yeah, afternoon. They have these cockeyed rules about where they live and sleep. Some of these dubious girls have to leave town early to get back to

(117)

their concentration camps.

"Well, on that street in the afternoons each whore seems to have her regular position. Like a rainbow trout behind his special rock in a stream. I guess if she gets swept up by the tide—or by the Fuzz—another trout moves in. And those dolls are every color of the rainbow too.

"They keep talking about apartheid in South Africa. But the color line fades between the sheets. It's only a matter of getting away with it. They make a fuss if an Indian wants to marry a black girl. But if a white wants to sleep with a darkie, who cares? Just so long's you don't talk about it. Or get caught.

"Well, I'll tell you. My first trip here after I broke with Mandy—that's the Libber girl—I ran into Yumyum on that street and asked her if she wanted a drink. She did. And how. You know, that's a woman who's proud to be a woman. She needs men. Yeah, really needs them. And knows what to do with them, what they're for.

"And she has great charm. She talks well and excitedly. About many things when she turns on. She may not be precise but she's sure a chatterbox. I guess you found out. No? Well maybe you were too busy. She can't tell left from north but she has other graces all her own."

I nodded in solemn agreement. At that moment Mr. Arik came back and the steward left. A sign flashed on asking us not to smoke and to fasten our seat belts. The plane began to lurch heavily down through clouds of mist and suddenly Dar-es-Salaam loomed into sight on the edge of a steaming lagoon.

We taxied to a far corner of the airport and got out, following a dark-skinned officer to a small building where we sat down, surrounded by fierce-looking black soldiers, carrying bayonetted rifles and moving the whites of their eyes as they stared at us, saying not a word.

None of our cargo was unloaded; no passengers left or

joined us; and, after a fuel truck had pumped gas into our tanks and driven off, we were mustered back on board, dripping from the humid heat.

When we had gained our flying height and turned back on course, we headed into a furious tropical storm. Although it was still afternoon, it became almost as dark as night and the lights were turned on. The plane bumped, swayed, creaked and groaned. Every once in a while we would drop with a sudden grunt that made the wings squeal when we came to the bottom of the air pocket. Lightning zigzagged all around us.

This process was repeated many times. Finally the strain was too much for the crates tied in the passenger compartment. First one, then another broke loose. The nice American steward got some of the Israeli soldiers to help him and tried to lash the boxes back. But they didn't succeed. Whatever they contained was much too heavy and the air was so rough that their combined strength was never effectively applied because of the lurching.

I tried to help, confident that my powerful arms and back would successfully manage the problem; but they didn't. I found my height a disadvantage and my strength inadequate. "Better go back to your seat, Curly. You're doing us no good here," said the steward. "You just go back there and dream of Yumyum. Of having her all to yourself." I returned but I didn't manage to dream. I was too scared.

Mr. Arik was sitting beside me peacefully, his eyes closed, a hint of a smile on his crooked mouth, his chunky hands lying together in his lap, thumb linked to thumb. He turned around, opened one eye, and said with a wink: "Never mind, Curly. It will get a lot worse before it gets better."

It did. One large crate burst open when we dropped several hundred feet and it came down hard on another box beneath. The wooden boards splintered and all of a sudden strange metal things shaped like oval vegetables of gleaming black metal started rolling down the aisle. "Good God!" said Mr. Arik. "The Crotale ammunition."

He explained to me that South Africa was making some kind of French rocket, with French permission, and had developed improvements which were being taken to Israel for testing to see if they were in fact more effective than the things France had already supplied to the Israelis. There were continual small fights along the frontiers, he said. Just called raids. Counterinsurgency. So the Israelis could find out how this weapon worked in battle, even without a war.

A South African military mission that stayed in Israel secretly would cooperate in the testing, he added. "Now don't you ever mention this to anyone. But I guess you have a right to know what these are so you don't grab one by mistake. Better leave that to technicians who know about such things. We've got plenty of them aboard."

The storm seemed to get rougher and rougher and there were flashes slicing through the clouds outside as electricity hummed around us.

Just then there was a loud crack as forked lightning struck our right wing. The plane staggered and suddenly fell into another deep pocket. I saw two unshaven, stony-eyed Israelis reach into their pockets and pull out little skullcaps which they shoved on their heads and they wound some long black strings like shoelaces around themselves. They shut their eyes, folded their hands together and began to pray, sweat trickling down their faces.

There was a loud bang and a flash of light. When I looked around I could see the back of the stewardess leaning over a man who was holding his head and screaming. I saw patches of bright red blood splattered on the side of the cabin.

"This is getting pretty rough," said Mr. Arik. "Worse

than I'd bargained for." He got up, heaved his way to the rear, and barked out some orders in Hebrew. I saw two men trying to gather up rolling cylinders and lay them together on two empty seats, attempting to hold them down with shirts and jackets laid across them.

Then there was another bang and when I looked out, to my horror I saw the right wing starting to bend visibly, up and down, like the wing of a bird flying heavily and slowly. The captain's voice came through to us on a loudspeaker, penetrating the noise.

"We are in bad trouble," it said. "I must insist that everyone, passengers and crew, strap themselves in to the nearest unoccupied seats. Immediately. This is an order. This is an order. For the moment you will have to let the loose equipment take care of itself. First things come first. I repeat, this is an order."

I guess the captain must have been excited or nervous or something because he forgot to turn the loudspeaker off and we could hear him communicating with the outside world. He kept shouting over and over: "This is K for Katy ninety-nine. K for Katy ninety-nine. Don't know where we are. Don't know where we are. Feels like a tornado. Can't climb out. Instrument fai . . ."

Once more I looked at the bending wing. Then, remembering the third wish that still remained to me, I unbuttoned my fly, drew out my penis, opened the amulet, took out the shikwembo charm, rolled it down on the wishing place, and whispered aloud in a panic: "Please save me. I wish that I may be saved." I kept my eyes shut, terrified.

The plane began to spin rapidly downward, in ever-widening flat circles. I could feel the weak wing pulling and dragging and fluttering but I didn't dare look. All of a sudden, there was a rustling noise, then a kind of breaking noise. "Prepare to crash," said the captain. "Emergency procedure. Everyone sit tight, bend forward and hold your hands tight across the back of your head. Take off your shoes. Loosen your ties. Ready. Ready. Here it comes."

I tried to lean forward and do what he had told us. But I was too large. I couldn't even squeeze myself loose enough from the tight grip of my seat. And when I shoved my head down in front it bumped up against the wall of the crew compartment. I was frantically wondering what to do when there was an absolute roar of noise, of breaking and banging, a splintering of wood and metal, and a rattle and rumble as loose crates pounded forward down the aisle. Then there was nothing.

How long I sat there I don't know but eventually I woke up and I hadn't an idea where I was. The steward was right. I had been dreaming of Yumyum and I had her alone to myself. I could smell something that seemed to be burning. Then everything hit me. I knew where I was and why: aboard an Israeli plane that had crashed in Africa. And it was loaded with various kinds of soldiers and, much worse, a lot of dangerous, loose explosives.

"Ah, Mutterl, Mutterl," I moaned aloud. "I wish you were here. Just to see you once again, Mutterl."

Suddenly I remembered. The magic ring was still in place. And, without realizing it, I had made the fourth wish. The third wish had saved my life. But now there would be disaster.

Wildly I pulled myself out of my seat and stumbled forward into the crew compartment, screaming. The pilot and the copilot seemed dead. They were jammed into their seats, their heads forward resting on the cockpit windshield of glass that hadn't shattered but that was filled with thousands of wrinkled fractures. Three other crewmen had been flung into strangely awkward positions and were at least unconscious.

There was a door marked EMERGENCY and below that EXIT. I grabbed the handle, pulled and staggered out into a mass of soggy, strange, damp green leaves. The ground was marshy and soft but I forced my way along it as fast as I could to get away from the plane before it exploded.

After what seemed to me minutes, I turned around and at that moment there was an orange flash, followed by a whoosh and a roar. Pieces of the plane whirled upward through the heavy air and some skimmed past me, smacking trees and branches. I gazed at the explosion with astonishment. I smelled roasting flesh and burning gasoline and I watched while a huge, intensely bright fire ate its way through the wreckage. Is this the disaster of the fourth wish? I wondered.

I looked about me and discovered why I was still alive. The plane had made its forced landing in a banana grove. The trees, with their long, heavy, gentle leaves and their pliant branches and trunks, had absorbed some of the shock of our crash. I sat down, leaning against a mound, and held my head in the position recommended by the pilot which I had been unable to achieve aboard.

Now, I wondered, what do I do? Sole survivor of a mystery plane. Alone in an unknown jungle far from anywhere. I didn't even know what country I was in. How could I possibly get out? Where should I try to head?

Absentmindedly I reached for a banana, stripped it and began to munch. Suddenly I heard a noise near me, just strong enough to sound over the pattering rain, the gusts of wind and the crackling of the fire. I looked around. Sobbing, unkempt, but otherwise intact, I saw the stewardess, dripping wet, pale, a wild look in her eye. I called to her and she stumbled over, weeping but not hysterical.

"I don't know what happened," she moaned. "But when we hit, the aft section broke off. I guess I was at the point where it split and it flung me into the jungle. I'm all right, I guess. But the others are all dead. I guess. How horrible, how horrible."

I got up, surprised to find I didn't even feel sore or have a bruise. I tried to take her in my arms. She looked up abruptly. "My God," she said. "It's Snarler. Of all people, Snarler. I didn't see you get on or even catch a glimpse of you in the plane. They just told me an American giant was along. Of all people, it had to be you."

For an instant I was startled. Then I looked closely under the tears, the smeared makeup, the torn uniform. It was Mildred, little Mildred of Ben Franklin High.

"Get your hands off me, you rapist, you. You black-Nazi-kike, you. Of all the people in the world. Of all the sons of bitches to be marooned with." But just the same she clung to me, sobbing.

I had not the strength nor the inclination to bandy words with her there in the middle of the jungle. What have you done when you have bested a hysteric in argument?

CHAPTER IX

The first we heard of it was a whick, whick, whick coming through the steaming cloud and stirring rills of water off the banana leaves. I had never before encountered such a strange sound but Mildred immediately recognized it, ceased glowering at me, looked up and started to pat her disheveled hair while smoothing out her wrinkled, sagging skirt.

"It's a helicopter," she shouted excitedly. "They can only be looking for us. In God's name, Snarler, take your shirt off and start waving it in the clearest place you can find. Otherwise they'll never, never find us."

I did as she suggested and managed to push over three banana trees, badly damaged by the storm, clearing just enough space so that I could stand in it and wave frantically into the mist. Both of us stared hopefully but doubtfully upward. Then, suddenly, through a hole in the bank of steam, we saw the ugly clackety machine, hovering overhead like an enormous metal dragonfly.

"He's seen us, he's seen us," Mildred screamed as a rope ladder dropped out of the copter's side. A moment later a man in light blue shirt and shorts climbed down the swinging staircase and squashed through the wet footing, looking about him with a grin.

"Well, well, well," he said. "So there are survivors after all." Mildred flung her arms around him and kissed him firmly on the mouth. "Now that's the nicest kind of welcome any rescue mission ever got," he added with an approving look at Mildred.

First he asked if we were hurt and we both replied we thought not. Then, before he could question us further, we told him our plane was totally wrecked and we were certain everyone else was dead.

"Well, we'll see about that," he said. "But first things first." He made a hand signal to the helicopter, still whirling motionless above us. Then he led Mildred to the rope ladder. "Can you make it?" he asked. "I can't imagine that crash did your self-confidence any good.

"Here, you just hold tight on that rung above you, put your feet there. Now climb. Slowly does it. I'll come up behind to help you if you get dizzy. Just look up all the time. At the whirlybird, not down at the ground. And you, big fellow. Just you stay there a bit. I'll be back for you soon." He had a strong British accent, much stronger than some Canadians and South Africans I had known.

When Mildred was emplaced within the bowels of the machine he slipped to earth again, spryly, and I took him over to the pile of smoking wreckage. As we walked cautiously around it, still too hot to approach, he remarked with a grim expression: "Hmmph, I see just what you mean. How you two ever managed to get out of this inferno is impossible to understand. You should each light a candle to the God you are accustomed to praying to.

"Now you just stay down here a bit more, old fellow, while I go back again and tell the skipper. Then he can radio a report to our ship and get instructions. We have to be damn bloody careful about giving a fixed position so either we or someone else can get back again. There's no hurry, I guess. This thing won't cool off for another twenty-four hours, no matter how much rain comes down. Now let's just crawl around a bit and make a racket. On the off-chance some other lucky devils were thrown out when it hit."

We hollered and we tramped all around and around, making great soggy sounds, but there was no sign of life. Just the skwushy noise of our steps and the drip, drip, drip of water pouring off the banana leaves. "All right, my friend," he said. "I'll be leaving you again for a few minutes. But don't get alarmed. We know where you are and we're not going to move until you move along with us."

We walked over to the little clearing I had made and he scrambled up the swinging ladder, agile as a monkey. I returned to the smoldering plane and stared glumly at the mess. What a nice group of friendly people, I thought. And now they're all gone. Even Arik, that sturdy and indestructible gentleman. I thought, at least the shikwembo's ring kept its value through the third wish. As for the fourth and accidental prayer: well, I was fated to see if the magic was as effective on the bad side as the good.

When the Englishman came back down he guided me up to his aircraft, pushing my big behind from time to time as I got tangled in the swaying rope. The machine seemed to bounce about as I clambered in. There, on the back seat, a long kind of padded bench, was Mildred busily jabbering away at two crew members, also dressed in shirt and shorts with visored flying caps and earphones shoved away so they could hear her gabble.

"Yes," she was saying, "I wouldn't be surprised if Snarler here had something to do with it. Sabotage or something. He was doing foolish things with rockets when we exploded. I tell you, I know that damn-fool giant. I wouldn't trust him as far as I could throw the Brooklyn Bridge. I'm sure going to file charges when we get to civilization."

All the Englishmen stared at me with puzzlement, including the pilot and the other two crew members sitting in a little compartment in front. The man who had rescued us moved between Mildred and me—I suppose to prevent any trouble—and then reached over to fasten seat belts around our laps. The ladder was hauled back aboard and we suddenly took off with a loud clattering whine.

As we bounced up through windswept clouds, our friend spoke to us in a shrill, penetrating voice that came through with surprising clarity over the steady drone of the engine and the great whacking propeller that kept us in the steamy air. Apparently they came from a Royal Navy rescue ship that was on station not far from Zanzibar where there had been some trouble. They received an alert from two airports ashore advising that our plane had suddenly disappeared from their radar screens. No warning. Just a blip one second and nothing the next.

But the two airports knew the whereabouts of the storm. They were able to work out from the blips and from their own respective locations just about where we had gone down. So several small planes and two helicopters had been assigned to search.

After a couple of hours we came out of the fog above a huge, silent, dark lake and then we slipped westward just over the water to a fine airport. I saw some immense fat animals munching grass and paying no attention to all the mechanical devices around them. "Hippos," said the Englishman, who had asked us to call him Bertie. "Sometimes they let us come in here for weekends and play golf. You get a free new lie if your ball lands in a hippo track." I didn't know what he was talking about.

There was a mumbled conversation between the pilot, talking into his face mask, and someone on the ground.

Then, when we landed, two cars drove over to our copter and several men in uniform, two of them with drawn pistols, got out.

"I'm sorry, old chap," said Bertie. "But this young lady has told us she intends to lodge a complaint against you. So we are turning you over to the wing commander here. He'll tell you what's what. Good luck to you, my boy."

The wing commander took me off in the first automobile, riding in front with the driver while I was squeezed in between the two men with guns. They had cold faces and looked very hard. When we got to a small building next to the airport, the officer ordered me locked up in a waiting room but gave me a beer and sandwich. I was glad that I had come to like beer by now. I needed encouragement. Mildred, I could see, had been taken elsewhere—to persecute me more, I guessed.

When the wing commander returned he was friendly but also very formal. In a quiet, cool voice he said: "There's nothing for it, young man, except to fly you on to Cyprus. Our bases there are the nearest British territory. We can't keep you here because we don't have either authority or facilities. And it seems your girlfriend intends to charge you with sabotage. What's she got against you anyway? She says she's known you for years. Apparently you don't wear well. What ever did you do to her, von Snarl? I see from your passport that's what you're called.

"In any case, now that we've got you we're stuck with you. Our embassy people have said that under the circumstances we must hold you in British custody until the legal arguments over you are settled. It seems the Israelis are hot after you because of this sabotage story. They've got a complex on that subject. Can't say I blame them either.

"But the Americans also want you since the outfit from which the aircraft was chartered is a U.S. outfit and anyway you're a Yank. And the insurance companies involved are both American and Greek. Therefore a British court must decide to whose jurisdiction you are consigned. Tough luck, my boy. From the frying pan into the fire, you might say."

I didn't see Mildred again. But a few hours later I was taken by one of the armed guards to a large British airliner. When all the passengers had been checked and marched aboard, my guard pulled handcuffs from his pocket and clamped them around my wrists. They were a very tight fit. My wrists hurt as the steel bit into the flesh. The guard didn't say a word. He just shoved me into the window seat of the last row in the passenger compartment, then slipped in beside me and pulled his seat belt tight. He did nothing about mine, I thought mournfully, as we lumbered off for Cyprus.

It was night when we landed. My guard turned me over to another pair of Englishmen who wore black armlets above their elbows with the white letters M.P. blazing out. One of them was given charge of my passport. He assured me it would be returned—"When you need it next, whenever that may be. No documents are necessary where we're taking you now."

After a long drive down a narrow road we went through a gate, patrolled by sentries, past strings of barbed wire, illuminated by searchlights, to an ugly gray cement building. Some kind of a jail warder then took over responsibility. Dead with fatigue and worn nerves, I was at last shoved into a large cell.

As the door clanged shut I could see by the dim light from the passageway that there were several other prisoners with me. Nobody said a word. Some of them turned over and the others just continued to snore. I fell asleep right away, wondering how much misery the shikwembos had scheduled for my unhappy, disastrous fate.

When I woke up I looked around at my cell mates. They were all munching half-loaves of bread and drinking what seemed to be black tea which they poured into chipped mugs from a jerrycan standing in the center of the floor. When they saw me open my eyes one gentleman, a very fierce-looking individual with a three-day growth of beard, said: "Okay, boy. Welcome to home of Aphrodite. She born in Cyprus from flake of seafoam. When she came know the place she went back to sea and disappeared. Knew what she was doing."

He chuckled and handed me a mug of tea and some bread. I noticed he had a peculiar accent. Very soon I discovered he was a Turkish-speaker named Refik. He was being held for murder. There were six of us, altogether. I was told we were the only civilians in a British military jail. They threw the lot of us into one cell to keep us from infecting the army with our bad habits.

Refik was the only one who talked at first. He told me he came from a place called Kyrenia, which was why he knew fluent English. He was charged with murder. "Hell, it was my wife," he muttered. "None this damned British business. Just family matter. You just wait and you'll fucked like everyone else. The limeys will give you all hogwash about justice and common law and uncommon case and then they'll hand you over with pious Billy-be-damned.

"In your case it will either to Jews who'll jail you for life—and their jails real tough and no escaping from them. Or to Americans who seem want you bad. Or, if you're real unlucky, to Tanzanians. I understand it happened over their territory. If you go those heathen they'll just carve you little pieces."

Another of our cell mates was a thin, long-faced Assyrian named Enlil, a Christian who came from a place called Lebanon across the sea from where we were. He was a very religious, solemn, poetic man who spent all his time quoting old poetry to us. He didn't care whether we listened or not. He had once been a professional soldier and fought with the English against the Arabs. Years later, when he was running a tailor shop, a customer accused him of cheating on his prices so he picked up a long scissors and stabbed him in the chest. Unfortunately the customer was frail and he expired.

"The lord speaks to her of intercourse, she is unwilling," Enlil chanted. "My vagina is too little, it knows not to copulate. My lips are too small, they know not to kiss."

"Shut up, goddamit, Enlil," came an American voice from the corner. "We've got enough trouble without all your dirty verse. Get your mind above your hips for once."

Enlil paid no attention. Mournfully and in a toneless voice he recited: "He stood up proudly like a rampant bull. He lifts the penis, ejaculates, fills the Tigris with sparkling water. The wild cow mooing for its young in the pastures, the scorpion-infested stall, the Tigris is surrendered to him as to a rampant bull."

"Hell with you, Enlil," Refik grunted. "All you ever think is fucking." Imperturbably, Enlil commented in his monotone: "It's not the heart which leads to enmity. It's the tongue which leads to enmity. . . . Tell a lie; then if you tell the truth it will be deemed a lie."

"Ah, don't mind that jug-eared old jasper," came the American voice. "He doesn't really have a mean streak in him." Then he added: "Enlil, pal. Leave us alone, won't you? Spare us for a while. There may be something educational in what you're always telling us but it sure ain't entertaining. You're a pearl of great price I haven't any doubt. But we get impatient with you, Enlil."

By this time I had finished breakfast and I introduced myself to my companions. But they seemed to know all about me, about my origins, about the Trotters, about my name, about my present troubles. I never did learn how they found these things out but I did soon discover that in this prison everyone managed to pass on information to everyone else. They were a very tough bunch but they certainly managed an honorable code among murderers.

The man with the American accent didn't have an American name at all. He was called Mavros, which means the Black One. He had lived most of his life in the good old U.S.A. but he was born in Cyprus. When he came back to his village to join the fight for independence from Britain, he was soon accused of killing a Turkish neighbor for informing against the patriots. Mavros and Refik both liked and hated each other, which I soon found to be a common relationship between Greeks and Turks.

"Damn all Greeks," said Refik with a scowl. "Mavros, you're just like rest. Maybe you can't described as salesman of poisoned snake-oil but you have many of traits. Only thing worse than Greek is Greek-Cypriot. Like you. You and your cursed Makarios. That damned archbishop. He thinks he's above God. Above Allah. He preaches everywhere that he's neutral and impartial. Yeah. But only to Greeks and members his religion."

I thought Mavros and Refik were about to strangle each other. But suddenly Mavros grinned quite amiably. "Ah, you Turks," he grunted. "You're a balanced race. A chip on each shoulder. One for Greeks. The other for Armenians. You like to blame others for your own stupidity, my friend."

At this point, and before I had learned the names of the other two cell mates, a guard came by and unlocked the door. He led us to the latrines and washbasins and afterward to the courtyard where we were allowed regular daily exercise. We walked round and round like those blind horses that drive Egyptian waterwheels. As we chatted, lazy sentries with tommy guns stared down upon us from watchtowers.

Enlil explained that the military prisoners were not allowed to mix with us. "They fear contamination. By free civilians," he said. I used to be Tommy myself and I understand now that I'm free civilian." I couldn't tell if he meant to be sarcastic. "Never saw such ignorant bastards," he continued. "They'll do anything they're told. But they've got guts, they have. Even mousiest-looking of them all."

As we shuffled along I noticed a very strange thing. At one or another time, each of my colleagues would walk unconcernedly with both hands in his pockets, sometimes two or three of the men at a time. Little, faint trickles of dirt filtered out behind them as they shuffled forward. The rest, without seeming to pay any attention, managed to kick the dirt around here and there so it mixed unnoticeably with the courtyard sand.

At first I didn't say anything because I thought this was an accidental thing but I decided it couldn't be because it went on and on. "Now that is very strange," I told Refik. "What are you doing with that dirt?"

"That kid thinks he's smart one," Refik muttered to Mavros out of the corner of his mouth. "Hey, Buster," Mavros snarled. "Ain't your eyes getting a bit nosey? Ain't they getting too big even for ya?"

"Well, Mr. Mavros," I replied. "At least, as my family says, I don't keep my eyes in my pocket."

"Nope, he keeps them in other people's pockets," another voice said gruffly. It spoke with stern authority and came from one of the two men I did not yet know. He told me his name was Faust and that he was a German who had fought in the French Foreign Legion. After he deserted he set up in the hashish and heroin smuggling business between Lebanon, Turkey and Greece. The British had caught him but they clearly hadn't undermined his bitter spirit.

"Look, von Snarl," he said. "I've heard something about you. We've got quite a grapevine here. And none of what I've heard makes sense. Let me just tell you one thing. These Brits haven't yet built the prison that can hold Hans Faust for long. Just mark my words. So it's all right if you keep your eyes open. I approve. But keep your mouth shut. Otherwise I'll shut it for you. Painfully. And for good."

He spoke with a thick accent but he spoke clearly and well. His voice was even more menacing than his words. I said nothing but continued ambling along with the other five, trying to avert my eyes, but they kept drifting back to the faint trickles of dirt.

Mavros looked up at one of the sentries who seemed to be a black soldier. "Goddamn jigaboo," he snarled. "We're starting to get them even in Greece, not just Cyprus."

"What's a jigaboo?" I asked.

"Nigger. Black bastard."

"Then I must be a jigaboo. Because I'm black and I'm a bastard. My grandma was an Oorlog Herero and my father never married my mother."

Mavros stared at me, startled. Then he roared with laughter. "Well, good for you, Snarler," he said. "Come to think of it, I may be a nigger too. Mavros means black or Moor in Greek. My family claims we first came from Famagusta. That's a town on this island where a fellow named Othello was governor once. And he was a Moor. My family claims we're descended from him."

"Hah, hah, hah," Refik exploded into laughter. "You'd ought bonk him, Snarler," he suggested. "For insulting the both of you. We've all heard of your bonk. I'd like see it demonstrated on swell-headed Greek."

"Shut up, the lot of you," Faust commanded curtly. "You're all a bunch of bastards and I suspect most of you are black. You're also all a bunch of idiots. I want no more of this—this gossiping." He had cold, milky-blue eyes and a deadly air of authority.

"Don't tell me I'm a bastard or I'm black," Enlil protested.

Faust turned on him. "You Assyrians only became civilized when you became Christians," he snarled. "If then. And as if Christianity mattered."

Enlil dropped back three paces so he was level with me on the endless circuit. He glared hatefully at Faust, spitting out: "You dolt, numskull, ignoramus, school pest, you illiterate, you ignoramus." Then he flashed a grin at me. "Ancient Assyrian poem," he whispered shrilly.

When we got back to our cell Faust, who was clearly in charge, stationed Refik and Mavros at the door and told them to fuss around with the broom and pan we were given to keep things clean and neat. Whenever they heard a guard approaching they should make a clattering noise.

Then Faust took me to the far end with the sixth member of our company, a grim, silent man, long and lean from many wars, whom he introduced as Smitty. Smitty, he told me, had been his right hand in the dope-smuggling operations and they were caught together. Smitty was an expert on all kinds of clandestine operations including jailbreaks because he came from the C.I.A.

"Clandestine?" I asked. "C.I.A.?"

"The C.I.A. is a secret organization," Smitty said in a strangely penetrating soft voice that came out of the side of his mouth without seeming to move his lips at all. "That is, it is secret until all its members blab about each other and their exploits, which is what they do. That's why I got out.

"But I learned things there. In addition to keeping my mouth shut I learned about infiltration and exfiltration and demolitions and the seventy-seven ways to kill a man without using a weapon. I went to the Farm and I've been in all covert services and I guess I can get out of any prison going, just like Houdini. And what I don't know, Faust here does," he added with a silent look of admiration. "Faust was in the Waffen SS."

"Ah, so was my Vati," I answered. Faust appeared to be

stunned. "You mean your own father was . . ."

"Yes," I boasted happily and explained. Faust and Smitty sat in silent admiration as I told them. "Well," said Faust when I'd finished. "Nobody could make up a tale like that."

"That's the tallest tale I've ever heard," was Smitty's comment. "And told by the tallest liar."

"Smitty is our technical expert," Faust explained, seeming to take me more into his confidence and according me a new air of respect. "He worked in Spain a bit for the C.I.A., infiltrating the urban guerrilla movement. He's read all the books on guerrilla tactics, on forgery, on escape, on evasion, on demolitions. He worked in Japan. He even speaks Jap. He got into the Korean rackets there. You name it, he knows it. When the Franco police broke the ring he was working with he kept his cover, told no one, and in the end busted jail. Busting a Spanish jail is not that easy, Curly." It was the first time Faust had called me Curly.

"He is a master of explosives. And he is a master of tunneling. He is a master of engineering and therefore can estimate weights, strains, distances without the need of equipment. And what we do need, he can show us how to make. He knows judo, karate and all the other dirty sports. He is also a master of disguise. You have no idea what he can do about false mustaches and fake eyebrows. You will learn.

"Although, Curly, I fear you are impossible to camouflage. Not at your size. In any case, you follow Smitty's instructions and obey my orders and you'll be out of this place. That must be understood. Wholly understood. This is a disciplined conspiracy. He who is loose-lipped will soon be dead. Unquote."

Faust summoned the others with a gesture. He whispered: "All right. Now he knows. He will work with us and benefit from what we have done. Do not mistake. He is a good Aryan. I vouch for him. His father was Sturmbahnführer. That is enough of a guarantee. He sees how urgent is his task."

"Thank God he is good Aryan, not Greek," quipped Refik. "When Greeks see situation as urgent they mean it isn't quite so pressing as tomorrow, *avrio.*" Then he added, on a more somber note: "Death will now bend our backs—and will silence tongues."

CHAPTER X

From that day on I was allowed to join the team that was digging our tunnel to escape. In fact there were two teams: Faust, Enlil and myself worked one shift and Smitty, Mavros and Refik worked the other. Faust and Smitty were the commanders; they gave each team orders.

Every evening, after supper had been brought to us in a bucket with a plate for everyone, a chunk of bread to go with the stew and a large aluminum spoon to eat with, we would go to work after our nighttime visit to the latrines. It really wasn't very hard to organize. The cell lights went out at ten o'clock; the light in the hallway was dim. The guard there walked the passage regularly until he figured all the warders were asleep and the officers wouldn't make any more inspections. Then he'd tip a chair, midway along the passage and away from the naked light bulb, back against the wall and snore with evident pleasure.

As soon as we had heard three or four snores Faust would signal everyone to start. One shift would pull back a camp cot in the corner and then lift from beneath it a rock slab constructed of long flagstones cunningly joined together. From these they pulled out three dummy figures, made of uniform cloth we had bought from military prisoners and stuffed with dirt. These were carefully laid on three of the cots and covered with blankets.

Then another single flagstone slab was pulled out of the wall at the far corner where it touched the floor. First either Enlil or Mavros (depending on which team was going underground) would reach in and get out the light tools. Most of these were knives, trowels or tiny spades shaped out of the aluminum spoons. Every now and then we would complain to a friendly guard that he'd forgotten one of the spoons. He usually gave us a replacement without comment. We never had knives or forks because the prison regulations considered these deadly weapons we might use for assault.

So we manufactured everything from the rounded aluminum—including some very sharp, pointed knives that were indeed dangerous weapons. Smitty and Faust used to do this in their spare time whenever one or the other was up in the cell with his shift, mounting guard for the three who were underground. It was easy, I saw, to shape spoons into almost anything once you learned the knack of spitting on a piece of limestone and rubbing them over and over again in a certain way.

The shift that went down to dig left their clothes in the entrance of the tunnel and climbed in wearing underpants, pulling small sacks of military uniform cloth behind them, fastened by strings around the waist. Like most things we used, they were bought with bribes or stolen. These were for loading up the earth we dug. The earth was dragged back to the opening, before we stopped in the early morning, and redistributed into even smaller bags. The bags were then shared out by everyone and tied under their trouser legs to be dribbled out discreetly during our daily exercise walk in the courtyard. That way we could get rid of the dirt without anyone seeing it. As I had already noticed, it was just about the same color as the surface of the yard.

While one shift was working underground, the other sat with their backs to the passageway, huddled over, sometimes talking in low voices, sometimes napping. This way it looked just like a normal group of six bored prisoners in case an unexpected face peered in: three dummy figures sleeping, three resting.

Smitty, who was the chief engineer of the project, was very clever about designing the tools we needed. He had somehow managed to steal two buckets and turn them into a set of four shovels. He found some old olive-wood trunks underneath the prison, as our tunnel progressed, and made spade shafts from them. He also made one stout and one long lever which we had to use occasionally when we found heavy rocks in the way that we could not burrow around.

The passage of the tunnel was very narrow and tight for me because I was so much bigger than the others. But I could manage it all right except at one sharply angled turn around an underground boulder. There, under Smitty's directions, they carved out more space.

"Since Snarler is now in on this—and he damned well has to be—" said Faust, "we'll have to give him a chance to make himself useful. Furthermore, I've got plans for that broad, strong back at the very end of the game."

It was hard work and, although the ground around us was quite cool and even moist, it was very hot. Either Smitty or Faust—whichever was on the working shift —would sit about ten yards from the entrance leading out of our cell and pump fresh air down the passage through a kind of bellows Smitty had put together from some canvas tent cloth.

And we had light. I soon found it was possible to get

almost anything for money and Faust and Smitty always seemed to have some, either Cyprus or British pounds. Eventually I discovered that this was arranged from the outside. One of their drug smugglers kept sending it in and it was passed along, at a price in bribery, by soldier criminals among the prison trusties.

Therefore Faust had obtained plenty of flashlights, four pocket compasses, and even a small Italian pistol with six bullets which he never let the rest of us touch. "I can't imagine anything so dangerous that would make me use anything so noisy," he would say.

With all this equipment we slowly managed to excavate a passage that must have run about eighty yards underground from our cell. It wasn't bad work either. It reminded me of my visit to that mine in Witwatersrand, except we were naked and made less noise. We only mumbled softly to one another and, when Faust wanted to get a message to us in the passage, he did it by jerking a string that was wound to the ankle of Enlil or me, depending who was the number two man and farther behind that day.

Each fifteen minutes the two diggers—Enlil and I or Mavros and Refik—had to stop, pull back a little, and sit to rest and suck in some of the air pumped in by canvas funnel. Otherwise we might faint. The first time this happened Enlil began to croon, as we sat naked side by side: "Bridegroom let me caress you. My precious caress is more savory than honey. Let me enjoy your goodly beauty. Lion, let me caress you."

I was very embarrassed. I thought of the Ukrainian primate and I wondered what had happened to Enlil. "Hey, hey," I said with a blush. "You have been away from women too long." But he looked at me and grinned. "Don't worry, you freak," he chuckled. "That's only the poem of King Shu-Sin. Nothing to do with Curly."

When Enlil was at the very end of the tunnel, at its face where he had to scrape out an inch-by-inch advance, he would sing to himself very low: "Pig-eon in a peee-ach tree; par-tridge in a pi-ine," over and over again. I said to him I was sure that was wrong. It was about a partridge in a pear tree. Mavros told me he had that same argument with him earlier when they were on shift together before I came. It didn't matter. That was the way he liked the song.

I heard Mavros complain to him one day when we were ambling round the courtyard on our daily walk. "God's mother," said Mavros. "Can't you get anything straight, you Assyrian limey?"

"How could God have a mother?" Enlil asked. "God made everything. How could he make his own mother? And why?"

"Sounds worse than incest," Smitty murmured out of the side of his mouth.

"Never argue with an Assyrian," Enlil replied happily. "Rule one."

"Nor a Greek," said Refik. "During war I volunteered R. A. F. ground services. Goddamn British send me North Greece help goddamn Greeks against Italians. There, in Epirus, we make airfields where no airfields possible. We all notice great big bird flying in and out mountain cave above us where he live with funny kind animal. Animal look something like man—like Greek man. Ragged pants and nothing above but hair. He sometimes climb up and down to cave on thick creeper rope. And bird sometimes sit on shoulder. They great friends.

"Well, one day goddamn British capture animal when he stealing food from cookhouse. He wearing just these ragged pants and whole body covered hair except for eyes. They round, not like human eyes. And his feet have six toes. While we looking at him bird fly circle and circle over his head making screams and monster he just hisses back. Suddenly he take big leap and jump practically over two our people surrounding him.

"One Greek, he pick up gun and aim to shoot him.

Britisher knock down his gun. 'You can't shoot him,' he say. 'That man human after all.' 'Not human,' say Greek. 'He speak just like Turk.' 'Well, I start strangle that Greek and get thrown out R.A.F. But first do one month prison. That how I start road to this goddamn place.

"And you know, at my trial, goddamn Greek swear he never did any things he did or say any things he said and other goddamn Greeks in unit swear same thing. Never believe Greek. Never argue with him. Just kill him. Like Alp Arslan, our big Seljuk general. He had mustaches so long he tied them behind head when mounting horse before going off to kill Greeks in battle."

Mavros heard all this with a calm air of boredom. I guess he'd heard it often before. It seemed to vex him only slightly, like an itch. He just shrugged his shoulders and muttered: "Those bloody British should have minded their own business."

When we reached the stage of preparing the tunnel for its final purpose, mainly specializing in buying and shaping old planks and props in the prison carpenter shop with funds obtained by Faust and Smitty, my participation was interrupted. The officials suddenly took me out and put me in a solitary cell where I was interviewed by a series of officials.

First I was visited by one Israeli and one British psychologist. It was explained carefully and sympathetically by my guard that these were gentlemen who are misfits in life and therefore try to find out why other people are normal so they can prove this is an unnatural state. One called himself something like "Freudian" and the other one called himself something like "Adlerian." They agreed that my background was unusual and might have accounted for my unusual physique. But they argued in front of me whether my behavior could be called "rationally insane" or "irrationally sane."

Then there were two doctors, one black—I suppose

from Tanzania—and one white and Greek. They stripped me, poked me, measured me, photographed all parts of my body, and showed particular interest in my tail. They agreed that this might represent a vestigial symbol of "an animalic killer instinct." But they disagreed on the implications of the bumps and measurements of my skull. "He is definitely part Negroid," said the Greek. "So were Aesop, Pushkin and Dumas," said the Tanzanian. "He is also quite evidently of a perceptible Jewish strain." "So were Einstein, Spinoza, Maimonides and Marx," replied the Greek.

But they were of one mind that I was an exceptionally odd physical specimen. The Greek said: "It is probably from an infection of the pituitary gland. That often comes among peoples with hereditary syphilis. Like his ancestors the Hereros. He will age prematurely, get progressively feebler at a comparatively young age, and die rather fast."

"You talk balls," said the Tanzanian. "Everyone knows syphilis is a white export. Indeed, you whites all blame it on each other. The French call it the Spanish disease. The Italians call it the French disease. The Germans call it the Italian disease. Why even the Japanese call it the Chinese disease."

"We don't know," said the Greek, "if he didn't inherit his syphilis from the Hereros, that shikwembo bitch he tells us of certainly fixed him fine."

Looking into my puzzled eyes, the Tanzanian concluded the discussion: "I went to Durham University in England, practically in Scotland. Don't you mind, boy. You won't die young. 'Grow old along with me; the best is yet to be.' Robert Browning. English poet. Maybe from Durham."

Finally two lawyers, one American and one South African, came to interview me. They explained it was merely part of the legal preparation to decide where I should be tried because of the contradictory claims concerning the charges made by Mildred and the question of jurisdictional rights.

"I am trying to have the venue shifted to New York," said the American. "That is where the charter company that owns the wrecked plane is headquartered. And there I stand a good chance of getting some Jews and blacks on any jury. Even some Nazis from Yorkville. Might help you when Mildred uses her pretty legs."

"That would be fine, sir," I told him. "Then I can see Mutterl and Borborigmi."

"Alas, I was unaware you had not been told," the lawyer said in solemn tones. "I fear they are both dead. Your mother tripped over your stepfather one night when going down the stairs during an electricity strike. He was quite small, I believe. In any case, he broke his neck and she fell through a rickety banister."

I began to weep and this embarrassed the American who began to weep also. People are usually emotional Faust had told me. I could only think: this is the real start of the disaster. That awful fourth wish. The thing that got me was the way it all fitted together: Mildred turning up to denounce me; the arrest; now the disappearance of my loving Mutterl and little Borbo.

"Yes, I'm afraid things don't look good for you," the South African said in a kind tone. "I was flown up here by Bram Jonker who wanted to help even if our country has no claim or wish to get involved in this new case. But it is obvious any prosecutor will dig out the evidence once used maliciously against you in Johannesburg, at least concerning the Screwhill, Tawis and Rupert deaths.

"And now your friend Mildred—I really suspect it is she who is a bit unbalanced. She claims she saw you deliberately throw a rocket grenade into the rear of the plane, as if you were so stupid you thought it would only kill other people without making it crash. She says this is part of your Nazi heritage which taught you to hate all Jews. Is she Jewish herself?"

"There is another thing," the American interjected. "That wishing ring the witch doctor gave you. It might be good for evidence in any trial. It might be used to confirm that you didn't know what you were doing for reasons of mental instability."

I didn't like that idea at all. But before I could object the South African said: "Or a victim of predestination. Good Calvinist predestination as we affirm in our Dutch Reformed Church. It's bad luck that we can't claim jurisdiction in this case and have another trial in my country. That would really make Bram Jonker famous."

"In any case," the American summarized: "The truth of your position will be legally ascertained only according to the law under which you are tried. For the bearer of truth has, before a court, only one virtue: that he carries the truth within him. As to the rest, it is merely a question of clever lawyers and jaundiced juries. But no decision on jurisdiction has yet been made. The British authorities must make this ultimate choice. Therefore, my boy, I suggest you make yourself always agreeable and respectful toward them."

My series of interrogations was ended when, after several days of cross-questioning, I was taken to a room where a man in a Royal Air Force uniform with four cloth bars on each shoulder received me. He was pleasant and informal. He dismissed the guard who had marched me in and offered me a chair and a cigarette. I said no thank you.

"Don't you smoke?" he asked, lighting up himself. "Lucky man."

"No sir. I don't know how to smoke."

He looked me shrewdly in the eye, to see if I was kidding him, I suppose.

"Look, my man," he said friendly-like, once he was sure I meant no disrespect, "yours is the most complicated and tangled legal case that has come before me since I assumed command of this base. We are in a peculiar position here anyway, a base in what is really a non-country. Everybody calls this the Republic of Cyprus and talks about the Cypriots—except the Cypriots themselves. They call themselves either Greeks or Turks. And we are supposed to safeguard this mess even if we can't stabilize it.

"The whole thing is rather like freezing chaos. And it produces plenty of legal claims and counterclaims, I can promise you, whenever it impinges on our base territory. But that isn't what I brought you in for. I simply wanted to say that until the various nations involved in your strange case have agreed which one among them is judicially responsible to try the accusations against you—and under whose laws—we can't reach any decision as to whether you are being falsely charged, whether you really are involved in—er, committed—a crime.

"I rather get the impression the Israelis want you badly. Maybe it's because your mother was Jewish under Nazi law and that makes you eligible to become a citizen of Israel. Or maybe it's because your father was an SS officer and they want revenge.

"But the Tanzanians also want you badly. Maybe it's because your father was half black and they'd like to go easy on you. Or maybe it's that German streak; you know they were once a German colony. No, you didn't know that?

"And the American lawyers want you badly. So do their psychology experts. They seem to think they'll get famous handling your case which is beginning to get some publicity. The South Africans, who have sent a pretty fine man, think if they are involved with you again some of them will get even more famous and launch political careers.

"Then there is the angle—if you'll permit me to be frank without intending offense—of whether you can be held mentally responsible. No Greek considers a Turk mentally responsible—or vice versa—except when a killing is involved. In such a case, and they are frequent, all

(148)

Greeks and all Turks pronounce each other sane and guilty. And there are no Cypriots in this republic: only Greeks and Turks.

"So, if you ask me, you may be here quite a while. Certainly for all the interested countries except us—and I don't think we want to go any further in this extraordinary case—the questions of race, religion, pigmentation and each nation's own special definition of sanity is at stake.

"Happily, if the Israelis gain eventual custody over you, there is at least no taint of Arab blood, as they would see it. Thanks to the anti-Jewish Nuremberg law of Hitler, you are eligible to declare yourself a Jew right away and become their citizen, because of your mother.

"But the problem is so intricate and fascinating that it has now reached the world press. Several journalists are due to arrive this week, as well as several legal scholars from various countries. Therefore, to convenience you, I have decided to remove you from your cell and give you new quarters: a room and bath all to yourself.

"Perfectly normal room and bath. Not even bars on the windows. You're too big to get through them. The only thing will be to keep your door locked and place a sentry outside. And you will receive regular officer's rations. Now, doesn't that please you, von Snarl?"

"Well, sir, thank you, sir, but, Mr. Officer, I'd like to stay where I am with my friends. You see I haven't had many friends in my life. Only my Mutterl and Borbo, who are now dead, and I suppose Tawis and Dave, some Trotters, and Mr. Jonker. But now I have all these nice fellows I live with: Faust and Smitty and Refik and Mavros and Enlil."

"But they're all hardened criminals. They're likely to murder you one night."

"Oh, no, sir. We get on fine. And it's nice to have a whole lot of friends. It's new for me. Like drinking beer the first time in Johannesburg. Please, Mr. Officer, won't you let me stay where I am?"

"I must say, von Snarl, yours is a very peculiar and unusual request. But I suppose there's nothing irregular about it. I shall simply have to remove you from time to time to your new quarters so that visitors can see you there and maybe even talk with you in special cases. That's all." Then, in a sharp, loud voice, he barked: "Sergeant. Come in now and take this man back to his cell." He regarded me strangely as I left.

When the guard flung open the door to our cell and I lumbered in stooping, my friends, who were sitting on the floor in a circle, looked up in amazement. "Well, Snarler," said Smitty, "we thought they'd taken you off for good. Off the island. We figured you were headed for trial somewhere but even the rumor circuit knew nothing." Mavros smiled and crossed himself.

"Goddamn Greeks," said Refik. "Always crossing themselves. What's matter with damn Christians anyway? Cross nothing but instrument of torture. Why not make sign of noose? Sign of electric chair? Sign of head chopper's axe? What so good about cross? Red cross. Cross of gold. Maltese cross. Roman cross. Double cross."

"Bloody heathen," sneered Faust.

"Shut up, everyone," said Smitty. "I was telling you a story and I damn well intend to finish it. Well, where was I? Yop, as I was saying, we steamed from Bali on to Lae and then to Port Moresby and from there down the East Coast of Australia where we cut through the sticky sea by the Great Barrier Reef and past Moreton Bay to Brisbane which rose suddenly out of the haze. And when we got to Sydney we had to adjust ballast after unloading most of our cargo. We docked next to the *West Ecock* which had run on a rock off the Great Barrier, and all day we could hear them hammering on her rusty plates. The rust flaked off like the scab on a large tattoo and wrinkled into the water.

"Well, in those days they had a pretty good aquarium in Sydney and somebody told me that a huge shark had been taken alive off the mouth of the Hunter River and it was well worth seeing, especially by anyone who'd seen the cruising fins sticking out of the waters of the Reef. So one Sunday I went to that aquarium and sure enough there was quite a crowd gaping at the thick glass window covering the inside face of one of the fish tanks and there was a really enormous white shark sort of swimming real lazy right up against the glass.

"Imagine, just as I got in front of him and looked that damn shark in the eyes he sort of nodded as if he knew me and then he opened his mouth real wide and vomited very slowly."

"Sure he knew you," said Mavros. "That's why it made him sick to see you again."

"Shut up, greaseball," Smitty snarled, but amiably. "First thing out was a man's arm. Very muscular. And then, after the arm came half a ship longboat's oar and then an empty bottle. Looked like a whisky bottle but the label had rotted away.

"But you see the interesting thing was that the arm had an enormous tattoo on the shoulder, running down almost to the elbow. It was the tattoo of a Chinese girl with three tits. And I recognized the tattoo. It was unique, at least I never saw another like it. And this one was on the arm of a Macao opium peddler who shortchanged me.

"I warned him I'd get him. And by God I did. When the fellow came down to Darwin to make a big deal I had a chum in our organization terminate him. He just disappeared. Until I saw him, or rather a piece of him, just a few days later in Sydney. That shark sure got around. It's a long, long swim."

"What 'organization' was that? " asked Mavros with a smirk. "National Maritime Union, greaseball," Smitty replied. "And don't get so snotty, either. My organization caught one of your Greek destroyers cruising in the

Aegean on NATO maneuvers and all her guns were stuffed with sugar being smuggled to Turkey from France."

"Goddamn Greeks," sniffed Refik. "Always screwing Turks."

With great dignity Mavros pointed out that he was a Cypriot citizen who just happened to be of Hellenic ances-, try. "It is too bad I must share my country with Turkish dogs," he added. Everybody laughed. Even Refik. "First Cypriot I ever met," said he.

The evening of that day of my return Faust took me into the far corner, after we'd shoved our supper bucket, plates and spoons to the guard when he came, following the latrine visit and when he'd slammed the door shut. "You're lucky you decided to stick with us, von Snarl," Faust said in a low rumble. His lips hardly moved but he spoke distinctly. "I told you these Brits could never build a jail to hold me. Well, tonight's the night we go. Just think how you'd feel if you'd traded off an officer's billet and a pack of silly professors against freedom. Jah, that's what you'll have by this time tomorrow."

After we had calculated the guard was as usual leaning backward in his chair against the wall and, by his snores, judged him to be comfortably asleep, Faust nodded to Smitty. Without a word Enlil and Mavros together lifted out the stone slab and started silently pulling out the tools, distributing them among us. I made ready, as had been my recent custom, to accompany Refik in the second shift to crawl into the opening but Smitty urged me forward, signalled to Faust, and he, our commander, stooped at the opening, pulled his pistol out of his pocket, and waved me inward.

"This time you go first," whispered Faust into my ear. "This is what we need you for. You crawl to the end of the tunnel; and I'll be right behind you with a flashlight. Nobody mans the bellows today—or any other day. While you were gone we shoved a little periscope just above the surface in an angle before the exit. That'll give us all the air we want.

"What you have to do is crawl right past it and jam yourself, head first, up against the rock face where the passage finishes. We have dug out a small kind of chamber there, with you in mind. When you arrive at that place—a little beyond the air periscope—jam your head up against the wall, set yourself firmly on your hands and knees, spread them apart, and the rest of us will crawl under you. You may wonder why. Well, the reason is the last two yards of tunneling come right under the usual patrol path of the sentry, outside the wall and wire, and we didn't dare make any unnecessary noise shoring it up. Besides, we've run out of bed slats and other wood. It would taken a long time to scrounge around for any more.

"So that's where you come in. We're going to reverse the usual order. I'll go second. After and under you, breaking the shallow earth at the exit by the rock face. Then I'll look around to be sure everything is in good shape before we move farther. We reckon all of us should be out and away within fifteen minutes, before the sentry returns.

"And we've made a small kind of metal toadstool covered with stuck-on dirt which we'll plug in the hole. Unless the sentry actually steps on it, that should hide the mark of our escape for a few more hours. After me comes Smitty. Then Mavros, Refik and Enlil. Once Enlil has crawled under you and is safely away, you can come out. But gently. We don't want to widen the hole if we can help it. Smitty will be waiting for you by that time. He'll take you down to the boat."

"Boat?" I asked, excited by the adventure.

"Yes, we're really going away. We've arranged a motor launch hiding out in a cove. I've been paying the skipper a daily rate for the past week, to come in each night and wait, loaded with petrol, water and food. He's also got guns. He'll take us to Beirut. Once we're there we split up.

Anything can happen in Beirut. And usually does."

All went just as Faust and Smitty had so carefully planned it. I found it barely possible to wedge myself square into the exit chamber, pressing my back in firm position to hold up the earth above. Almost immediately the dim light of Faust's torch shone through my spraddled knees and slipped carefully under my belly. Just in front of my face, his trousers scratching my nose, I could feel him cutting away the final segment. A cool breeze of fine fresh air suddenly showed me he had succeeded. Quickly he scrambled up through the hole, snapping off his torch and hauling the metal toadstool out of his shirt. I noticed it was a folding apparatus.

Behind him came Smitty. Then Mavros and Refik. I remained steady so as not to shake the dirt above. Finally I could feel Enlil worming his way beneath me. But when he got to the hole and stuck his head out, he stopped. I heard Smitty angrily whispering he should hurry up: "Move along, you damn gook."

"Get along," hissed Smitty again, sticking his head right down to the edge of the hole. "You're holding up the works."

"No," said Enlil firmly although in a low tone. "I just wanted to smell what freedom like. Freedom is only smell of it. Not really exist. One breath freedom. Then return to security. Back to prison of my life. Never worry, Smitty. I go back carefully and slowly, ass end first. You close getaway hole and when I get back I close up entry to tunnel. I tell no one nothing. Better for you. Better for me. You have what you think freedom. I have what I know security. That what tunnel mean to me. A breath of what doesn't exist."

With this, before Smitty could whisper another word and before I understood what was happening, Enlil scrambled backwards under me, something like a crab. As he retreated I heard his labored humming in a soft tone:

"Pig-eon in a peee-ach tree; part-tridge in a pi-ine."

Smitty angrily whispered: "Okay. Get cracking, Snarler. Time's getting short." I eased myself gently forward and then, coached by Smitty and assisted by his competent hands, gradually extricated myself from the hole without greatly enlarging it. He jammed in the toadstool. In the dim starlight I could see it even had leaves and branches growing out of the lid. Then Smitty beckoned to me and I followed, crawling at first. Once we were behind the blocking ledge of rock I stood up. I was so stiff I could almost hear all my joints cracking like the breaking of twigs.

Always behind Smitty, I trudged as well as I could, my eyes getting swiftly adjusted to the clear, moonless sky. Finally, after about an hour, we came down a steep slope and there, tied up in the shadow of a rock, was a rowboat, the kind of long, wide boat I had seen fishermen use near Grande Comore. There was only one man in it when we scrambled aboard.

"Where are the others?" I asked Smitty in great surprise. "Don't worry, kid," he said. "I've made our own plans. For you and for me. I never did trust that bastard Faust. As for you. I've got a great future in mind for you. And I've got the contacts to work things out. Don't think I've wasted my life doing nothing. You and I are going to be rich, kid."

Smitty sat down beside the man in the fishing boat and they began to pull away from shore, saying nothing, and rowing together with strong, easy strokes.

The night was beautiful, cool, dusted with the Milky Way. Just over the eastern horizon I saw a crescent-shaped moon climbing imperceptibly upward, tailed by a bright star. At least Enlil has that as part of his breath of freedom, I thought. The water that slipped behind us or was stirred up by the straining oar blades, curled by with ripples of bright little phosphorescent light.

CHAPTER XI

Well after dawn, when the sun had changed from soft red to a burning white fire, we drew up beside a tubby little ship flying a flag which Smitty explained was that of Panama. *"Regina,"* he said with unexpected pride. "I've used her before. Arms smuggling. Captain Nikolaos is an old pal."

"Nikolaos?" I asked. "Is that a Panamanian name?"

"No, you idiot. He's a Greek. Just like Minodoros here, the man who's been rowing this damn boat. They only fly the Panamanian flag as a convenience. Saves on taxes and makes it easy to arrange deals when they're caught."

"Caught? Are we going to smuggle arms?"

"Well, not this time, Snarler. You're the object of this particular exercise. I went to a lot of trouble setting things up from that crummy jail without having Faust catch on."

"But how am I the object of an exercise, Smitty?" I asked in some bewilderment.

"Climb aboard. You'll learn soon enough." And while Minodoros held the bottom of a rope ladder dropped from a gangway hanging partly down from the plump ship's deck, first I, then Smitty, went up. The ladder was hauled back, the gangway was lifted, and then Minodoros, staying inside his rowboat, was hoisted up to join us by a clinking small derrick.

"Hi, Nikolaos," said Smitty. "Here he is." And then he turned to a sturdy, scowling, pockmarked man with a yellow and obviously Asiatic face, adding: "This is Pak Sin Man. He's a Korean from Osaka in Japan. And he's really big in the rackets there. We've done some pretty fair deals in the past, haven't we, Pak, old fart? That was when I was with my former organization," Smitty explained to me.

I was real puzzled by all these very efficient arrangements but before I could ask any questions Nikolaos gave some orders in Greek, the anchor was hauled up on a squeaky winch, and then the captain led us down a narrow stairway on which I had to both stoop almost in half and at the same time proceed sideways, in order to squeeze through.

"Better you should all stay below until we reach Turkish waters at least," said Nikolaos. "Sure would be easy to identify this young man from a helicopter." And, indeed, within two hours I could hear that same rattle, whooshing noise Mildred and I had heard beside the airplane wreckage in Tanzania. "British don't like people skipping their pretty little hoosegows," said Smitty with evident satisfaction.

For hours, as we chugged slowly in the direction of a port named Iskenderun and I sat uncomfortably on a sofa in a small room called the saloon, Smitty proceeded to explain his plans for me while Mr. Pak Sin Man listened with a frowning, silent, impassive face.

"When I was in the company," Smitty began, "I had

many jobs in Osaka, which is the most important Japanese port facing China. And I had some dandy contacts there including Pak, here. You know, most of Japan's crooked operations are controlled by Koreans, and Pak is the number one bimbo of the lot. He can handle anything from breaking strikes to whorehouses to fixed gambling games like pachinko to murder, any way you want, and dope, any kind you can think of. He also knows every damn thing that goes on in Japan. Most other places as well.''

Pak said nothing. He glowered and didn't even seem to blink.

"Now this guy you're looking at here is deep in betting, as you might imagine, and the big national sport in Japan is sumo wrestling. He even is a member of a group that runs a big stable of sumotori—that's what these wrestlers are called. And when I sent word out to him about your size, your bulk, the fact that you were an athlete and still young enough to learn things, he decided to go along with me on my idea.

"It's what you might call a joint venture. I knew plenty about judo and karate as well as more than a little bit about sumo. Also about the amount of money you can make in Japan on well-placed bets. Therefore Pak here, who respects my knowledge and trusts my judgment, agreed to join in the party. He fixed up the transportation. But that's just the start."

All this time I had been sitting in great confusion. I didn't know anything about any kind of wrestling and I had started to wish I had been able to go with Faust and the other group. Even, maybe, to turn backward with strange little Enlil who loved to smell freedom but taste security.

At that moment a small man with bandy legs, sweating and smelling of garlic and wearing a filthy shirt and pants with the sleeves and legs cut off, entered and murmured something. "My second mate," said Captain Nikolaos. "He says we'll be off Iskenderun in an hour. Don't worry about not having papers. Everything's fixed." He rubbed the thumb against the first two fingers of his right hand and nodded at Mr. Pak. "Good man, that," he announced admiringly. "Hats off. No wonder you're a kingpin in Japan. How come the Japanese ran Korea for so long if Koreans like you seem to run Japan?"

"You bet your life he's good," said Smitty. He pounded him on the back. "Old Pak. I'll bet considerable life he's sold everyone who bought him—at one time or another."

"Who will cast for him a gold pizzle whip?" asked Mr. Pak dourly. "Translation of old saying well known in Korea. Think it over."

"I guess what he means by that," Smitty rattled along, "is how are we going to make the tallest basketball player in history into the sumotori champion of Japan? Also, how are we going to get the title for a non-Japanese and keep your talents—which you ain't even got yet—in hiding long enough to make a financial killing in the operation?

"Well, I've got my plans and Pak knows most of them. And you'd better come up to expectations, Snarler. There's been a big investment in you. Think of the transportation costs alone. To say nothing of baksheesh and arranging false documents for you which we'll pick up along the way."

From Iskenderun, a little old port in a bay, a truck loaded Smitty, Mr. Pak and myself plus Mr. Pak's bags into its rear section which could rapidly be covered by a furled-up tarpaulin drawn forward in a few seconds over a series of metal hoops above us. The others shared a bench and I lay on piles of empty sacks spread along the floor.

"There are two troubles with him," said Mr. Pak, looking at me with that same unhappy, blank expression.

"Trouble one is he don't know how to wrestle at all, much less sumai. Trouble two is he don't weigh enough. And what he's got is in all the wrong places."

"Don't weigh enough," snorted Smitty. "Why he goes about two seventy pounds."

"Got to fatten him up," said Mr. Pak. "Should be at least four hundred, with his built. Got to fatten up his ass, his butt. Got to give him stronger legs. And quick. Then, this here bonk I've heard about. We might develop that into effective tsuki-taoshi. You know, the thrust-down and slap-down technique. There ain't many sumotori who use that nowadays. Might help our surprise effect."

In a city called Adana we unloaded at at airfield and pretty soon we boarded a two-engined plane for Teheran which is the capital of Iran. There we were joined by a tiny Jap they called Fungo and we slept in a hotel by the airport where Fungo had arranged rooms. Since he was the smallest, he shared my accommodations. I had to sleep on the floor on my bedding because I couldn't fit in the cot. By next morning, when we climbed on a huge Japan Airlines jet, I was scratching all over. "Fleas and bedbugs both," Fungo explained helpfully.

The jet was only half full so I was able to make myself comfortable on a strip of three seats because the pretty little Japanese lady in a kimono who served as our stewardess removed the arms that normally divided the space. Then she brought us breakfast, Japan breakfast for Mr. Pak and Fungo, fine Western breakfast for Smitty and me.

I ate all there was: ham and eggs, toast and butter and jam and rolls, fruit, coffee, cheese. "Now it's time to start," said Mr. Pak. "Young lady, bring that man a second breakfast please. He's got a very large appetite and I wanna keep him happy."

"Hai, hai," said the pretty little girl, with a smile and a curtsey. She brought me another tray and I ate all the second breakfast too. It's lucky the prison food was so bad, I thought. I see it's given me quite an appetite. But how am I going to put it all in the places desired by Mr. Pak? I soon found out, when we finally changed planes at Tokyo and flew to Osaka where we disembarked.

It seemed that Mr. Pak had a large financial interest in a heya or stable of sumo wrestlers which was situated on the outskirts of the city. Fungo, who proved to be a Nisei or Japanese-American from Hawaii, worked there as a sort of fixer, arranger, coach and general handyman. He was a nice fellow and just as proud as I was of being American. He had no foreign accent at all and explained to me that he was a veteran of the Puka-Puka Battalion, a military unit of the Niseis who fought in the American army at a battle called Cassino and, he said, were very, very heroic.

The stable master, who was the big boss but in fact always kowtowed to Mr. Pak, was called Hatanaka and had once been a high-ranking sumo wrestler himself. He was devoted to the sport and to all the ancient traditions and legends that accompanied its formal practice still, and he was very dubious about the possibility that some-one like myself, who was not a Heaven-descended Japanese, could ever become proficient at it.

Moreover, he thoroughly disliked Mr. Pak's idea that I should be trained and fattened up in secret so that, as an unknown surprise entry, I could win my very first impor-tant match and clean up a massive fortune on the care-fully placed bets of the handful in the know. These bets, Mr. Pak assured Hatanaka, could be well distributed by the Korean crime syndicate which, for the entire Osaka area, was entirely in the hands of his Korean friends and associates. Mr. Pak also explained, as Fungo confided to me later, that Hatanaka would make a very good thing out of all this if he played along.

The result was that I was not actually placed directly in

the Hatanaka stable but was sent some miles away to a property owned by his brother-in-law where a very small and well-screened heya was created especially in order to train me. Fungo was placed in direct charge of the operation although Smitty and Mr. Pak often dropped in to check on how I was developing. A trainer named Wajima was effectively in charge, however.

Assigned to train with me and to work out together were four other sumotori aspirants none of whom were Heaven-descended but all of whom looked more Japanese than I did: a Tibetan, two Koreans named Kim and Ko, and a Lobo giant from southwest China who was only sixteen inches shorter than I and had been impressively nourished, presumably since joining Hatanaka's heya. Fungo told me that the Lobos were savages, reputed to be cannibals and slave owners, and were the largest in stature of the Chinese peoples.

As soon as we had been installed in the secret heya a serious hitch developed in Mr. Pak's and Smitty's project. The first time I took a bath, settling myself in a huge round tub after carefully washing away the soap with which I had lathered myself, my fellow wrestlers promptly noticed my small tail which had hitherto escaped the attention of all the brilliant planners, starting with Smitty. "Why didn't you tell me?" Mr. Pak, Fungo and Wajima all screamed at him in different languages.

"Well, how the hell should I know? We didn't go in for public bathing at the Cyprus clink. Good God, we hardly ever had a bath of any sort. Not even a shower."

"It's all right," I tried to reassure them. "This is not a problem. Why when I was with the Harlem Globetrotters I always wore two jockstraps, one in front and the other turned around backwards. Yes, really ass-backwards. You need not fear that I'll be hurt."

"Be hurt, you fool," said Fungo. "Don't you realize that every sumotori wears only a mawashi. That is a kind of belt of heavy silk which is almost thirty feet long. It is two feet broad but when it is folded and wrapped around you the part that comes up behind and is attached to the rear section is only a couple of inches wide. A jockstrap would show. You'd be laughed right out of the profession. And us with you."

"We'll have to think of something else," said Smitty, calm as usual. After a while he came up with the idea of a kind of flesh-colored wrapping that would hold my tail tight against me pointing down and in along my ass. This in turn would—or should be covered by that narrow piece of mawashi and we'd hope for the best. The big trouble was that in some throws the opponent grabs the main mawashi sash and tries to drag one out of the ring with it.

Our heya was in the courtyard of what some people said had once been a temple destroyed during the wartime bombings. We were given bedding called futon and we spread this on rice-straw tatami mats laid out on the floor. For me, the biggest concentration (once my tail case had been manufactured and successfully tried out) was on increasing my weight and seeing to it that every pound I gained was concentrated in my legs, hips, ass and belly so as to shift my center of gravity downward; and also on strengthening all the lower portion of my body, especially my thighs and calves.

It was explained to me by Hatanaka, on one of his frequent visits to our special quarters, that the ultimate secret of a sumotori's success lay in the power of his legs and hips. This was so even though all hope for my eventual success would lie in my successful mastery of the thrusting technique of tsuki-taoshi, the sudden attack supposed to fell an adversary and to be developed around my famous bonk.

When I began my training I was eight feet six inches tall—almost two feet higher than any successful sumotori had ever been, I am told—and weighed two hundred and ninety pounds. The plan was that my weight should be increased as rapidly as possible to a minimum of four hundred and fifty pounds, all of which would be concentrated below the line of my bottom ribs.

This would make it harder for other wrestlers to lift, unbalance or dislodge me by one or another of the seventy kimarite or winning methods that are officially listed as permissible and useful in the Japanese national sport. These were divided into thrusting, pushing, throwing and tripping techniques, many of which involved grabbing the opponent's mawashi, regarded as my great vulnerability.

However, up to a point I might be protected here because grabbing the mawashi's actual thin strip between the buttocks was regarded as an automatically disqualifying foul as were attacks on the sex organs, pulling by the sumotori's topknot hairdo which I had to start growing, deliberately trying to break bones, gouge eyes or smash ears. No fisticuffing was permitted but this did not discourage openhanded slaps on which, in the form of a new, orientalized bonk, my future reputation and the financial well-being of Smitty, Mr. Pak and their friends all depended.

From the first moment, even before I was permitted to start learning the rules and also some of the great variety of holds, I was subjected to forced feeding like a backyard Harlem pig before Christmas and to a course of very tough exercises. At first the exercises provided less difficulty for me than the food, which I found most untasty.

With Fungo always directing activities for Wajima, because he could speak American and Japanese equally well, I was shown how to strengthen my legs and harden my hands. There was a stretching exercise in which I had to sit on the ground with my legs spread out flat at right angles to my body and then I had to lean forward time and time again and touch the ground with my head. When I failed to actually reach the earth, the Lobo forced my shoulders down from behind. I don't mind saying it hurt so much I often yelled.

Another thing I had to do was walk slowly around and around our training place carrying the Lobo on my back and stopping, when ordered, to do deep knee bends over and over while that great, fat, smelly weight clung to my shoulders. Other times I had to drag the two Koreans, sitting together smiling, up a steep hill on a kind of sled Hatanaka had invented made of thick bamboo slats.

Finally there was a whole series of heavy stomping and endless hopping exercises and a group of tests called teppo in which sometimes you had to push as hard as you could and for a long time against massive wooden posts and other times you had to slam your hands against them or down hard on smooth boards, until they almost bled. But that was the only way to get tough and I accepted this as an unhappy part of my new career.

What I could accept less easily was the need to eat enormous amounts of the food that was shoved at me twice a day, almost always based on a kind of stew called chanko-nabe which was supposed to be full of vigor and calories but which stank like garbage. It was served in a vast pot from which we all ate.

This, together with heaping piles of rice and soy sauce, was supposed not only to add rapidly to your weight but to distribute it in the parts that were considered most desirable. They made the stew of fish or meat or chicken and filled it up with bean curds and vegetables but it always smelled bad, the worst being the fish chanko. I could hardly keep it down, and it was difficult at first even getting it to my mouth because I had never become used to chopsticks. But all the coaches and the other wrestlers bullied me into taking it by mocking me, sneering at me, slapping me or boxing my ears while Fungo and often Smitty stood by calmly warning me not to strike back.

As a result of all this, and despite my problem in sleeping cold nights that were even worse than those I'd known sometimes in Ontario, I rose rapidly in weight until I had actually reached four hundred and fifty by the end of the year. At that point Hatanaka, assuring Mr. Pak that he was certain I could still gain another fifty pounds and it would be to our general advantage, started personally teaching me the minimal number of defensive and offensive techniques he held necessary to successful accomplishment of my mission.

By then my whole shape had changed. I had the appearance of an enormous pear, it seemed to me, but although mine was one of the biggest potbellies in the world I felt quite sure that not even a heavyweight boxing champ could hit me there and make me wince. In fact, he'd probably hurt his hand as soon as it penetrated the outer inch of blubber. As for my thighs, they were like round, muscular casks.

And I was even beginning to like the diet as this huge new body of mine craved increasing amounts of food. The thing I couldn't stand was the constant stench of garlic (which Lobo and the two Koreans fancied), the heavy, sickening smell of rice, and the stink of sweat all the time, despite the numerous baths we took.

Kim, Ko, the Tibetan and the Lobo were taken away from the heya at various times in order to gain experience by participating in local sumo tournaments and seeking, by winning often enough, to advance the status of their ranked skill. Nevertheless, it was decided not to expose me and thereby risk conceivable knowledge of my power and ability until I could be entered as an unknown but at a very high level which would enable large wagers to be placed on me at the most favorable odds. Although such a procedure was contrary to the highly formal rules of sumotori procedure, Smitty, Mr. Pak and Fungo were all confident the corrupt Korean criminal apparatus would be able to bribe the necessary authorities and make this possible.

In preparation for that eventual occasion, I was given the professional wrestler's name of Toratora and the heya barber saw to it that my hair was allowed to grow long in the center of my skull so that an impressive topknot could be wound there. This was not only a long-established tradition but also ensured some protection when head-butting was attempted by tough opponents.

Hatanaka argued that a splendid Japanese name did not alone suffice to make me Heaven-descended. My pigmentation, the color of my skin, was all right, but it was perfectly obvious from my features, above all my eyes, that I was not of the right race. How, he asked again and again, could a non-Japanese, someone not even an Asian like the Lobo and the Koreans, aspire to the championship of an ancient, honorable, godly sport? After all, even Kim, Ko and the Lobo could contend their homelands had been occupied by Jap soldiers so they might have some divine blood; but I was patently inferior.

Hereupon Smitty developed a logical argument, which when translated by Fungo, finally convinced the stable master. He told Hatanaka that I could claim pure Aryan descent through a Nazi SS Sippenbuch which was at present in the possession of British prison authorities in Cyprus. "Ah, Nazis very honorable allies," said Fungo, translating Hatanaka's words.

"Well," Smitty continued, "the Nazis proclaimed all Japanese honorary Aryans. You were their blood brothers which means you came of the same honorary strain. Therefore you must now consider Snarler here—I beg your pardon, I mean Toratora—an honorary Japanese. That's simple, isn't it? Hatanaka was persuaded.

Once the heya boss acknowledged I had just claim to participate in this kokugi or national sport, he made no difficulty about the crooked aspect of fixing a surprise match which would enable him, as well as the others, to gain great wealth through the operations of Mr. Pak's Korean gang of crooks. He became increasingly enthusiastic as I continued to gain weight and strength, pointing out that I need concentrate only on basic defensive tactics while perfecting my tsuki-taoshi bonk for the sudden assault that would gain me unexpected victory.

Hatanaka stressed that most sumo fights are of very short endurance, generally lasting little more than a minute and often just a few seconds. Once the formal pantomime that preceded a match had been finished, it was simply necessary to force an adversary to touch the ground with any portion of his body other than his feet or to push, throw or force him out of the ring. This was a mound of hard-packed earth covered with sand, on which the sumotori themselves scattered salt during prematch ceremonials.

I had to avoid giving my opponent a chance to rush or lift me out and then, suddenly, surprise him with my new form of tsuki-taoshi, a technique that was used but very rarely. The enormous extent of my reach would help this strategy, and the fact that I had attained a weight of nearly five hundred pounds seemed adequate insurance that not even the strongest sumo could overbalance me if I merely remained alert and on guard.

By this time I was having increasing difficulty in sleeping at night. Smitty came up to me one day and said: "Fungo thinks it'll do you good to get some sex. Between jail and the heya you've been without tail a hell of a time, fella, and I guess Fungo's right. So we've fixed up a little party for you tonight and we'll see if that doesn't help."

Mr. Pak, Fungo, Smitty and I were taken off that evening in an enormous German automobile that had no less than six doors and three complete rows of seats. I was allowed one row all alone. We were driven for about an hour and a half to a series of little buildings with a small gate in the entrance through the main wall. I had tremendous awkwardness getting my height and belly past it but I managed.

Several little Japanese women, smiling and bowing in their pretty, bright kimonos, welcomed us in and made us take off our shoes. I had been given an immense new gray kimono and sandals to wear but the others were in European clothes. Fungo told me he had explained to the lady in charge that I had been a Japanese soldier in the World War who, heroically, had never surrendered. He had explained I managed to stay alive in the remote mountains of New Guinea by wrestling with native Papuan strongmen who were of superhuman stature. As a consequence I was now a remarkable sumotori although as yet not well known.

The little women, simpering and chattering gaily, led us to the largest room in the establishment which became crowded as soon as I wedged my immense bulk into it. We all sat cross-legged on cushions laid on the tatami mats. I had three cushions and had gotten quite used to this position, especially after much practice and all my leg-spreading exercises. I just let my vast belly hang out in front and tried to move my chopsticks around it. Smitty, who was not accustomed to the posture, kept shifting uncomfortably around.

"These are geisha girls," Fungo explained. "They will talk with you, sing to you, feed you, keep your cup full of hot saki wine, play music, invent games and even make short plays. But you must not touch them. It is only later, when our hostess thinks the proper time has come, that you will be introduced to other charming ladies. Geisha are very proper but this is a special kind of place, and for special customers like Mr. Pak special services are arranged as a matter of generosity and hospitality."

The lovely girl who kneeled beside me, constantly filling my saki cup, of fragile porcelain and shaped like an egg, was named Hopeful Angel; at least, that is what it meant in Japanese, a language I could now understand although only a bit. She was very nice and her eyes looked at me with admiration. She patted my huge stomach and said in broken English: "Oh, very nice. Very strong. Very big man. Big man all over."

Our dinner lasted a long time and the food was quite an agreeable change from the usual chanko-nabe I ate. Also, I drank a lot of saki. It made me feel happy and ready for anything. Mr. Pak, Fungo and Smitty were all drinking whisky, I noticed, each of them with a bottle on the table in front of him and they had big glasses which their geisha companions kept well filled. They also seemed to be smiling and relaxed, which made Mr. Pak belch loud and often with pleasure.

Finally, the other geishas gathered in a corner, looking very old-fashioned with their hair done up even more formally and smoothly than a sumotori's topknot, and they began acting out a play and singing gentle songs while one of them plucked a long-stemmed instrument with strings running over a kind of bowl. Hopeful Angel touched me gently on the sleeve like a timid butterfly. "You come me," she whispered softly.

She minced out with delicate steps and I managed to rise without upsetting the whole dinner and stumble heavily behind. I followed her in my slippered feet through a garden, stepping on flat stones laid along a path, until we came to another dull-colored building with a tilted Japanese roof. It was larger than the rest. When we arrived the door opened and there was another beautiful young lady, quite a bit larger than Hopeful Angel. "This Pearly Gate," she said, introducing her to me. "She Korean. Kaesang girl. Korean kaesang like Japanese geisha. Except she do more. She more experienced. She speak much good English because many American soldiers Korea. By-by mister big boy."

Pearly Gate was just as lovely as Hopeful Angel and her voice was just as sweet and soft. But she was much bigger, the size of a tall American lady. She took me by the hand, shut the door, and led me to a room as big as that where we had banqueted. "Now," she said, "take off your clothes, lover, and I'll start proceedings by giving you a bath. We got the word from Pak Sin Man that you were a giant but I had no idea how much of a giant you really are. And I've seen some big ones in my time.

"They use me for the very large men, foreigners and Sumo wrestlers, when they're allowed to come. Not many Japanese girls can handle them. But I can take anything, even you, lover. Once you get inside me you'll know why they call me Pearly Gate. I've been told by experts there's not another like it this side of Heaven."

We began when she sat me down, legs what they call akimbo, handed me a double-sized cup of hot saki, and tenderly went about the business of removing my clog-slippers, socks and kimono while I remained seated. Suddenly I found I was naked on top of a pile of heavy silk. Then she undressed swiftly, almost in a single motion, and conducted me to a good-sized pool that was set at the end of the room in the floor like a huge bath. It was very hot but very comfortable, especially as she began to rub my back.

Pearly Gate was of a happy nature. She applied herself smilingly and enthusiastically to her job, talking to me softly all the time. She was quite pleased when she inspected my private parts but suddenly amazed when she discovered my bony little tail. "What's that?" she asked in some astonishment. "I've never seen one of them on anybody. Do you have any feeling in it? Is it a kind of second prick?"

I assured her it had no feeling but was simply something I had been born with, perhaps because of my Oorlog Herero ancestors, and that I did not use it for the purposes about which she had inquired.

"Ah, you carry your own harigata as it were," she said. Then she explained that a harigata is a kind of artificial gadget that many Japanese ladies use to excite themselves or even to make love to themselves, all alone, when their husbands are away. "Some are of ivory. Some are of finely varnished wood. Some have peculiar shapes and are employed for unusual purposes.

"But you are the only man I ever heard of who is equipped with a working prick as well as his own personal harigata. I will learn to amuse myself with both. This must be the very important secret that Pak Sin Man sent word about. You know what I was told? I was told that if I breathed a word concerning you to anyone I would be strangled. But I was also told that if I breathed a word concerning one particular secret I discovered, I would be strangled very, very slowly. Pak Sin Man is powerful. He has a big say in the rackets."

She shivered. I looked at her with horror. Mr. Pak, I thought, must be a most evil person, even more evil than I had thought.

When she finished bathing me she made me lie down on my back on thick, soft futon bedding spread on wide tatamis along the opposite wall from the pool. Then, with much tenderness and skill, she began to show me how to kiss properly, something I realized that neither Mildred nor Yumyum had ever truly understood. And then, with me on my back and Pearly Gate sitting astride me below my belly, we made love. "This is the only sensible position," she explained. "If you were to roll over on top of me, you'd break every bone in my body."

We made love several times and I had never known how wonderful it was. Each time she squealed and moaned with pleasure. Finally she got up, poured saki for each of us, and then, after a while, whispered gently: "Turn around. I wish to use your harigata." I managed to lurch over on my massive belly and she did exactly that. It gave me no pleasure at all but such was not apparently the case with Pearly Gate.

I don't know how many hours we had been there when a shy tapping sounded on the door and there was Hopeful Angel again. She spoke in a low voice to the marvelous kaesang girl who explained in turn to me that Smitty and Mr. Pak had decided we must go because it was almost time for the sun to rise. Pearly Gate helped me dress and then stood on tiptoe, putting her arms around my thick neck.

"Lover boy," she said, "I like you better than anyone on the whole earth. Better than anyone I ever met or hope to meet. Will you please try and get permission from Pak Sin Man to come here as often as possible. I know you are in training. But at least three or four times a month. I'll do you good. Tell that to Pak. No matter what I am supposed to be doing, I'll make myself available to you. I promise. To you and your harigata."

Hopeful Angel looked puzzled and embarrassed.

"You know," Pearly Gate said in English to Hopeful Angel who clearly didn't understand: "When you look at naked men they quickly change shape. But lover boy changes in two directions."

CHAPTER XII

B ack at the heya during the next few weeks I
worked with such speed and expert knowledge,
above all in my encounters with Kim, Ko, the
Tibetan, and the Lobo, that (urged by Fungo) Mr. Pak
agreed to let me visit Pearly Gate every ten days. We fell
very much in love. The fact that she so obviously cared for
me and I adored her somehow helped me because I
wanted to prove myself worthy of her affection.

This suited both Smitty and Mr. Pak, once they saw
that my talents as a wrestler were becoming truly super-
lative. The rest of the heya only knew that as a favored
sumotori who had arrived at Hatanaka's stable in the
company of the two top bosses and with Fungo as a kind
of personal coach and attendant, I was entitled to special
privileges.

In return I trained hard, ate as much as I could cram

into my tummy and worked vigorously at all exercises, especially the teppo which would strengthen my arms, toughen my hands and thereby improve my bonking tsuki-taoshi. Consequently, it was agreed by my managers that a campaign of fake propaganda should be started on my behalf; but only sufficient to gain registration for me in the Niho Sumo Kyokai or Japan Sumo Association.

This made me eligible for public matches, but not well enough known to arouse the suspicions of those who were to be induced to wager large sums against me. At the same time, Mr. Pak's racketeers were both belittling my prowess, describing me as an ignorant fat man in the bars and gaming parlors of Osaka and also trying to work out preliminary bets at odds incredibly favorable to Smitty and Mr. Pak.

It was widely rumored that as a gaijin, or non-Japanese, I could never be expected to master the essentials of shingitai (spirit, technique and strength) to achieve important successes. Nevertheless, some specially paid photographers were allowed to visit the heya. They watched me work out in restrained circumstances and confirmed with their lenses that at least I was respectful, had carefully trimmed fingernails, a proper topknot and knew the rudiments of the sport. Neither photographers nor sportswriters were allowed to speak to anyone at the heya save Mr. Pak and Fungo; not even Hatanaka or Wajima, whose judgment and tact were considered insufficient for the job.

The story that had been told to the madam at the geisha house about my heroic experiences in Papua after the war was carefully amplified in order to stir interest in me as a person who was physically remarkable even if obviously not of championship quality. It was said that I too was of Lobo ancestry and even had some obscure Japanese strain. Anyway, I had volunteered to serve the emperor in the last war and therefore was spiritually and psychologically no gaijin, though my blood might be polluted.

Since very few Lobos had ever been encountered by Japanese, this tale went over extremely well. Moreover, the feats of strength attributed to Papuan giants were exaggerated as a means of explaining how I had acquired certain wrestling techniques, even if most of these could not be acknowledged or tolerated by the Nihon Sumo Kyokai.

Mr. Pak and Smitty, after many consultations with Hatanaka, had worked out a plan that called for me to be given forged certificates of military service, forged documents from nonexistent Japanese officials who had "brought me back" from New Guinea and sufficient forged testimonials from the government's Nippon Budokan to qualify me as one of the Maegashira, or Senior Wrestlers, class in Sumo's Maku-Uchi. This was the special championship division of five different categories, all eligible to participate in the most important and therefore financially the most rewarding tour-financially the most rewarding tournaments.

Of these, of course, the Emperor's Cup conferring the Grand National Championship in the Tokyo sport stadium or Kokugikan was the obvious trophy to aim at. However, Mr. Pak and Smitty decided such a goal was too high and involved too much trickery and risk. It was therefore resolved to make our big coup in the annual Osaka tournament of March, one of the big four annual competitions. Also, in Osaka the Korean underworld could most effectively use its broad money-making network.

Just to take part in this event it was necessary to be recognized as a sekitori or one of the acknowledged experts of the profession. Hatanaka, however, was able to schedule a series of exhibition bouts and minor competitions where, with his shrewd coaching, I managed to win sufficient victories for promotion although never appearing to be more than an oversized, awkward bumpkin whom any of the Maegashira, or Senior Wrestlers, would have no difficulty in defeating. Also, to avoid any chance of accident, Fungo had arranged that my mawashi would be imperceptibly broader in back, even if the difference was unnoticeable, and that my embarrassing vestigial tail was strongly bound in its well-fastened case.

I survived a series of regional contests called basho. Each of these lasted several days. Furthermore, I succeeded without displaying any special talent except sheer strength, which the expert commentators promptly decided was more than offset by my inexperience and clumsiness. Training in the mountains of New Guinea against Papuan wild men was cynically scoffed at as inadequate preparation for a Japanese martial sport at least the peer of bushido and judo.

Only once, in a local match, was there a moment of potential embarrassment. My opponent sought to defeat me with sudden application of the hidari yotsu, a hold which inserted his left hand abruptly inside my tightly bound mawashi, in an effort to unbalance me. Fortunately my secret was not exposed and I swiftly disposed of him by accomplishing an ashi-tori or leg throw with my long and powerful arms and hands.

"Toratora, Toratora," shouted Kim and Ko, who had been brought along to assist and encourage me, but few in the small group of spectators even bothered to applaud. Hatanaka roundly scolded me afterward: "You are supposed to be only a huge lump of an oshi-zumo wrestler who pushes and not one who grapples, grips, thrusts or throws. Everything else must appear unknown to you, or at least unfamiliar. Pak's gamblers have stressed that this is very important. Don't forget again."

For the last weeks prior to the Osaka tournament I trained against the Lobo and the Koreans only in the various forms of tsuppari. That is a kind of fast, hard pugilism but with the hands open, almost like bonking except without the fist. I also practiced even more vigorous teppo than ever before so that I hardened my hands to the degree where I could smash fair-sized beams in two.

Both Kim and Ko were adept in the Korean sport of karate, which requires much practice in splintering wood with the outer edges of the palms. Both were also big, strong men. But I could shatter chunks approximately twice as thick as they were able to crack with the fiercest concentration. Moreover, in addition to perfecting the knowledge of the tsuki-taoshi I had not yet disclosed in my few public appearances, I extensively experimented with hataki-komo, a deadly method of whacking an opponent on the back or neck when he had been maneuvered off balance, something rather difficult to accomplish against a well-versed sumotori.

Finally the big day arrived. The evening before, Smitty and Mr. Pak visited the heya. They told me Pearly Gate and the madam who ran the geisha and bath establishment were coming to watch me fight and would be sitting together in their box in order to encourage me. Next morning, after a light workout and tea, I had an early nap on my futon. Afterward Fungo and one of the junior wrestlers in Hatanaka's stable oiled and combed my hair before winding my thick and curly topknot in the center of my skull, somewhat behind the axis of my ears.

I was clad in my best dress kimono. This was then hung with a kesho-mawashi, a brocaded apron of heavy silk which is customarily worn by the two competitors when they begin the solemn ceremony of entering the ring and preparing for combat. Then, after my big bosses had departed, Fungo and a young sumo apprentice from the rather low jo-nidan division, who had been assigned to be a kind of second for me, climbed into the vast black Mercedes that seemed to be at Mr. Pak's disposal. Off we drove to the bout that was to make my reputation and the fortunes of everyone brought into the plot that Smitty had so cleverly hatched in a Cyprus prison cell.

All sumo encounters are accompanied by a series of rituals that have descended from many centuries of custom. While these solemn affairs take place, the spectators gather in rows of boxes and seats where they jabber at each other, gulp down quantities of saki, holler the names of their own favorites and have a general good time getting into the proper mood for excitement. I noticed Pearly Gate, the madam, Mr. Pak and Smitty all jammed into one box near the ring when the ceremony of blessing the combat area began according to the ancient ways of Shinto, the warrior religion of the Heaven-descended people.

Three gyoji, the professional sumotori priests and referees, were there. It was already midafternoon and several preliminary encounters to ours, the main match of the day, had taken place. My opponent, a chunky, self-confident young man of the Ozeki or championship division, with thick arms, legs and neck and scowling eyebrows that lifted away from the top of his nose like heavy bird's wings, was just stepping over the packed-sand mound in the center of the arena. I lumbered up with a grave expression on my face, accompanied by Fungo and the jo-nidan second.

There were shouts and squeals and claps as I approached him. "They're hollering how big you are," said Fungo. Pearly Gate smiled with approving, loving pride. I noticed that Smitty, who was puffing a large cigar, had an absolutely blank expression. Sitting just behind Mr. Pak, in the second tier of boxes, a one-eyed man identified to me by Fungo as a very important Osaka Korean who served as the chief of a koenkai, or support group, formed to sponsor me in this match, glared fiercely at me. He had tattoos on his hands and his little fingers missed the last joint. "He's a big shot in Yamaguchi-Gumi," Fungo muttered. "The biggest crime syndicate."

I felt his stare so strongly that, much as I wanted to gaze around or to smile lovingly at Pearly Gate, I just had to look back at him. From time to time runners, some of them mere youngsters, scurried down the aisle and handed him written messages. Often he leaned forward after reading them and muttered to Mr. Pak. "Bets," whispered Fungo in my ear. "More and more and more bets. You just do what you know how to do, bimbo, and we can all retire. Why you'll be able to buy the entire island of Cyprus with the cut you get. As for me, I'll buy Hawaii."

The gyoji began to recite solemn incantations while several grave-faced judges, whose decision on the outcome would be final if there were any disagreements among the referees, seated themselves about the ring, their backs straight, their knees apart. Saki was dribbled around the four corners of the hard clay mound in which we would fight. One of the gyoji inspected the well-packed bundles of earth and straw which fixed the border-line beyond which neither contestant could move without being declared the loser.

Then, while the judges solemnly sipped cups of saki, I and the Ozeki, whose fighting name was Kimaro, allowed our seconds to remove our kimonos and also our ceremonial aprons. We bowed with much formality to the judges, the audience and to each other, after we had been officially introduced. We slammed our hands together thunderously, successively regarding the four corners of the wind. Then we scattered salt on the earth further to purify it. Each of us sipped a ladle of water to give ourselves additional strength, rinsed our mouths and spat it out. Finally, we squatted low opposite each other in the middle of the ring, prepared for the fierce and ponderous charge called tachiai that would open the bout with a sudden clash of fiercely trained monsters together weighing almost half a ton.

The gyoji supervising our particular bout was dressed, as is the custom for his profession, in magnificent old-fashioned robes and wore the black head covering once usual among ancient nobles at the imperial court. He carried a large fan which served as his signal to start the contest and also to warn the sumotori against any possible infringement of the rules. While awaiting the flick of his fan as a signal to crouch in preparation for the final assault, we arose from our previous squat and stood with arms crossed over our chests frowning into each other's faces with gleaming eyes.

At the critical moment we dug our fists in the earth, leaning toward each other like bulls, our eyes still locked in frightening glares. Then, as the gyoji tipped his fan, we charged. For what seemed a long, long time but was actually only a matter of seconds, the referee kept shouting "hakkiyoi, hakkiyoi," which meant that we should get things going, keep things moving. For a moment there was silence in the arena. Everyone was embraced in an awed hush. Then the shouting began and I noticed that practically all of the applause was for Kimaro.

I pretended to use my considerable advantage in size and weight to apply a yori-kiri hold, working my long arms under the Ozeki's and starting to push him slowly, inch by inch, toward the straw and dirt bales placed along the outer limit of the ring to make the frontier clearly visible. Pearly Gate and the madam both cried shrilly for me to keep on pushing but as I glimpsed them swiftly, noticing that Smitty had suddenly started to eat his cigar, I felt Kimaro's big hand reach behind me, grabbing for my mawashi in a yotsu-zumo grip, trying to force me down toward my knees from the rear and thus to bring me to a lower height level where his compact power would be more effective.

As we strained against each other his stubby fingers groped upward along the flesh of my behind and closer and closer to my testicles. Just before the gyoji started to lift his fan, apparently in doubt still as to whether Kimaro was in the process of forfeiting the match by an illegal foul, I reacted with the tsuki-taoshi for which I had been so long and carefully trained.

In fact, I was so angry that my openhanded slapdown was as close to my normal bonk as it could be without patently breaking the rules. I slammed him with a kind of karate blow and I am sure my hard hand would have broken his cranium had it not landed flat on his thick topknot. As it was he tottered, stumbled backward, and just as he dizzily tripped and fell over the bales and almost into the lap of Mr. Pak, he muttered something over and over, then collapsed.

Fungo and the jo-nidan second seemed to rush me out and toward the dressing room with an unusual amount of haste. When a mob of reporters and photographers, their flashbulbs blazing, tried to squeeze in with us, Hatanaka and Mr. Pak joined the jo-nidan and forced the crowd away, slamming and locking the door. Fungo explained: "The son-of-a-bitch found you out. He just kept muttering that you've got a tail. I suppose he felt it when he applied his yotsu-zumo. He was certainly fouling you. Even the gyoji was about to call a foul on him and award you the match when you bonked him out of the ring. But now I don't know just what'll happen. They claim anyone with a tail isn't a real man. That he's disqualified. There's never been a case like this before."

Mr. Pak added glumly: "Kimaro's manager and the leaders of his koenkai, his financial supporters, are now protesting the gyoji's decision in your favor to the dohyo, the judges who were stationed around the ring outside. My God, we can't take any risks." He turned to Smitty, who still had an inch of dead cigar working its damp way into his mouth. They muttered something to each other and Smitty nodded, disappearing with Fungo. Then Mr. Pak said to me: "You not goin' change, bathe, nothin'. You come quick me."

We went through the back door of my dressing room, past the bath, along a dark corridor that seemed to run beneath the arena, and when we got to the end Smitty and Fungo were waiting in the big black Mercedes. Weeping, large tears streaming down her cheeks, Pearly Gate was sitting beside the driver in front. Hatanaka pushed me in and disappeared as we drove off.

Fungo explained: "Because there is no precedent of a sumotori with a tail, Kimaro is claiming no foul was involved on his part because his hand never moved forward from the base of your tail. He also claims you aren't a qualified real man. His manager agrees. At the same time he is insisting that your karate-bonk was an illegal blow and the Ozeki should therefore be awarded victory under any circumstances. Hatanaka is arguing that it is ridiculous to talk about any tail; that you have been so seriously injured in your privates by Kimaro's foul that you had to be rushed to a hospital for emergency treatment."

I was so bewildered by everything that I let them do whatever they wanted. "We're gonna chop that damn tail so quick you'll never know you had it," said Smitty grimly. "Then if the dohyo reverses the gyoji's decision, we'll produce you and any necessary doctors to give evidence to the Sumo Association."

Fungo added: "In the meantime Hatanaka is arguing that the judges should be aware that although your father was a Lobo, your mother had Ainu blood and came from the Kuriles, that everyone must know the Ainus are not only large but hairy and some of them have lots of hair around the ass. Since Loboland is part of Communist China where Japan has no relations and the Kurile islands are occupied by Russia and no Japanese are allowed to go there, we can insist there is no further means of investigating your ancestry.

"In the meantime, one of Mr. Pak's best forgers is rushing through a fake birth certificate, old paper. It will be dated from Shana which Moscow now holds. Hatanaka will delay the argument long enough, by threatening legal action, so that this certificate can be added to the military papers and other records we prepared for you and that have all been accepted. The Japan Sumo Association won't dare lose face by risking a court case."

"There's about ten million bucks in bet money involved," said Smitty grimly. "Off with your goddamn tail."

"Fortunately," Fungo told me, "the boss of your principal koenkai, the supporters who have been financing you and Hatanaka, has lots of pull with the dohyo of Osaka."

The only one who seemed at all concerned about me as me was Pearly Gate. "Poor Curly," she sobbed. "I hope it won't hurt too much. Mr. Pak has said I can come along."

After a three-hour drive we drew up at a door in a high wall that seemed to be guarded by a whole pack of dogs, judging by the chorus of barks and howls. Someone must have been waiting for us because the door swung inward as the car drew to a stop. Mr. Pak pushed me in first and everyone else followed. Mr. Pak, Pearly Gate and Smitty waited at what seemed to be a front office. Fungo came along with me to interpret.

All the men and women we saw, even the dog handlers, were wearing white suits or smocks and had white skullcaps and white masks tied over their mouths and the lower part of their noses. I suppose they were doctors and nurses but they looked like a collection of spooks. Much to his surprise, Fungo was made to put a smock over his suit and to have a mask tied over the bottom of his face. This didn't help his interpreting because the words came out in a mumble. All I could understand was: "Real sanitary, these goddamn Japs."

In a rather small bedroom I was stripped of my kimono, towels and increasingly uncomfortable mawashi and then they laid me out on a large bed. "This place run for big-shot Koreans," Fungo said, lifting the mask away from his mouth. "Lots of them are plenty big too. But these guys have never seen anything in your class before."

They turned me over on my belly and fiddled with my tail at considerable length. It appeared to cause them great astonishment. From their hemming and hawing and also from the delicate touch of their little fingers I judged that the nurses were even more fascinated than the doctors.

While this examination was still going on, a kind of broad table on wheels was brought up to the door and I was instructed to climb on top, belly down. I did so, with much straining and creaking. Thank goodness the tabletop, frame and wheels were all steel, the wheels being tired with solid rubber. The last thing I remember was the deep jab of a needle in the back of my neck and another jab, that I hardly felt at all, near the base of my spine.

It must have been a lot later that I started to come to. I was still lying on my stomach but now I was in a regular bed, I suppose in the first room where they had examined me. I had a terrible pain in my behind and a kind of weak sensation all over. My face was turned sideways on a regular western-type flat pillow and when I opened my eyes I saw Pearly Gate, right close, looking softly into my face. "Curly, Curly, Curly," she said in her soft sweet voice. "I'm so glad it's all over. The doctor says it was easy and that the operation was a great success.

"The only complication is that they had to cut away a piece of your scalp from the part that is covered by your topknot. A plastic surgeon grafted that to your bottom at the place where the tail stump used to be. They explained to me this is to confirm the story Hatanaka is telling the dohyo and also the Japan Sumo Association. About Ainu blood. You are so healthy that everything will be pretty well healed in a week, they promise me.

"They have good plastic surgeons here because they have plenty of practice with wounds—knife wounds and gunshot wounds—and also with changing the features and the fingertips of people wanted by the police." Pearly Gate said all this as if it were the most natural of things.

A few days later, when I had been allowed to shift positions to lie on my back, just so long as my legs were kept apart, the chief nurse came in and handed me a glass bottle in which my amputated tail was carefully preserved in alcohol. "Ahhhh," said Pearly Gate. "My harigata. May I have it?" she asked. "Sure," I replied. "What for?" "Oh, I'm going to dry it out completely and then keep it as my dearest souvenir of you. The finest harigata any woman ever had."

Mr. Pak finally called for me, Fungo and Pearly Gate at the end of ten days. My missing tail section didn't hurt at all although the new patch of hair was somewhat tender and itchy and the place it had come from, right behind my topknot, was sore. Mr. Pak made me take off my kimono and the loose kind of diaper thay had given me and he carefully examined the results of the operation.

"Fine, fine," he said. "Won't have no trouble. That Kimaro crook already being kicked around public press for sending you hospital because twisted your balls half off in foul. Public now wants you declared winner. Wants dohyo accept gyoji decision. All except those lose money. They lose plenty too, boy. You do fine job even if you lose tail. Maybe that good luck."

Everything went exactly as Mr. Pak predicted. I was given a medical examination by approved physicians of the Japan Sumo Association in the Osaka offices of that body. Ozeki, his coaches and chief koenkais were all present as were my principal friends and supporters except for Pearly Gate. A doctor who (I was later told by Fungo) had been given a generous tip by Mr. Pak very quickly and gently inspected the new clump of hair inserted just beneath my ass. One of my balls had actually been bruised by Ozeki's yotsu-zumo and the doctor took great pains to point out that it still was swollen. The decision was entirely favorable. Kimaro was demoted from the Ozeki to the Maegashira division of the Sekitori class and was also temporarily suspended from competition because of his foul.

That night Mr. Pak and Smitty gave a huge geisha party at the madam's establishment where I had first met and fallen in love with Pearly Gate. Smitty told me I was being paid fifty thousand dollars in U.S. money for all my successful efforts. That seemed to me to be very generous considering that only about ten million dollars had been won by the Korean betting syndicate and they had also taken care of all my medical expenses.

"I am keeping the money in a large envelope for you," said Smitty, "and you can have it whenever you want. Just give me twenty-four hours notice to get it out of the strongbox where I've put it. Now, Snarler, why don't you run along to Pearly Gate? She can hardly wait to see you. Hopeful Angel will take you there again."

I had wondered why my beloved Pearly Gate was not at Mr. Pak's party and felt puzzled to find myself waddling after the delicate little geisha as she tripped daintily over the flagstone path to the bathhouse just as she had done the first time, so many months ago. She simpered admiringly at me as the door opened. There was the faithful Korean kaesang, smiling, beautiful and completely naked. She flung her arms about my neck as I stooped to kiss her. "Ah, Curly," she cooed, "my black Jew, my American Ainu, my Lobo from Papua, my man, my primate. I adore you and want only to spend the rest of my life with you."

"I'm no longer a primate, you know," I told her.

"Yes, I have the evidence. I have my harigata. See," she

said, removing it from a little silk pillow in the corner. "I have dried it and polished it so now it is firm and smooth and beautiful. I have even used it when I dream of you. I shall never give up this sign of your primacy. I love it better than anything in this world except for you yourself."

Pearly Gate was very sentimental and she insisted that just like the very first time she should begin by bathing me, massaging my shoulders gently and every tender art she had taught me that night we met. The bath was hot and delicious. When, afterward, I lay on my belly, she even tickled the patch of hair that had been sewn to my behind. She took down my topknot and inspected the bald patch underneath from which my Ainu-ness had been removed by the helpful surgeon.

Finally, she asked me to turn over on my back and, while I fondled her breasts, embraced me passionately. But nothing happened to me. I did not rise. There wasn't the faintest change. She tried everything, all the arts I suppose she had learned in the kaesang school. But nothing happened, nothing at all.

After a long, long time she ceased her efforts and just kneeled beside me looking yearningly into my eyes. "I don't know what they did to you," she said. "I don't know how long it will last. But, Curly, do not worry. We will try again. And again. Meanwhile I shall always be with you, wherever you wish to go."

Much embarrassed, I said to her: "But Pearly Gate, you knew already that I was no longer a primate."

"Yes," she answered. "But I had not thought that maybe also you were no longer a man." On her cheek was a drop of something that was not rain.

CHAPTER XIII

From that day on I began to lose weight very rapidly and with the weight I also lost my strength. I tried hard to eat, without succeeding; and I became more and more weak as soon as I resumed the regular program of exercises. Despite the fantastic propaganda about my triumph over Kimaro, which was a subject of discussion all over Japan, according to Mr. Pak, it was becoming clear to everyone, including myself, that my career among sumotori was at an end. Only six weeks after I had defeated the Ozeki my hands and arms were getting soft, my belly had started to hang in great folds over my apron, and I had already lost sixty pounds.

One morning Fungo came to me and said: "It's tough luck, pal, but Hatanaka says you're finished. Something's gone wrong with you since they chopped off that tail. Says you'd better get out while the getting's good. So you're gonna have to hang up your mawashi. Hatanaka has fixed it. There'll be a small ceremony at the heya tomorrow. Lots of your friends will be there. It's what they call a danpatsu-shiki. That means they'll cut off your sumo topknot. Then you'll be like everybody else. No topknot."

"And no tail," I added.

"Don't worry, kid," said Fungo. "There'll be a little party and I'm sure the Koreans'll fix you up with a job. A good job too. That's the least they owe you."

So the following evening I was seated on a stool in the practice ring which had been all cleaned up. There were even chrysanthemums placed in pots near the corners. I was wrapped in my best kimono and sat looking sadly at my few friends: Pearly Gate, who was weeping, Mr. Pak, wearing a hat and smoking a cigar, Fungo and all the other wrestlers of the heya as well as the trainers, masseurs and cleaning people.

Hatanaka climbed up behind me and then signalled to my stablemates. One by one they came up and, using a scissors Hatanaka handed them, each snipped off a small piece of my topknot. This, it was explained to me, was as a keepsake, a reminder of me; rather like Pearly Gate's treasure, my tail, I thought.

Then, when they had each been given a little lock, Hatanaka quickly snipped off all that remained, exposing the raw bald spot once covered by the tickly tuft on which I was sitting. As he made this final, fatal cut, the people around the ring began to sing funny songs and clap but I saw that Pearly Gate could not control her sobs despite the general merriment.

After the ceremony Mr. Pak, who scowled all the time he chewed his cigar, gave me a large glass of whisky and said: "Curly, now you no longer wrestler. You no longer train. Drink, drink, be merry. You be glad to know too that you owe nothing for all that expensive medic treatment. Your yorokin, your retirement allowance, just big enough to cover cost. Almost big enough that is. I make up difference. So you don't owe me nothing."

That was good news I thought. I considered Mr. Pak a very generous man although he was not always tender and agreeable.

At the party Hatanaka was very nice and poor Fungo did everything he could to try and cheer up Pearly Gate. He asked Mr. Pak if he couldn't go and get Hopeful Angel to come and help comfort her but Mr. Pak didn't answer. He seemed to be thinking deeply about other things. Finally I decided to ask him what had become of Smitty. I was surprised he wasn't there. After all, Smitty was my old friend from the Cyprus prison. He had arranged my freedom and he had promoted my great new career.

"Smitty, he go away," said Mr. Pak. "Days ago he discover wall-eyed Chinaman in Kyoto and now he take him along to Burma. There been even more murders than usual in Rangoon this year. So Smitty take this gook along as the Man with the X-Ray Eyes. He supposed to look at fellow and tell right off if he murderer or not; or if he gonna be murdered or not. Kind of insurance racket. I hear Smitty he doing well. Rangoon great town for murder. National sport."

"Oh," I said. "That is very interesting. I am surprised Smitty left so suddenly and without saying goodbye to me. But he is a very enterprising man. Could you tell me, Mr. Pak, where he has put my money? He told me you were being very generous and I have been paid fifty thousand dollars U.S. as a result of your investment in my success."

"What money? You big liar, kid. I already tell you I plenty generous and pay your medic expenses. There no more money."

"But Smitty! That's what Smitty told me."

"Well, you go Rangoon find Smitty. None of my affair look after washout sumotori."

I was furious. I raised my flabby but still powerful right arm with the intention of bonking Mr. Pak whom I could barely see through the mist of my rage. But he simply twitched his cigar up to a high angle and I suddenly felt myself seized from behind. Then, while four of my companions in the heya held me and Mr. Hatanaka stood in front, giving specific and painfully scientific instructions, I was thoroughly beaten up.

When I came to, later on, I was lying in the rain outside the little geisha and bathhouse where Pearly Gate worked. She, Hopeful Angel and the nice madam who ran the place were carefully wiping my cuts and bruises with soft wet cloths and stinging ointment.

For two days my tender lady friends looked after me carefully, but then the madam told Pearly Gate it was impossible for me to stay there anymore because that might give the place a bad name and the madam valued her good name very much indeed. A rapidly fading former sumotori who had already received the danpatsu-shiki represented the past and not the future.

I was not even yet an ancestor. Nor, did it seem likely from what Pearly Gate had told her, that I was ever likely now to qualify as an ancestor anymore. So to her regret and with most tender affection I could no longer adorn her unworthy establishment.

Pearly Gate was very downcast but she made every attempt to cheer me up. Finally she took me to a sailors' hiring hall in Osaka port which was run by a retired Greek sea captain whom she had known during his happier days. She told the Greek, whose name was Mitsotaki (and everybody thought this sounded Japanese although he came from Crete) that she would pay him her life savings if he could get us aboard a ship that would go far, far away. Then, together, we would forget the past and journey hand in hand to the future.

"That'll cost you plenty much, Dolly," he said. I don't

know why but he always called her Dolly. "Despite, however, in memory of good old times, I fix you. Any papers?
No papers! Neither of you. He can't leave on fake
forgeries? Well, that will cost you plenty much more,
Dolly," he said.

"But Mitsotaki good friend. Mitsotaki stick to word.
How much money you saved up, Dolly? That all? Well, I
know tramp steamer heading Dokkos soon. That Greek
island. Very pretty. Very quiet. Very nice people. My
cousin he used be lighthouse keeper there. You give me all
money you got saved, Dolly, and I see to it that both start
off for Dokkos. Long, long way. Suez Canal closed but you
go round Africa and through Tangier and Gibraltar and
Sicily, wherever we take cargo, in fact, on the way to
Piraeus."

"And what is your cargo?" Pearly Gate wanted to know.

"Well, let's put it this way, Dolly," said Mitsotaki.
"You've heard something about that Man with the X-Ray
Eyes whom Smitty he now pals up with in Burma. You
know where Burma is? Part of Burma is in Golden
Triangle. And what do they grow in Golden Triangle?
They grow happy-juice there. You squeeze it out of
flowers and you cook it, sniff it, become happy. And Man
with X-Ray Eyes can see them pretty flowers miles away.
Smitty, as always, he knows what to do with it. How to
get away with it." I thought of my fifty thousand dollars
as a good example.

Pearly Gate took charge of everything. She bought me
two rumpled, secondhand European suits made for a circus giant who had outworn them. I had by then lost so
much weight that they fitted. She bought herself two
European dresses in which she looked very strange, especially when she had all her glossy black hair cut short like
western ladies wear it. Then, one evening, after saying
goodbye to the madam and Hopeful Angel, she took me
to a seedy hotel in the port, left me in a room that was far

too small for us and our cardboard suitcases, kissed me and said she had to go and spend the night with Mitsotaki; it was part of the arrangement she had made. We were sailing the next day. When she came back in the morning she was crying. "He said I no good anymore," she sobbed. "Just make same movements like busted grandmother clock."

The steamship *Herakles* was not very pretty to look at. It had paint blisters in various colors all over it. It was small and had a filthy smokestack that looked as if it might blow away in the wind. It had a hoist in front of the bridge and another one behind which I was told were to load and unload cargo; but all the cargo seemed to be on board already.

At the rear fluttered a Stars and Stripes but I soon learned that it was not American, as I had first thought with excited pride, but Liberian. I didn't know where Liberia was. I supposed it was just another one of the big United States, like Texas. In Ben Franklin High School they told me Texas also had only one star in its flag but that it was part of the U.S.A.

Mr. Mitsotaki was not on the ship when we lumbered up the squeaking gangway. There was a greasy fellow named Barbayanni at the top, who wore a captain's hat and gold rings around his sleeves and greeted us: "Mitso told me you'd be along. Everything oke. Or oka as we say in Greek. All paid for. This my last voyage and, by Saint Christopher Doghead, am I glad. I have sat on this damn tub for thirty years and now my dolphins have hatched out and they need me no longer."

I found that Captain Barbayanni and his crew were very interesting and experienced gentlemen. Although they made eyes at Pearly Gate they still respected what was left of my once impressive size and strength enough to treat her with courteous if jovial respect. There was a ship's doctor aboard who told me he was from Corsica, which is a part of France. He had been sentenced to the guillotine which is the way they chop off the head of murderers in a prison called the Santé. He was very proud that his was the only case in history when the falling blade got stuck halfway down. His sentence was commuted to life imprisonment and he broke out of a train transferring him to jail in Marseilles.

He was extremely interested when I told him I had had a slightly similar experience in South Africa and from then on he regarded me with respect. I asked how he had become a doctor. "I'm not really a doctor," he said. "But I was in the dope-peddling business so I learned something about chemistry. Also, I guess I'm a bit of a surgeon too.

"You see, the man I killed; well, I did it by slicing his head off very slowly and neatly after first cutting off his ears." He explained this gave him a certain reputation for the administration of drugs and the practice of surgery and of course I could easily understand. "Actually," he confided, "nowadays I prescribe whisky for everything. And it makes everybody pleased. Personally, I never drink. Fatal," he said. "It's my liver." When I repeated this admiringly to the first mate he guffawed. "Steals a bottle a day from medical stores and fiddles the books," he contended.

The first mate, Mr. Okla, was a man with skin the color of a tangerine and a gray cast that entirely covered his left eye. Pearly Gate was afraid of him and said she could tell he was wicked from the way his hands moved, all by themselves, it seemed, like long, thin, scaly snakes not connected to the rest of his body at all except by shabby cuffs, ringed with tarnished gold. He told me he became a professional seaman just before the partition of India in 1947. "I ran a sambouk from the Baluchi coast of what is now Pakistan down through Saudi Arabia, Oman and the Hadramaut. We did a very good business."

"What did you sell?" asked Pearly Gate. "Slaves," he

said. "Young slaves. Some were sold us by their parents 'cause they couldn't feed them. Others we stole. But the bottom was already dropping out of the market."

"But you must be quite old then," Pearly Gate said.

"Oh, no, I have a great capacity for rest. I shall live for years yet."

When we were three days out at sea Mr. Okla invited Pearly Gate and me to have a beer in his little cabin. He was drinking something brown that smelled very strong. "Liver medication," he explained. He was not wearing any of his normal uniform but leaned back in pink linen trousers which he said he had bought in Aden and a funny jacket covered with naked girls which he said he had bought in Miami, Florida. "The only way to rest," he told us, "is to relax. These are my relaxing clothes."

He was a very interesting man to talk to. He collected money and kept it in a large can that had once held navy beans. Now it was filled with Japanese yen, Belgian francs, Italian lire, Iraqi dinars, Canadian dollars, and a great many postage stamps which, he assured us, were very valuable. There were also dozens of very, very small shells he called cowries.

"What are they for?" I asked.

"Wampum," he said. "What my ancestors used."

"Oh, is that old Indian money?"

"Yes, exactly."

"Can we buy something with shells like that when we get to Calcutta?" asked Pearly Gate.

"Not that kind of Indian, silly," he replied. "I'm Choctaw. One of the five civilized tribes. Okla's my name. Get it? Okla falaya. The red people. Oklahoma. The red land. Not this brown scum," he added, looking out of the porthole as if the whole population of Calcutta were peering in.

"Why are you all so civilized?" I inquired.

"Just because that's the way we're born," he said with satisfaction. "Not brown scum. Red people."

There was one other officer, the chief engineer, and also a gentleman they called the supercargo who, I gathered, represented the owner, Mr. Mitsotaki. The chief engineer was a red-faced Irishman who seemed to suffer many physical complaints, all of which were treated with the same medicine by the steadfast Corsican doctor. "There's a man who knows his arse from his tits," the Irishman used to say when he returned from a treatment. "By the willow harp of Brian Boru, High King of Ireland, I respect a professional who understands his business."

The supercargo, Mr. Skoufi, was known to everyone aboard as Goofy Skoufi because he seemed to have a head crammed with harebrained schemes. He had once persuaded another Greek, who was in the oil tanker business, to sign a contract with an Arab petroleum sheikh, using a special brand of ink that faded away entirely within a month. At the signing, Mr. Skoufi was treated like a prince and given a golden dagger and a platinum Movado watch. But he had not yet managed to leave when the sheikh saw the contract vanishing in thin air so he took his revenge by chopping off Goofy's right hand because he said he was a thief.

Mr. Skoufi then sought to recoup his fortunes when he heard that the Shah of Iran paid great heed to mystical voices which advised him on policy decisions but which could be heard by no other living being. Goofy went into partnership with a medium-astrologer, who had earned considerable acclaim in Swat, and with a dealer in secondhand airplanes. When the two of them visited His Imperial Majesty, Goofy swore he could hear a prophet named Gabriel telling the Shah the only way he could insure the strength of Iran against its enemies at a reasonable price was by mass purchase of secondhand aircraft. "They're more experienced," he added. Fortunately, both Goofy and his new partner left the country before all deliveries had been finished so Goofy was still able to eat with his left hand. "There are few attractive

(197)

cities I have known," he used to say, "and Teheran is not one of them."

Sometimes when Pearly Gate and I talked with Mr. Skoufi on the rolling deck of our little ship he would assure us solemnly: "I'm just about to corner the cardominium business. You know, like condominiums. Movable dominiums. Joint owners will share all cars and I'll make my fortune at last—before the auto industry frames me. By the time they realize what's up I'll have a different face, a different name, a different passport and a brand-new right hand." Other times he would say: "What we all need is world kinocracy. Government by dogs. Dogs are kinder than men. Even I could thrive in a kinocracy. Would be afraid of nothing."

Once the Corsican overheard him on this subject. "You," he spat out. "You'll always be afraid. You fear everything. You fear for your life but you're not really even alive. You just crawl about on the surface of the world without any object, any purpose. You're lucky to have one hand left—to pick your nose and wipe your ass, the way the Arabs do it."

Our first weeks of rolling down the southeast coast of Asia, through the Malay straits and into the oily approaches to the Indian Ocean were not eventful save for the day the doctor got angry at a Javanese seaman who sought to swat a large fly, missed, and hit the Corsican instead. He was promptly heaved down the ladder of the bridge where the doctor had no right to be except that he was pondering the effects of his cough syrup.

When we finally reached Calcutta, Mr. Okla invited Pearly Gate and me to accompany him to what he described as "a pleasant harborside restaurant" and which I can only imagine he favored because it allowed him ample excuse to boast of the superiority of the five civilized tribes. It was a very smelly place. The odor of curry was unable to disguise the odor of sweat and defecation. The owner or manager was a very considerable woman with heavy lipstick on her mouth, a figure like a thawing Canadian snowman and a dress that was almost entirely open between her breasts and between her thighs. Pearly Gate said nothing. But I noticed that she pulled her shawl tightly about her although it was desperately hot.

On the wall above the flyblown bar were large signs in various languages. The ones I recognized said: "Get Hot Baby" and "Do Not Waste Your Time" and "Plenty Girls Here" and "We Take Dollars And Even Pounds." One said: "No Dogs Or South Africans Allowed." There were seamen from many countries present, some arguing feverishly and some (mainly American) sitting quietly around tables with bored looks, most of them chewing gum. White, black, brown, yellow and every other kind of girls were doing their best to sell drinks to the customers or help to consume them rapidly. Pearly Gate was very uncomfortable and I wanted to go.

"Whatsa point?" the first mate asked. "Have another beer, Curly. These ladies aren't any worse than babes are anywhere. Soon as you leave them they scram off with the nearest drugstore cowboy. They wave farewell at the pier and next thing you know they've dropped another baby only eight months after collecting their regular allotment. And at that the baby's often the wrong color. From the husband's point of view, that is.

"Never worry," Mr. Okla continued. "Five trips ago the skipper brought his wife along when we shipped from Norfolk to Perth. Had a big poker game, head to head, and he lost. He offered to double the stakes. Know what I won? A written certificate that I had first rights to his missus all the way to Port Lousy in Mauritius?"

"Port Lousy?" asked Pearly Gate in wonder. "Oh, they call it Port Louis, he explained."

"He doesn't sound so civilized to me," I commented, taking Pearly Gate by the arm and leading her through the noise out into the steaming night.

It was a very long trip so Pearly Gate used it to improve

her knowledge of Greece. We stopped in Hongkong, Saigon and Singapore on the way and she spent some of the little money she had hidden from Mr. Mitsotaki buying English paperback books about the ancient Greeks. They seemed to be mostly gods and soldiers. There was a very long book by a man named Homer who I told her must have been a pretty good baseball player at least.

Also, because she had a talent for languages, she persuaded Captain Barbayanni and Mr. Skoufi both to talk to her a lot in their native tongue. The captain soon showed he was interested primarily in investigating Pearly Gate's more intimate secrets but she rebuffed him. She warned that although I was slightly out of condition, I was a renowned sumotori and famous throughout Japan for my bonk which could knock down a six-inch-thick pine tree. From that moment Barba regarded us both with respect but he was nice enough to keep on helping her to improve her Greek.

Mr. Skoufi, as we found out later, tried to make fun of Pearly Gate by telling her the wrong Greek expressions and dirty words for very proper English words. When we were in Rangoon taking aboard a load of canned foods with funny-looking labels that were eyed suspiciously by the customs authorities until Goofy ostentatiously paid them off, an honorary Greek vice-consul came aboard because he reckoned logically that any vessel flying the Liberian flag and named *Herakles* must be Greek. Pearly Gate, wishing to be especially polite when the captain invited us to have a drink with the diplomatic visitor, said a Greek phrase that sounded very pretty and poetic in her soft, musical voice. The honorary vice-consul seemed horrified and embarrassed.

After he had left, Barba asked Pearly Gate: "Where you learn that nasty phrase, Pearl?"

"Why nasty? Mr. Skoufi told me it means 'It is an honor to make the acquaintance of so distinguished a gentleman.' "

"Well, Pearl, that Goofy'd better watch out or he'll be wiping his ass on his elbow. For your information what he told you means something entirely different and not at all nice. I am going to warn him he'd better never make that same mistake again. Also, that from time to time I'm going to examine you on what he's taught."

We had a long, long trip around Africa and even stopped in both Grande Comore and Lourenço Marques. I didn't see anyone I knew but I told Pearly Gate about my adventures there as a young and innocent traveller on the road to glory and distinction.

Finally we turned northwestward and waddled up the western coast. Captain Barbayanni shouted to me one day: "You say, Curly, that you're interested in South West. Well, there's Walvis Bay. Walvis, pronounced Vahlfish. Means whale. We ain't stopping there but thought you'd ought to know."

"South West?" I said. "Why that's where my family comes from." Everyone except Pearly Gate looked at me as if I were mad. I had told her all about the Oorlog Hereros and about Vati and about how his fellow soldiers tried to send him home—and failed.

Once we had entered the Mediterranean life aboard the *Herakles* became much more active. We stopped in a whole series of ports—Tangier, Oran, Marseilles, Palermo, Naples—and I noticed that Mr. Skoufi did a great deal of entertaining. He banned everyone, even the captain, from the main saloon where the officers used to eat.

When Pearly and I sometimes walked past on the deck outside I noticed that he kept agitatedly waving his left hand, patting his visitors on the back, pressing them to drink from a cluster of bottles and glasses he had spread out on the table, and occasionally taking out a pad and pencil, scratching down all kinds of figures and calculations. Once or twice I saw thick rolls of money exchanged.

Meanwhile, outside, there was a coming and going of small boats, launches and lighters, always at night and always rather dimly lit. Among the roster of guests I often noted men who must have been port officials of one or another sort because they wore differing kinds of uniform. Mr. Skoufi was especially polite to them and this may have helped us to achieve our frequent nightly business transactions with a minimum of fuss and a complete absence of red tape.

I knew the cargo was always the same: cooked, canned flowers from the mysterious Golden Triangle. But I was surprised when I saw it being brought up from the storage holds, sometimes in little nets hoisted by our derricks but generally just carried up in suitcases or duffle bags: the tins in which everything was packed were of different shapes and sizes and bore labels in various languages and pictures of cows, birds, noodles and all kinds of things but flowers. This didn't seem to bother any of the people who came aboard to buy.

It was only after we had gone southward through the Strait of Messina, under a smooth sky glittering with stars, that Captain Barba told me we were on the very last lap. Piraeus was the final stop of the journey, and the day before the *Herakles* was scheduled to arrive there we would go past Dokkos where, Mr. Skoufi said, Mitsotaki had arranged that Pearly Gate and I would be picked up by a sailor in a small boat, just large enough to hold us and our suitcases. These included our western clothes, Pearly's few books, and her harigata which she valued far more than I now esteemed Mwagulane's pickled vulva. Although the British prison authorities in Cyprus had allowed me to keep the shikwembo's talisman as harmless, while withholding my other possessions, I no longer wore it around my neck for fear of any further accidental misfortunes. However, when Pearly Gate had first discovered it among my effects she put it aside in a pretty little Japanese lacquer box containing my polished, amputated tail.

At dusk, a few days later, we rolled comfortably along a silent sea with mountains and craggy islands outlined beneath the light of a sun setting like a fiery tomato behind us. I saw Captain Barba gesture to the mate, who flashed a series of signals from the bridge with a powerful hand torch. Almost immediately a beacon began to shine in a lighthouse at the very foot of a barren cliff ahead of us. We seemed to slow down; then, as we watched, a tubby boat, round at both ends and equipped with one ragged, flapping sail hung slantwise from a low mast, took out from the shore below the beacon.

"Get ready," Mr. Skoufi said. We already had our possessions in a little heap on the deck at the point where the narrow gangway went down. Just before two sailors loosened it, all the officers, headed by the supercargo and the skipper, came by, shaking me warmly by the hand and kissing Pearly Gate with affection. Mr. Okla and the Corsican doctor produced a large tin suitcase and Mr. Skoufi explained it contained presents from our colleagues: good things to eat and drink in cans and bottles that didn't come from the Golden Triangle, a book with pictures of Greek temples for Pearly, a book about basketball for me, two woollen sweaters, two flashlights and even an envelope with coins jingling inside.

"Gold," said Captain Barba. "Only money that counts in Greece. It is just for good luck and the pleasure of your company. There's nothing on that damned island. But Mitsotaki sent us a radio message. Said that in memory of Dolly he has arranged that Curly here can take over his cousin's former job as lighthouse keeper on Dokkos. Who's Dolly?"

"It used to be me," said Pearly Gate.

"Let me warn you again," said Barbayanni. "There's nothing on that island. Nothing. Just nothing. Not even the sailor who's arriving to pick you up. He only comes by once a week from Hydra or Hermione in that scruffy little boat, bringing fuel oil for the lighthouse, food and water. If you need anything special you must tell him. You'll have no company. Not even goats. It's a big island but the only other things alive on it are passing birds. Every month the Aegean Islands administration from Piraeus will send you a very small pay envelope which Mitya the sailor brings. I hope you won't be too lonely. There isn't even a radio."

"Ahoy, the caique," said Mr. Okla as the sailboat grated along our side. The rickety gangway was lowered. First two sailors carried down our baggage, including the suitcase of presents. Mitya waved up with a grin, detectable only by the flash of his eyes and teeth in the rising full moon. We clambered awkwardly aboard. "Lovers meet in journey's ending," said Mr. Okla mysteriously. Suddenly we were alone, drifting rapidly from our home of all those weeks, as Mitya guided us to Dokkos.

CHAPTER XIV

The lighthouse was terrible and the island was worse. Mitya took us around the first, from the little tower where, on top of a winding stair, the oil-fed beacon revolved.

There were two stone rooms below. In one was a stove where some driftwood was piled. "You have to gather it after each storm," the sailor said. "One must be thrifty here. The water comes from that cistern," he added, pointing to a deep cavern in the rock, covered with cement and slanting sluices that gathered up the autumnal and winter rain. "There's one eel inside," he explained. "From Porto Cheli. If he dies, let me know. He eats the algae. Without him water goes rancid. But you can't have more than one. If there are two eels, within a year there's a million. They breed."

He said all this in Greek to Pearly Gate who seemed to understand everything. I could tell from her face. Tears kept running down her cheeks. Was there any water tap?

she wanted to know. No, only a pump by the cistern. Was there a toilet? "Where do you think you are?" asked Mitya in astonishment. "You think you need an archbishop's chamber pot?" Poor Pearly Gate. The capital of her dissatisfaction had no limit.

When finally Mitya had helped bring up our few possessions and store them near the stove—where Pearly decided we'd sleep as well as eat, because at least the food we cooked would produce warmth—he left us cheerily. As the night breeze sprang up, we watched him hoist his slanted sail and head off around a point that blocked the view.

"I hate him," Pearly Gate whispered into the wind. "But who is more responsible, the judge or the executioner, Mr. Mitsotaki or Mitya? I suppose it's not the fault of that Mitya. But you can't expect me to love the hangman as he adjusts the rope around our necks." Above us, in the black night, the beacon kept turning round and round. It seemed to go faster and faster as we watched, using the sun's own energy to twirl us toward the sun itself, like some crazy instrument trying to cheat time.

"You know," said Pearly, "in one of those books I read on the ship it says that the length of time since human beings first started to live in this world is no thicker than a postage stamp on a very high pagoda tower compared to the length of time other forms of life dwelled before in this world; and that all of these together are even thinner than a postage stamp compared to what went before and will come after. "We simply don't exist," she added. "We never have. Death is the only permanent thing. It is eternal. Therefore there is no life."

I didn't understand anything she said but I was puzzled to think that a sweet kaesang girl, mixed up with Osaka crooks, could come to a stony Greek island and understand such difficult thoughts and also be so tender and kind with me. "I hate death," she continued. "Once you cease remembering death you are too old—and ready to die." It occurred to me I never thought about dying anymore. I looked at the distant, honey-colored moon hanging between the humps of a saddle-backed island opposite.

Next morning Pearly made us some coffee with sugar and canned milk and she found some ship's biscuits and jam in the suitcase our *Herakles* friends had given us. Then she told me I must climb and put out the beacon, as Mitya had instructed us, because otherwise we should soon have no more oil. While I was shuffling up the stairway she unpacked everything and when I came down I saw that she had placed our books and the polished harigata and the shikwembo's magic ring, now in a strong square little bottle, all together on the mantel of a fireplace where some old fir cones were piled.

There, in the place of honor, were the symbol of my thwarted life and the vestige of my primacy. Pearly Gate had found a broom of twigs bound together and was vigorously sweeping dust and trash through the open door so it fell down a few feet right into the darkening sea. An ominous bloodred sun that seemed pregnant with disaster was working its way through a mattress of clouds above the spit of rock at the island's southern tip,

We started that day to explore Dokkos. It was very difficult, stern and rugged. There were no trees and no bushes, only clumps of tough weeds here and there. It was steep and high and we found it hard to move from one peak to another. There were flocks of seabirds and also others that were smaller and looked like pigeons and even smaller ones that made a funny whirring noise when they flew in brief spurts. Occasional hawks flung themselves like hooked sharp weapons from the sky. A glow fought its way out of the cloud bank proclaiming the imminent and brilliant sun. Below us, looking down from the mountain comb, spread the sea. Every now and then a sudden, unexpected gust of wind would whip snatches of dust around us, both enveloping and ignoring our unexpected shapes.

The first time Mitya came by with a little money and our supplies, Pearly said he must bring us a few chickens so we would have companions and occasionally we could eat or breed their eggs. She also wanted two goats but the Greek said these were too expensive. Also there weren't enough weeds on the whole island to keep even one goat alive. But he did bring the chickens and we used to save our bread and biscuit crumbs for them. We let them wander wherever they wished and they seemed to know how to keep away from the hungry hawks, always staying near protective ledges of rock.

The chickens made Pearly Gate very happy. "I would have preferred a dog," she said, "since it has become clear we can never have a child. Why is it people like to insult each other by calling them 'dirty dogs'? Any dog is nicer than a human and a dirty dog is happier than a clean dog. Thus a dirty dog is not an insult; he is a happy superhuman.

"In one of the books I bought in Singapore there is the story of a Greek saint called Kinokephalos, Saint Christopher Doghead. He was a handsome young man from Alexandria who liked to frolic with the girls and drink a lot so God changed his face to that of a dog and when none of the girls would look at him anymore he became a saint. Now that was a very stern thing for God to do but don't you think it's nicer being a dog anyway? So maybe God's wisdom is really infinite."

She looked at me with her warm, affectionate eyes, spread her frayed skirt and sat beside me on a ledge facing across at the saddle-backed island called Trikkeri. Yes, I thought, it might have been nice being a dog. Already I was becoming bent over like a crab with pains that Pearly said must be arthritis.

I had shrunk into a kind of quarter-moon shape, a huge

bent old man. My long hair, occasionally scissored by Pearly, was growing white with a broadening bald spot in the middle where my topknot once had been. My skin was becoming ever darker and had burned spottily in the sun and wind. I had a dirty, matted beard, tufts of which had started to fall out. I had turned from walking to shuffling like some immense crab and Mitya told Pearly that the fishermen who sometimes laid their nets in the waters off Dokkos referred to me nowadays as The Old Man of the Sea.

All I did each day, while Pearly busied herself about our little house, tried to add to our rations with fish she caught off the point and by pounding nettles she found on the mountain, was to pump the rock water from our two cisterns and to feed the chickens with crumbs, a bit of grain, and occasional insects I carefully trapped on the barren hills.

I loved being with them, listening to their chatter, watching the hens hatch their eggs while the roosters boasted, fondling the little yellow soft ones when they pecked through their shells into the strange new world about them. Always above I was aware of the hawks watching with fierce eyes but I never lost one—except on rare occasions when Pearly Gate decided we should eat a member of our flock. I always insisted she must kill it. Each time she did so sadly, sighing like the sea at dawn.

The seasons passed and each September the first rains came tumbling out of leaden clouds and filling our linked underground water caves. Mitya—and, nowadays, often his son—would arrive with an eel in a covered bucket. One or the other would climb down a ladder after we'd pulled out the covering lid by its iron handle, and fish around in the remaining shallows for the old eel which he would dash against the cistern wall, and then hand up to Pearly for our supper. Then Mitya would let the replacement slither in, with a splashing dive.

They knew their weather so well that invariably within

a week the September showers had started and the eel's hidden pond would gradually start to fill. That was the time of year when fragile, purplish cyclamen flowers would appear from nowhere on the crags and in the gullies, their seeds perhaps borne by the south wind, and there was a sparse resurrection of the asphodel stalks that once, it seemed, filled the island passes.

Sometimes—and nobody, not even Mitya, could explain from where they arrived because, unlike turtles, they can't swim—tortoises would lumber along the comb. When I found one I would bring it home and Pearly cooked it for hours and hours but my teeth were beginning to wobble and get rotten and it was hard meat to chew.

Although I had gone to Ben Franklin High, I never learned to enjoy reading, even despite the fun I had turning over and over again the pages of the book on basketball our *Herakles* friends had given me. Pearly tried to read to me each late afternoon or evening (by then we had two kerosene lamps) but I preferred it when she told me stories from things she had learned in her collection of Greek books.

She told me about the huge treasures the Hellenes had stolen from the Persians, great camel-loads of darics and siglos which they had brought back to these islands, fighting all along the way. She told me about a Greek man named Socrates who was almost as great as Hwanung, the creator of Korea, and indeed might actually have been Hwanung, and what he said when he died. He said he owed a man a rooster and then committed suicide. We had lots of roosters by then and I never wished to kill myself.

She told me lots and lots of things I found very difficult to understand until she assured me I wasn't supposed to understand them and that she didn't either: that love is the only important thing of the mind and that among physical things all that counted was matter, motion and mass and that mass contained both matter and motion. Once I could comprehend this, said Pearly Gate, I would cease to regret such inevitable decay in life as the loss of my tail, my strength, my power, my faith, my confidence in good fortune. God, she told me, is luck—and therefore prayed to. Death is time, relentless, impassive and impervious. There is no such thing as the present, said Pearly Gate; the future becomes the past and that is all; there is nothing in between.

She told me that what some people called infinity was just as hard to understand as God because it always thrust out and became ever-bigger or it always thrust in and became ever-smaller, backward to a beginning that never was and forward to an end that never would be. She told me that I should no more worry about my wizened, flabby, bent-over and distorted shape than a beautiful woman should regret the way she faded. I then looked closely at Pearly Gate and noticed that she had faded and was covered with wrinkles but I saw none of this in her warm eyes and gap-toothed sweet smile.

"A slow rotting away," she said, "is the way to compose yourself for the sudden shout of eternity."

When a dead little seal came floating ashore one morning, its bloated, half-rotten body sogging against the rocks, I wanted to hide it beneath a pile of stones because it looked so pitiful. "No," she said, "graves are for the living, not the dead. The living put flowers on graves to do penance, to salve their own consciences, or as a form of political protest. The dead don't care if they are idols. Nor do they know it." She pushed the small animal gently into the water with her foot and watched a school of minnows play around it as it floated away in an eddy.

Those were beautiful days and I found great peace and happiness as I withered away on an island as bare and hard and remote as the moon. I did small, mean things every morning, afternoon and evening, content to be beside the woman for whom I had once been a splendid giant of magnificence and was now but an aged, overgrown crab—except she couldn't see it.

One spring day I had painfully climbed to the very apex of our jagged comb, which meant slowly going around from behind where an ancient galley ship was supposed to have sunk, and then crawling inch by inch upward toward the sky. I sniffed the fine air with its hint of newness and cleanness and I gazed across at the towering mass of Hydra across the channel. I thought I heard the echo of a faint shriek but I paid no attention as an unusual number of gulls was wheeling and circling overhead, playing with the air currents.

Late that afternoon, when I descended and limped homeward in order to be in ample time to light the evening beacon, I saw from a distance hundreds of little furry creatures that seemed to be disappearing from our small stone house and leaping heedless into the sea. When I drew closer I discovered they were great brown-gray rats and they were indeed jumping into the water, fearlessly and by droves. They seemed to be able to swim but a limited way. In long lines and clusters they were busily paddling out in the direction of Trikkeri and then, a few hundred yards from shore, they would disappear.

First there were innumerable rats, furiously swimming forward, side by side, in clusters. Then there were lines, only occasionally filled out with tiring groups seemingly pressing together. Then, farther forward, there were just a few heads. Then there were none. Nothing was urging them onward from behind but none of them hesitated or sought for an instant to turn back toward shore. They simply swam forward into destiny—and vanished.

As rapidly as I could manage I scrabbled forward—and found nothing. There was no sign at all of Pearly Gate. Only days later, on Mitya's next visit, he told me some night fishermen, out in the predawn hours with their pitch-lighted rowing boats by which they attracted fish into their nets, had found the swollen corpse of my beloved and given it a sea-burial, wrapped in an old net weighted with rocks. One of them, a former priestly acolyte, had said a few words from the Greek Orthodox service. Apparently her body was untouched by the rats but her eyes had impressed them as being swollen with fright. I suppose the poor thing had jumped into the sea in hopes of eluding sudden terror.

I stumbled everywhere in our house, not even remembering to climb the spiral stairway to our lantern until it had been dark for over an hour. I never knew where the rats had come from, since there were no animals on our deserted island. They had no origin and they had no destination save drowning, like thousands of old Greeks.

Every chicken we possessed had disappeared; even every egg but one. There were a few scraps of bones and feathers, pieces of eggshell, mostly strewn along the ledges beneath which the wary hens hid from the hawks and the occasional small owls that sometimes flew suddenly, hungrily out of the night.

All our souvenirs were gone: Pearly Gate's shoes and underclothing; my sparse wardrobe; the food that wasn't in cans, but had been placed in plates upon the window ledges; the bowl of soaking weeds where Pearly had been making a salad; the platter I had fashioned from driftwood and where she used to keep the fish we dried in sunlight and salt; even the few books we owned, torn into thousands of meaningless fragments.

I saw the sturdy bottle where the shikwembo's ring was kept. It had fallen to the stone floor and was marked with tooth scratches; but the bottle had not broken and the souvenir of my misfortune was intact. However, the harigata, my brightly polished tail, had vanished. Days later I found an unmistakable fragment of it lodged in a crack stuck just below the entrance of our doorway. I flicked it into the water below.

The only living thing apart from myself and the cistern eel, which Mitya's son discovered sluggishly thrashing about that September when he came to prepare me for the autumnal rains, turned out to be a single egg, curiously wrapped in some wool that Pearly had been knitting and had left on a shelf beyond the reach of the rats even though, judging by scratch-marks on the wall, they had sought to climb up and devour it.

When I found the egg I felt that it was still warm, kept alive perhaps by Pearly Gate's dear love and the fact that the woollen wrapping was on the shelf where the sun's rays last lingered on lengthening spring afternoons. Immediately I resolved to cherish this last remaining bit of energy. I knew, since childhood, that an egg contained life while it was warm and that it could be hatched into a living being if it was heated and cherished by its mother. So I resolved to be its mother, to keep if possible, a final thread linking me to life.

I made a nest for the frail oval object in Pearly's wool and left it in the sun each day, moving it continually from place to place so that it would be neither overheated nor underheated. When dark came, I held it tenderly in my hands and sometimes kept it between my legs, in my lap, being fearful I might accidentally crush it if I put it under my arm. I rarely, if ever, slept because I became so obsessed with that precious egg.

I began to feel that if it failed to hatch, everything still alive would die. When I carried it delicately in my bent fingers, limping with the lengthening shadows of the sun, I had visions that were I to drop it with one great yellow splash, specked by a single fertilizing drop of red, I would be the murderer of mankind, of all life.

The egg hatched. One morning, as I held it in my gnarled open hand, exposed to the early sun, I felt it throb inside. I watched and watched, not daring to move and then there was a fluttering little stir, a tiny peck, and then a crack. The fragile beak came out, the shell began to fragment, and suddenly, before I had truly become accustomed to the idea for which I had so long waited, a skinny birdlet, with wet, soft, yellow feathers lay quivering in my palm. All day I sat there, feeding it occasional tiny seeds and, from our wheat bin, pellets of flour slightly mixed with olive oil, while the bird looked up at me with anxious loving eyes. Soon it took a few tottering steps and eventually it was running about, investigating the huge world about it.

My Friend, which is what I named the bird, grew to be a strong active cock and liked to preen himself on a flagstone I placed upon the ledge above the cola-colored sea. Sometimes I would sit with him for hours while my warm chicken huddled beside me. I would remember how, in my own way, I had helped create him. Strangely it made me feel, in my great unhappiness, like some kind of god.

Now you who have read this, remember: it is not that I tell lies but that you may refuse to believe what you do not already know.

One day, when it was cold and storming and the loneliness of existence stormed about me, I took down from its shelf the bottle containing the rubbery vulva of Mwagulane, origin of all my triumphs, all my disasters. Recalling its only dreadful function now, I extracted it, fitting it to me and clutching My Friend as I did so.

"Kill me," I said. "That is my final wish." I quaked in fear lest my prayer be granted.

Nothing happened.

I wish especially to thank Linda Lamarche of Paris and Peter Hawthorne of Johannesburg for their help on parts of this manuscript.

I also wish to acknowledge my debt to *Go, Man, Go!* by Dave Zinkoff (with Edgar Williams) published by Pyramid Books, New York, 1958, as well as *Takamiyama, The World of Sumo*, by Jesse Kuhaulua (with John Wheeler) published by Kodansha International, Tokyo, 1973, for its helpful information on the sport of sumo wrestling.